The Best in the West

Books by Kathleen Walker

Fiction

The Best in the West
A Crucifixion in Mexico
Life in a Cactus Garden

Nonfiction

San Xavier: The Spirit Endures
A Place of Peace: San Juan Capistrano
Desert Mornings—Tales of Coffee, Cactus & Chaos

The Best in the West

Kathleen Walker

Black Heron Press
Post Office Box 13396
Mill Creek, Washington 98082
www.blackheronpress.com

The Best in the West is a work of fiction. All characters that appear in this book are products of the author's imagination. Any resemblance to persons living or dead is entirely coincidental.

ISBN (print): 978-1-936364-25-1
ISBN (ebook): 978-1-936364-26-8

Black Heron Press
Post Office Box 13396
Mill Creek, Washington 98082
www.blackheronpress.com

"The great sadness of my life is that I never achieved the hour newscast, which would not have been twice as good as the half-hour newscast, but many times as good."
—Walter Cronkite, CBS Evening News anchor, 1962-1981

OPEN

"Tits up!"

The shout hit her as the red light flashed on, the hand came down, and her lips began their rote movement. Son of a bitch.

"Good evening," she said.

Son of a bitch.

"I'm Jean Ann Maypin."

The son of a bitch did it again. Well, he wasn't going to get her. Not this time.

He picked up the toss.

"And I'm Tom Carter. And this is the news."

Back again.

"A major fire in our valley tonight. We'll have a live report." Her look was concerned, urgent, his equally so as he took it back.

"And the governor may have to call a special session of the legislature to help our highways."

He allowed the faint hint of a smile to curl the corners of his mouth. They could see that Tom Carter knew the highways needed all the help they could get, that help better be on the horizon, and that the governor was not a favorite of his.

She let her eyes linger on his face for a split second of silence. They were in this together, partners. Together they had it under control. Together they cared.

"We'll have that news and all the news of the valley and the state, coming up next." She smiled gently, no wide flashing smile, only the assurance that they, together, would be back soon.

She had it under control without that son of a bitch trying to throw her with that tits up thing. They were watching her, loving her, trusting her, Jean Ann Maypin. That's why they were watching The Best in the West.

She straightened slightly in the chair, legs crossed demurely at the ankles. She knew the moves. She was the star and the son of a bitch wasn't going to be allowed to forget it.

No mistakes, no mistakes so far. She held the smile. No mistakes.

Thirty seconds gone, another twenty-eight minutes to go. She had it made.

With a flash of a hand, she and the son of a bitch disappeared. The screen would now fill with the music and clipped motion that announced what it was she did so well, the six o'clock news.

*

Ellen Peters did not have to look through the windows or walk past the patios of the other condos to know the news had begun. She didn't have to see the blue-gray flickers of a hundred screens chopped, divided, quartered then boxed into eighths and finally sixteenths. She didn't have to hear the buzzing music of the helicopter as it sliced through canyons or see the familiar worried faces of men and women rushing, typing, talking, running. All familiar, all worried.

They registered though, those flickers. They had registered in some way every night for over two years. They had to. That is what they were designed to do, to register. That thirty-second flash of movement and music had taken ten days to produce, to shoot, to edit, all to catch her ear and eye and mind.

She opened the trunk of the car. One last bag, one last trip to be made and it was done. She fumbled for a cigarette from the pack in her jacket pocket. She leaned against the car and smoked. There was no screen she could see, no masculine voice to be heard singing out like the town crier of old. Alone in the parking lot, she rested and she smoked.

"You know what I want to be?" Debbie had asked her. "I want to be this great reporter pounding out stories on an old typewriter, smoking a cigarette, my hair all messed up. You know?"

Ellen wondered then, as she did now, if Debbie realized that her dream was to be the person she was telling it to and it wasn't much of a dream or all that original. It was, however, a strange vision for this tall woman with her soft blond hair and beautiful skin.

That is how Debbie first came into the newsroom, all soft and young, all ruffled and hot.

"Gosh, it's hot," she had moaned and they all laughed. It was only April.

She had a Garbo look, skin so white and clear you could almost see through it, with the barest hint of pink on the checks. She was twenty-four.

Ellen wondered that day if Maypin was watching from some corner or office, trying to see down the maze of cubicles to the young woman with the gentle blue eyes.

"Got a new reporter coming from Bakersfield," Carter told them at the last meeting. No one rolled their eyes or sighed dramatically at yet one more proof of Carter's insanity in hiring. They didn't need to hear the story of how he heard her read the news or saw her report one story.

All he said was she was coming from Bakersfield. He did add that she was young and pretty, sneering across the room. They expected that from him, one of his sick jokes, but Bakersfield brought no snickers or groans. They all started in someplace like Bakersfield, except those few who had started with The Best right from the beginning.

Yes, that's how she came to the station, young and pretty.

"Probably how she left it too," would have been Ellen's aside, had she found a place to use it or cared less about Debbie.

She thought about it now. Was that how Debbie left, all innocent and hopeful and wondering at the relentless heat. Did she simply step out and float away?

The reason it was a sick joke, that thing about her being pretty and young, was that Carter made damn sure all of the male reporters he hired were married. And, he wanted them more than married. He wanted kids, lots of kids. Like he told Ellen, a good Mormon boy was his idea of a reporter.

It had to do with keeping them and scaring them. Men with kids were scared, hungry and scared. Carter knew that. He had no children. If he ever had a wife, no one knew about it, not even Ellen Peters, and he always told her more than he should.

"I can't stand those good-looking blond guys," he once blurted at her.

"What?"

"You know, guys like Adkins. I can't stand them."

"Why?"

"I don't know. I never liked blonds. Too many sissy boys are blond."

He hesitated, turning his salt and pepper head of hair away from her and looking toward the bookcase with its folders and piles of tapes and résumés. A row of award plaques and citations hung on the wall above them.

"Shit, they got everything going for them. I don't know. Maybe I'm jealous."

It was the kind of thing that threw Ellen about Carter. Right when she had lived through weeks of good reasons to despise the man, enough reasons to shoot him, he'd say something like that, flat and sad. She'd wait though, for that glint of meanness to return to his eyes. And, it would.

Carter picked Debbie Hanson from those piles of tapes and résumés and she came to them ready to start on the next set of steps on the path of television news.

Of course, Maypin was watching from somewhere. She wouldn't miss any tall blond under her own age of twenty-eight or was it thirty. Ellen thought and said often enough that Jean Ann Maypin had been twenty-eight for the last five years at least.

Jean Ann and the weekend anchor Scott Reynolds shared their own windowed office. Unlike Tom Carter, they had no dark blinds that could be dropped down and tightened shut. They could be seen by anyone going in or out of the newsroom.

Ellen could see them from her cubicle, at least a corner of their glass room, enough to see the purple sheen of fluorescent light on Jean Ann's black hair.

1

She was born a blond, dishwater blond which turned darker with the years but never, of course, black. That came later. Blonds were a dime a dozen in television news or would be. She was smart enough to figure that out. They were white blonds or golden blonds or soft blonds like Debbie Hanson. Soft and fluffy and gentle blonds or they were hard blonds like that weekend anchorwoman Across the Street.

That's what they called the competition, Across the Street, which it was, about a half a mile down. It held the number one slot in the ratings. The other network affiliate was so low they never bothered talking about it. As for the public television station, they might as well be off the air. Across the Street was number one but not, they reminded themselves, a strong number one. Slick, they were slick, but The Best was better. The Best gave the viewers basic, solid news. The Best won the awards. The Best was there when you needed them and with a black-haired anchorwoman. Now, that was unusual.

She started as a brunette at the station in Virginia. The color went well with her dark eyes. That too was unusual. Anchorwomen, the few there were, and reporters, men and women, had blue eyes or light-brown eyes.

You did have to be careful with blue eyes. Sometimes they were too piercing, too snapping and, for some reason, the audience didn't like them. Oh, they'd take them at six-thirty in the morning or at noon but not for the big newscasts, not for the six or the ten. That's when they wanted, they needed something gentler, blue but not too blue.

Jean Ann's eyes were dark brown and not that deep endless brown that makes you want to fall into them. Hers were a dull dark brown.

However, the right makeup and lighting gave them a sort of luster that made them almost perfect with black hair. And, so unusual.

She was born Virginia Susan Maypin. Like the hair, the name would have to be changed. At the beginning though, at the first station, she made it an asset.

"Please, let me try," she begged the producer. "I think it would be good. Don't you think so? Couldn't it be good?"

"Sure, sure," he said. "Go ahead." He didn't care. He wanted to get the newscast on the air and grab a couple of beers before going home.

That night, as she ended her report on-set with anchorman Jackson Hale, she said with a chirp in her voice and a girlish smile, "And so for Virginia, this is Virginia, Virginia Sue Maypin."

"What the hell was that?" Jackson Hale yelled when they went to commercial. "Virginia for Virginia? What the hell?" Then, he laughed.

"Oh well," she sighed sweetly.

She did real well, real well indeed.

She went to that station armed with a degree in English from a state college so she could work and a few months of sex with a journalism professor so she could get a job. He made the call to the station. Better them than him was his thinking.

Only a handful of women reporters sat in television stations across the country. One of them left the local station right around the time the professor made his call. Virginia Sue Maypin was nothing if not lucky.

The reporter she replaced did a silly little female job created by station management and the news director. They needed someone to take care of the annoying calls they got from viewers who wanted help without offering any news story in return. They decided they needed a consumer reporter.

It was supposed to be a sort of on-air household hint column – removing wine stains from rugs, blood from lace. People called wanting to tell someone about their problems. Virginia Sue Maypin's predecessor took the calls and the job seriously and moved it, story by story, into real consumer complaints.

The questions about rug stains turned into investigations of shaky used car sales, dishonest repairmen and leaky new roofs. Still, a lot of the work involved listening to those little calls and equally small problems. Virginia Sue Maypin was not happy with the job she inherited.

New car batteries died for no reason, trailer parks had no heat or water. Mail-order companies, carpet-cleaning companies, car-towing companies, nobody doing what they were paid to do. And one of the people who couldn't have cared less was Virginia Sue Maypin.

About the only thing she liked about the job was the men in suits who ran or represented the offending companies. They stood when she entered a room and reached for her hand and her chair and her smile. She liked them.

She wasn't exactly sure what she disliked so much about the rest of it. It couldn't be the old ladies who cried and prattled at her over the phone because they also called the station and told everyone how wonderful she was and how she had saved their lives and said over and over, "I don't know what I would have done without her."

It was their problems that made her crazy, the new stoves that didn't work and the refrigerators that made no ice. Why did they call her? Didn't they know anyone else to call?

Every morning she found the little pink message squares waiting in a pile or taped to her desk in lines. They had names attached like Mattie Swanson, Mabel Hicks, Mary Wilson. They had notes about broken pipes and dead batteries and electricity being turned off and the numbers she was supposed to call.

No, it wasn't the old ladies that made her dread beginning each day at the station. It was those pink slips and those problems, never the old ladies. Virginia Sue made it a point to love them. After all, they loved her.

Her starting salary was barely above minimum wage. By the end of the first year it had tripled. At least three times a week Virginia for Virginia gave her report from the news set and the next day the phones would ring with a female chorus of how wonderful she was and could she help them. Management recognized her value and she earned her money.

She was in by six-thirty every morning. They saw her working at her desk when they rolled in at eight or nine or ten. She was still there at seven or eight or ten at night and nobody asked why. Had anyone known why, it wouldn't have made a bit of difference.

Virginia Sue Maypin had a problem. She needed at least three hours to write a two-minute story and that didn't produce good, solid writing. The good writing came later, from the producer who reworked her scripts.

After one year she had management and the audience in the palm of her hand. She was pleasant, hardworking and not annoyingly smart. The director she slept with happily assisted her in the creation of a résumé tape. Less than twenty thousand dollars and endless lines of pink slips weren't going to do it for her.

The fifteen written résumés and six résumé tapes she sent out resulted in three strong letters of interest and one phone call offering a paid-for trip. She made sure the trip ended with a job.

One year and five months after she first set foot in a television station, she was on her way to New Orleans where Virginia Sue Maypin would prove to be an unquestionable flop.

Right off the top, it was the voice. In Virginia, she had added a happy hint of southern charm to her level Maryland-bred tone. For New Orleans, she stretched it to nearly a Carolina twang. It wasn't going to work in this city of voices blurred by elegance and education.

Then, there was the hair. She dyed it a deep chocolate brown, admittedly different in a city with a growing collection of blond reporters but not different enough. She would have done better as a blond. The brown looked too flat, the shoulder-length cut too long. The hair and the voice and the bright smile might have been fine for a consumer reporter. As a weekend anchorwoman, none of it worked.

And, Virginia Sue made another change, her name. She gave it a great deal of thought and many hours in front of a mirror. She mouthed all the combinations of names that might enhance her smile as well as look good printed on the screen beneath her.

She hated the way Virginia looked. Too much like virgin and it sounded a little old. What she needed was something perky, as she thought of it, a name that could place her between twenty-one and twenty-five.

She ended up with Jeannie. It was close enough to have been a nickname and she could go back to Virginia whenever she needed to sound formal and important. Her own childhood nickname was Ginny. That obviously wouldn't do.

"Good evening, New Orleans. I'm Jeannie Maypin with your weekend news." Perfect, bouncy and not too young or too old. So thought Virginia Susan Maypin. New Orleans did not agree.

Darker hair, different voice, Virginia for Virginia Susan, Ginny, Sue, Jeannie Maypin wasn't the New Orleans type. That's all and the only way to deal with that was to leave town as soon as possible. She did, in less than a year. What wasn't right for New Orleans, that sultry, persnickety, stiff-nosed city, proved absolutely perfect for her next choice, a gritty new city baking in the sun.

The hair was now jet-black and cut in a bob. The drawl became a little more west Texas than Carolina. The name underwent another change as well.

She spent more hours in front of the mirror, more testing, smiling, holding the pose to see how each syllable of each name would work against the next one. How would the face would look as it was being said? What expression would be left after that last sound? It was all so important.

"Well, my real name is Jean, Jean Ann," she told news director Jim Brown. "I think I should use it, don't you? I mean, I think that would be nicer, to use my real name. What do you think?"

The Ann came from a *Name Your Baby* book she found in a bookstore. There was no reason to go beyond the a's once she heard the Ann with Jean and Maypin. It worked and made it, as she told Jim Brown, her real name.

If there was one thing to be said about Virginia Susan, Ginny, Sue, Jeannie, Jean Ann Maypin it was that she believed devoutly in her own press.

2

Tom Carter hated faggots. They were faggots, not gay. He hated that they used that word, a good word and now look at it. He also hated most women, old women especially. He hated cats and birds. He would tolerate a mean dog but he hated the small, simpering breeds as much as he hated puppies of any breed and as much as he hated children. But, he really hated faggots.

"Artsy-fartsy," he would sneer every time someone did a story about artists or dancers or actors in the valley.

"They are all faggots," he leered at photographer Jason Osner.

"Along with about ten percent of your newsroom," Jason said with a smile.

Carter stared.

"Yup, ten percent of any population. That means you've got about four or five right here in your newsroom."

"Who are they?" Carter shouted. "Tell me who they are."

Jason laughed. "I don't know who they are."

"Well," Carter took a deep breath, "I know you're not one. You've got balls. I know that."

"You sure?"

"Shit. I can smell those sissy boys. You ain't no queer."

"No," Jason agreed with another smile, "but they are everywhere."

Carter thought about that. He did have doubts about that artsy· fartsy guy Harold Lewis, the arts reporter whenever there were any arts. Carter wasn't sure about him being a faggot. Sissy boy, yeah, not a queer. There was a difference.

Tom Carter also had some strong feelings about niggers, spicks, kikes, Polacks, hunkies, wops, greasers, wetbacks, jungle bunnies, Jew boys, frogs, smelly frogs and they all smelled, limeys, dumb micks, injuns, uncles, chinks, slant eyes, and gooks. That was a good new one.

To prove to anyone listening that he had such feelings, he would use those words in conversations with people in his newsroom. Morning producer Chuck, that dumb mick, Farrell kept a list of his pronouncements on race, religion and sex.

"Read it and weep," he said to Ellen and handed her the sheets.

"The only good niggers I ever knew," she read out, "were the ones that looked almost white." Next to the sentence was a date.

"Jesus."

"Someday it will come in handy," Chuck said as he put the papers back into his file drawer and locked it.

One night, as the cameras pulled back, Carter said, "God, I can't stand to be around those kids." He waited until he knew the shot was far enough back before speaking. Some of those bastards out there could read lips.

"What?" Jean Ann smiled and straightened her papers for the benefit of the closing shot.

"Those cripple kids," he said about the last story on the Easter Seals drive. "I can't stand to be around cripples."

Carter had nothing to worry about. As the most respected, the ads often claimed, news anchor in the state, he didn't have to go anywhere or be with anyone unless he so chose. That made him a prized speaker at men's business and service clubs throughout the city.

"The Cronkite of the Southwest," is how the president of one downtown luncheon club introduced him whenever Tom Carter joined them. "And Tom Carter was here first, even before Uncle Walter," he would add.

The men laughed at the way he said Uncle Walter, with a sneer and a snort. Then, they roared at his, "And we like Tom Carter even better than Uncle Walter because everybody knows Uncle Walter's a Democrat and I think we all know where Tom Carter stands even if he doesn't say so himself."

The clapping would be strong, the nodding gleeful. Even the Democrats approved. In this state, the closest thing to a Republican was a Democrat.

Tom Carter never argued with the description. He was there first, before Cronkite, before television. Tom Carter was the voice of the Southwest back when the Southwest was just desert and sky. It was his voice that brought the news into the living rooms every night, a booming, strong voice that could be trusted.

He could stretch that *s* of Thomas across seconds. *Thomasss* Carter, a radioman, a newsman. He covered the news, as much as there was, from the stone courthouse to the capitol a mile or so down the road. He knew the good old boys who ran the state. He talked like them, looked like them. He was tough and mean and foulmouthed. He told the state exactly what they told him to tell the state.

In those days, you didn't have to search out the news. They told you what they wanted said. Who could say whether or not the state was better now with all these reporters and photographers flying around? Not Tom Carter, that's for sure.

He too made a change in his name, a slight one, to fit the new world of big boxy cameras that was forced upon him. Thomas, with that long stretched out *s*, sounded lispy, like a sissy boy. Tom was better, short and tight, the same as his news. He liked to think he talked the way Hemingway wrote. He read a couple of his books. He liked old Papa, a gutsy guy.

Carter let his hair go gray at the temples, let the streaks move through the brown. He had gray, empty eyes. They gave no warmth, no joy, but when he smiled just right, the corners of his eyes would crinkle as though he was a good, kind man.

To Carter, smiling right meant a lift of the muscles at the corner of his lips. No full-toothed grin, he never had a need for that. Only a short, lip-curled, eye-crinkled smile with a quick nod to the side and move on. The audience, men and women, loved it. They loved the lift of an eyebrow that showed he knew and they knew the story was stupid or the reporter sounded dumb. That's what he did so well. He shared the straight scoop with them and they loved it.

It wasn't enough. He was still number two in the ratings. Real close. Across the Street, the name he gave them years ago, they had a silver-headed real Uncle Walter, Midwest variety with a couple of decades in the state. Boy, he pulled them in. He also had the head of a javelina mounted and hung on the wall behind his desk.

To Tom Carter, the white-haired man was the enemy, pure and simple. He seldom acknowledged his existence with even a glance much less a handshake unless forced to in a public setting. If the subject of the javelina came up, he would quip, "Shit, that's not the part of a pig I'd have stuffed."

His office was a glass square that looked across the newsroom until he lowered the blinds and closed them to brown slits. When they were set at the perfect angle, he could see out but no one could see in.

He had no family pictures on his desk, no blond wife smiling, no college graduation shots of post-pimpled big-faced boys or straight-haired, mortarboard-headed girls. Divorced was the consensus, divorced a long time ago.

However, there was one picture on the credenza that lined the wall behind his desk, a picture of an Asian child. Carter could not see it without turning almost a full one hundred and eighty degrees. Everyone sitting across from him, everyone standing anywhere in his office could see the picture.

"One of those Care kids," he told visitors. "You know, the ones the blond with the big jugs tells you to rent."

Most people would simply stare, thinking they had missed something, misunderstood.

The picture was carefully kept free of dust by the secretary, Mary, or by the never-ending work of the handyman, Augustino. Carter never thought about the picture until someone mentioned it or he caught them staring at it. The people in his newsroom tagged the kid, *Tom's One Fling Wong.*

Someone gave him the picture at a speech or an award ceremony. Something was said about his support for the children of the state, something about a child of his own. They mentioned letters, something about sending money and him getting letters. All was going to be done in his name. He never read any letters and if replies were sent in his name he didn't know about them. He certainly never sent any money. None of it mattered anyway. He only kept the picture because he liked that line about the blond with the big knockers.

He used it on Ellen Peters during her interview. It was his standard interview, questions about sex and marriage and when the babies would come. Nobody called him on it, never. Why should they? They all wanted a job.

"I guess you think you're good enough to work here."

"I'm good," she said with a small smile.

"So says you, missy," he snickered. "Everybody thinks they're good enough. I'm telling you this, missy. They ain't."

He waved to the bookcase, the credenza, to the piles of tapes and résumés.

"See those?"

She nodded.

"Those are from one week. I get a hundred people a week applying here. Everybody in this country wants to work here. They want to work for The Best.

"There's a man right here," he thumped the pile of papers in front of him with a thick middle finger, "who'd leave his network job making seventy thousand to come here and we ain't paying no seventy thousand dollars, missy."

He leaned back in his chair and put his arms behind his head. There were no sweat stains on his shirt.

She nodded again.

"So?" he demanded, jerking forward, once again straight in his chair.

Her eyes widened.

"What do you have to say?"

"That I would like the job."

"Yeah, well, we'll see about that."

He didn't like her. Right from the beginning he marked Ellen Peters as an uptight, smart-mouthed bitch. Right from the beginning he knew she was going to be trouble.

As she walked to the door, he called out, "You got good legs. I'll say that."

"Like Lincoln said, as long as they reach the ground."

He didn't bother with a comeback.

The way he figured it, the way she figured it, she'd be damn lucky to get the job.

3

They were all damn lucky to get their jobs. Carter wasn't lying when he said there were a hundred people a week applying for work at the station. Okay, maybe it was only twenty or thirty, and maybe some of them were repeaters, the ones who wouldn't stop trying. But, add the phone calls from around the country, the feelers, the friend asking a friend, and Carter's figure was low. Hundreds of people a week were trying to get a job in his newsroom or talking about it. It was the same at every other station in the city and in the state and in the country.

Television news had replaced Hollywood as the golden road to fame and fortune. Parents swelled with pride when a new reporter was born. The opposite sex fluttered with excitement, the same sex stewed with jealousy. Hollywood agents now advised new clients to try television news. The work was steady and if they made it to the big time, to that anchor seat, the agent's cut was nothing to sniff at. Rumor had it William Morris was taking on news reporters as clients. At The Best reporters were now making shadowy calls to talent agents on the East Coast who specialized in television news.

"Damn lucky," Carter would tell them as a group or individually. "Damn lucky."

It wasn't the money that drew them. There wasn't any, not really. If Carter had a hundred tapes on his desk and piled on his shelves, he could pay whatever he pleased and they took it with a nod of relief and appreciation. This was usually their second or third stop on the way to the real glory hole. Nobody, nobody good, planned to stay. Two years was about the limit. More than that and you were in trouble unless you were an unattractive street reporter, male, with two kids and a wife who stayed at home or held a low-paying, part-time job. If you were, you kept thinking this was the place to settle down because the choice had finally been taken away from you.

At the beginning it was the ego, the excitement of being there with the cops or the politicians. It was the thrill of being almost as important as the people who moved and shook the city, the people who made news. Eventually, with the help of consultants, came the realization that you too were important. You might even be more important than the stories you covered. After all, you were the one deciding who was going to be on and for how long and most of the time you were on camera more than anyone else in the story.

You did stand-ups. You stood in front of the camera and talked. You added some information or repeated, in slightly different words, what the person you interviewed said only seconds before.

You closed the story with "Some things will never change," or "Things will never be the same here again," or "How this will all end remains to be seen." You said your name and the station's call letters or the consultant-designed sign-off and the last face they saw before the anchor's was yours.

"Reporter involvement," news director Jim Brown insisted. "That's what they want, reporter involvement."

That meant shots of the reporter walking in the field, down the road, talking to people, driving a car, riding a horse, holding a dying man's hand. It meant, and no one made any bones about it, the reporter was as much a part of the story as the person or event he was sent to cover. That's what they wanted, the management boys and their consultants Back East. That's what they told Jim Brown and that's what he told his newsroom.

To the reporters, it meant more work, yes. It also meant more airtime. Out of a minute-thirty story they would take at least thirty seconds of it either talking to the camera or doing those walking, driving, handholding shots.

It all depended on looks, looks the audience liked. For the most part, that meant reporters who were solid American, non-threatening, happy and attractive. It meant someone like Frank Kowalski had a problem.

*

More than anything, Frank Kowalski wanted to be an anchor. He wanted that one moment when all the cameras moved, froze, a hand sliced the air in front on him, and he could say, "Good evening. I'm Frank Kowalski and this is the news."

He never got close. He did get to give a few, "Thanks, Tom," or "Yes, Jean Ann." That was it.

"Workhorse reporter," Ellen Peters described him to Debbie Hanson. "You know, day in and day out, covering the stories. Every newsroom has to have one. A good, average reporter. Consistent."

He was balding with small dark eyes. He was of average height and had a strong, square jaw but the face was also small and the forehead's only height came from the loss of hair. And, his shoulders were too narrow.

He did win awards, at least one spot-news award a year. He figured it as the law of averages. He did two or three stories a day, five days a week. He had to win at least one award a year.

He made twenty-two thousand dollars. Across the Street he might get twenty-five or twenty-six but nobody was making him any offers. He wasn't about to call. He wanted anchoring. At The Best, he had a chance. Across the Street he had jack shit even if they were interested, and they weren't. Like Carter said, reporters were a dime a dozen.

He adjusted his tie. It was wide, bright blue with big pink flamingos. He liked to make the guys laugh and to give Carter a reason to swear and shout that they all needed to "dress like professionals." He kept a dark tie in his desk for the times, the few times, he went on-set with that prick Carter and Jean Ann.

Jean Ann was okay. A bit of a bimbo, that was true, but most bimbos were blond. Look at Paige Allen. Now, there was a bimbo with great tits. He gave his crotch a pat, then a scratch. He wondered about her bush. It couldn't be blond. Paige was a bleached blond. Nevertheless, he wondered about blond pussy.

God, he wanted to be an anchor. He worked his way through college in Scranton, PA, busing tables, working fast-food kitchens, delivering pizza. He copped a few hours every weekend doing college radio and damn near sucked dick to rip the wires and write copy at the local TV station for minimum wage. They agreed and damn lucky, damn lucky, they told him.

Damn lucky in Wilkes-Barre, damn lucky in Ohio. Definitely damn lucky in Missouri with that Polack name and now, finally, damn lucky here.

Tom Carter saw him in Missouri, one stupid report on some two-bit fire. He really beefed it up that night, wearing his yellow fireman's jacket, holding the puppy they carried from the tenement.

"This little fellow made it," he said as the puppy tried to lick his face. "He was the lucky one."

Two people died in the fire, another was rushed screaming to the county burn unit. Three days before Christmas and thirty people were out in the street. The phones at the station rang all night with people who wanted to take the puppy.

"Nineteen-five," Carter said. "Everybody wants to work here, Kowalski."

It was one thousand more than he was making in Missouri. He made the move with his brown-haired wife and their boy. Their girl came later.

That was three years ago and he still had a chance at anchor work and goddamn it, it was a long way from Wilkes-Barre, PA. Shit yes.

He patted his crotch.

Maybe Paige Allen bleached her pussy. Hell, maybe it was even bald. God, would he love that. God, would he love to anchor.

*

They all came from somewhere else, Des Moines, Topeka, Bismarck, Fresno. Bakersfield was a big feeder for the station because Tom Carter often stopped in Bakersfield on his driving vacations in his big Chrysler. He made a point of watching the news coming out of that city. He never had a problem getting a reporter to leave Bakersfield.

Sure, his station might be number two but they loved them in New York. The reporters did the kind of hard-hitting, in-depth reporting that was often picked up by the network for the national newscasts. Across the Street it was all flash and trash, that's what they told each other. That they happened to be number one was answered with a shrug and a no-accounting-for-taste eye roll.

Once Carter brought you in, you did what you were told to do. You were the ingénue, the new kid. In the morning you would find your two assignments on your desk, usually combined with articles clipped from the morning newspaper with notes attached from George Harding, the assignment editor, or from his assistant Kim Palmeri. You could get a news conference in the morning about yet another delay on a forever-being-built freeway and an afternoon story on illegal dumping in the desert.

You might pick up some spot news, a fire or accident, on the way back to the station. That was the low-rung work, two stories a day and whatever you were passing.

Second rung up and you were on a beat. Jack Benton handled cop shop and the courts and the legislature, when in session. Richard Ferguson covered medical and science. Paige Allen, who knew nothing about them, worked energy and environment. Harold Lewis was on arts and entertainment. That didn't mean those were their only stories.

If they didn't turn up their own beat stories, they too would find themselves out on the street, at lunches and press conferences. They fought those assignments, usually at the top of their lungs.

*

"What the hell is this?" Richard Ferguson demanded from his three-sided cubicle. "What the hell is this, George?"

George Harding hunched over his silent black phone, the receiver held to his ear.

"I said, what the hell is this, George?" Ferguson yelled.

"It's a story."

"A story? A story? How the hell am I supposed to do this? I have a series I am supposed to be working on. Do you know that? Do you, George?"

"I know. I know."

"What?"

"I said I know," George yelled in exasperation. "I haven't got anyone else. Nobody else is here. I got three people out sick and two photographers out of town. I need that story."

"Not from me, George, not from me," came the taunt.

"Yeah, yeah," George turned to the cards of his middle Rolodex.

"Do you hear me?" Richard Ferguson was now standing on his chair so he could see over the cubicles to the assignment editor's desk.

"I hear you."

"I said I am not doing it, dickhead," Ferguson yelled.

A snicker came up from Jack Benton's cubicle.

"Do you hear me?" Ferguson demanded.

"I hear you." George stood up, now shouting as well. "And you will do it. You will. I can't run a goddamn newsroom with no reporters. Shut up and do it." He stomped out of the room.

"Sure, sure," Richard Ferguson said, and then broke into a wide grin.

"What a schmuck," he proclaimed for the benefit of all those who were listening.

*

What the beat reporters were protecting was their sweet little niche that made them almost as important as the anchors. They were semi-stars. People would stop them in checkout lines, would hover over their tables in restaurants.

"Oh," they would say. "I watch you on the news."

The beat reporter was guaranteed a seat on-set at least once a week, maybe more. They introduced their stories and answered a question or two from the anchor team. It gave them a chance to talk directly to the big cameras, to the audience. They had time for a friendly nod or a knowing wink. It was that precious gift of time that would make them remembered and, when pushed, they scrambled and kicked and screamed for every second of it.

"Don't I see you on television?" was the puzzled query the street reporters heard.

"I watch you all the time," was what the beat reporters heard and those people knew their names.

Oh, they knew the names of the sportscasters and the weathermen but, for most reporters, what those guys did was hardly worth the effort. How many weathermen actually got to New York or LA or even Miami? The only way to break into sports was to be some old jock twenty years away from a college bowl game, or some kid with manicured hair. Even then, you had to wait around for some old sports fart to die.

As for any new guys moving into weather, even if they wanted to, you might need some kind a degree in meteorology and about the only time you ever got out of the station was to stand outside when there was some sort of freak weather with your hair blowing and your eyes squinting. Come on, who needed that? Old ladies and middle-aged men knew the sportscasters and weathermen. Who else watched them?

The old-time weathermen and sportscasters looked at the whole business differently. They didn't think of themselves as stars, never had. Most of them were genuinely surprised that some piece of luck put them in such an easy job.

At The Best, it was John Devlin on weekday sports and Art Novak on weather, older men. Behind them, if they had been the type to sniff the air like the older reporters did, they would have smelled that coy scent of youth, cologne and hairspray.

Devlin and Novak were a dying breed, guys who had been there, who knew the game and didn't overdo the science. But, for right now, they were enjoying every surprising minute of where they found themselves.

Tom Carter wasn't worried about any sweet, sticky smell. He knew the young punks were taking over. Hell, he was hiring them. He put them right close on the necks of Devlin and Novak. He liked it, waiting and watching for that moment when the old dogs knew it was over. For their backups, he hired pampered models of men. He got the ones with the glittering black eyes and white teeth. Slightly seedy in the newsroom with their looks of used car salesmen, they somehow fit the camera perfectly at night. They had no aspirations for anchoring or even reporting. They had it made, a little smile, a little tooth glitter, and the bucks rolled in.

Youth couldn't carry the evening anchor slot. Only Carter could do that and he knew it would be at least ten years before anyone would even dare suggest they find a backup for him. Carter also knew that when the time came he'd pick the man. He'd find him out there in Fresno or Bakersfield and he'd watch as the balding, aging reporter boys in his newsroom died a little each day, knowing if he ever left his seat they wouldn't be the one to sit in it.

He earned seventy-three thousand a year plus a brand new Chrysler, top of the line, every two years. He read one newspaper a day, starting with the sports section and working his way quickly through the rest of the paper. He subscribed to one magazine, *Sports Illustrated*. He did check the wires twice a day and he kept in touch with the men who ran the city from their downtown clubs and restaurants.

He never watched a television documentary from start to finish. He did not watch public television. He went to no art or charity event unless it was to be in a front table seat with the men who ran the state. He did not own a tuxedo. He dressed down. He was, after all, a humble man, a man of the audience, a mean, racist, sexist, son-of-a-bitch man of the people. And, thought the salivating male reporters, if that son of a bitch could do it, so could they.

"Hell, he doesn't even know where to wipe his ass," Jack Benton shook his head.

"They love him. They sure love him," said Richard Ferguson. "Damn."

It was Tom Carter who coined the phrase *The Best in the West*. By that he meant his station first, his news team second, and himself a humble third.

*

On her first story for The Best, the construction foreman asked her, "What do you think of television people?"

Debbie Hanson smiled, slowly winding the mike cord in the prescribed manner, from hand to elbow and over again in neat gray circles.

"They're great," she said.

"I don't know," he said wiping the sweat off his forehead. "I once was at this party with a bunch of TV people and they all acted like they thought they were real important, you know? Like they were better than everybody else." He hesitated.

"I mean …"

"I know," she smiled, her blue eyes pained in the sun. "I guess we can be like that. But, we're really like everyone else."

SEGMENT ONE

"A major fire in our valley tonight," Tom Carter told them. "Jack Benton is live at the scene with that story. Jack?"

Behind Tom Carter and Jean Ann, Jack Benton appeared on a large screen. Behind him were flashes of red lights and the movement of passing figures.

"That's right, Tom, Jean Ann. I am standing here at what's left of the Allied Tire Warehouse."

With a punch of a button, he was full screen and Jean Ann and Tom Carter were gone. As he spoke, the words *Allied Tire Warehouse* materialized beneath him. Beneath them was an address.

"The fire broke out at about three o'clock this afternoon and may have been the largest and smokiest fire in this city in many years."

Then, he too disappeared but his voice continued as the tape shot that afternoon rolled. The fire at the Allied Tire Warehouse at Desert Way Industrial Park was dead but on tape it burned bright.

Jean Ann searched her script. Wasn't there a question she was supposed to ask? What was it? She bit her lower lip. Didn't she write it down here somewhere? Arson, that was it. She was supposed to ask it if was arson.

She had to ask the question the right way. There had to be that note of care and interest, like she didn't know the answer. Well, she didn't know the answer but she could guess. Why else would they tell her to ask the question? The producer always gave them the questions to ask. It was safer that way.

4

Ellen liked Debbie Hanson right from that first day. She liked the tallness of her, the innocence, the laughter. Right from the first day in her flower-print dress with the bared arms, Debbie had been fine. The blue eyes, cornflower blue, Ellen imagined, were wide with excitement and, Ellen thought, a touch of fear.

"You came here because it was cold or wet or something back there and this is the flagship of the network and ...," she teased.

Debbie laughed.

"I wanted the job," she said. "I love reporting. You search for the truth. It's what I want to do."

"Really?" Ellen asked.

"Yes," said Debbie. "And, gosh, it's hot here."

"This is nothing," Ellen told her. "Full-time reporter?"

"Yes, and they said I might get some weekend anchor work."

"Yeah?" Ellen searched Debbie's face for the hidden gloating or greed that usually came with that promise. She didn't see either.

"That's what they tell everyone," she said. "They tell everybody they might be able to anchor."

That wasn't completely true. They hadn't told her that. They didn't need to. She was a street reporter and, as she told Carter, a good one. She came to The Best because it had all gone to hell in New Mexico. By the end of her first day at the station, she had the feeling she had probably made one of the biggest mistakes of her life.

That was over a year ago. Now she felt that it really didn't make much difference. Here, there, it was all the same, for now.

"Same people, different faces," she'd tell the others in the newsroom.

A couple of things shot worry through her that first day. There was Jim Brown, a big man with a soft belly and a sweet smile but whose words did not seem to match what she saw in his face. There was the harried George Harding who had no time for anything but a quick upward glance at her before reaching for the phone. There was Jack Benton asking her for a date.

"Good party Saturday night. How about going with me?"

"Aren't you married?"

Carter told her about his preference for married male reporters.

"Yeah. So what?"

"I don't go to parties with married men."

"What are you, a prude?" He laughed. "Hey, Ferguson, we got ourselves a prude."

Great start. A few minutes later, the photographer with the baseball cap and the sloppy wet unlit cigar yelled at her.

"You don't drive my fucking van," he shouted when she asked him if the photographers usually drove. In Albuquerque the reporters sometimes did the driving.

"Well, I didn't mean …," she stumbled to explain.

"Nobody drives my fucking van but me. You got that?"

"The last thing I want to do is drive your fucking van," is what she should have said. Instead, she said nothing.

"What's wrong with your voice?" Carter demanded after her first story hit the air. "I didn't hear that thing before."

"What thing?"

"You talk through your goddamn nose. You talk like this," he twanged in a high nasal imitation.

"I don't think so."

"Yes, you do, missy."

"Well?" She was at a loss.

"Sounds like shit." He stomped away.

She was Brown's choice, not his. He got to another Brown choice early on as well. Two years ago a strawberry blond from Des Moines had somehow been hired for reporting and that possible weekend anchor slot.

"What's wrong with your nose? It's a real beak, isn't it," he laughed at her.

She swallowed hard. She was twenty-six. She needed this job, that's what the agent said. If she paid her dues at The Best she had a chance at the top markets. She needed that weekend anchoring.

"You ain't going nowhere with that beak, missy."

After one year, she took her vacation days and had the job done. The nose came back shorter, thinner.

"You're not good enough, not good enough for The Best," Carter told her after her one fill-in at the anchor desk.

"Maybe you could anchor in a smaller market," he told her. "But, not here."

Jim Brown cocked his head and clicked his tongue in sympathy when she finally asked to be taken off weekend reporting.

"I'd like to at least have my Sundays free," she told him.

"No can do right now," he said.

"But that's not fair. I've been on weekends for more than a year."

"I know, I know, but that's the way it has to be right now."

She resigned and went to a station in South Carolina, somewhere around the ninety-fifth market. Carter smirked over that. He was right all along. Shouldn't have been hired in the first place.

Ellen Peters didn't change anything. The voice stayed the same, sharp, nasal and, often, loud.

"So, why did you come here?" Debbie returned the question.

"Needed a job," Ellen said.

"How long have you been here?"

"For fucking ever."

The newsroom began to fill with reporters and photographers.

Monday noon marked the time for the weekly staff meeting. Debbie would be introduced as Ellen had been, as they all had been.

"Grab anything. They are all terrible," Ellen said of the pile of plastic-wrapped sandwiches from a downtown cafeteria.

"No such thing as a free lunch," she muttered.

Jim Brown walked to the center of the room. He hitched up his pants and smiled, including all of them in his good mood.

"We'll try to make this short. I want us to take a look at a few tapes from last week and I have a few announcements to make.

"But first, Tom, you have a few things you want to talk about. Right?"

"Yes, I do," said Carter who moved next to him. "We've got a real problem here and I want it corrected and I mean now."

Most of those in the newsroom came to quick attention. The row of photographers standing near the back door folded their arms across their chests in unison.

"Now, I want to know what the hell is going on here at night," Carter demanded. "I want to know and I want it stopped."

No one made a sound. Each person wondered what it was they had done to bring this on. Slowly, the glances were passed, from reporter to reporter, producer to producer.

What went on at night was reporters and photographers copying tapes to send out to other stations. It was silent, furtive work, looking for another job, pirating their own work in order to get one.

"I want to know," Carter gritted his teeth, "who the hell has been playing around and leaving spots on the sofas and chairs around this place."

Heads shot up. More wide-eyed looks were exchanged with exaggerated shrugs and grimaces.

"I know something is going on here at night. I know it. And, I want to know who the hell it is who thinks he or she can come down here for a little fun and games at night." He turned quickly, including all of them in his glare.

Ellen looked across the room to Chuck Farrell who was pulled down low behind the chest-high partition of the producers' area. All she could see of him was his tousled red hair and his brown eyes as they peeked over the cloth-covered panel. Suddenly one eye winked at her and she knew she was going to burst out laughing.

"You think it's funny, missy?" Carter swung on her.

She shook her head, holding back the smile.

Jim Brown slowly munched at his sandwich.

"I want it stopped and I am going to make sure it is," Carter said. "I am having these chairs and couches taken out."

"Ah, Tom," Richard Ferguson moaned. "It's the only place we have to sit around and eat lunch."

"I don't give a damn about your lunches, buddy. I am not going to have that filth going on in here."

Richard Ferguson put up a hand as though to hold back the words. It didn't really matter to him one way or another.

"Turn those goddamn things off," Carter yelled as the charter and squawks of the police and fire scanners broke through his audio time. "I can't hear myself think."

"So, what else is new?" came Charles Adkins's stage whisper.

"Ah, Tom," George Harding looked up from his desk, "the problem is if we turn them off we miss the stories."

"What we need is a dispatcher," a voice came out of the photographers' row.

"We aren't going to have any goddamn dispatcher," Carter spat out.

"And that's why we miss the stories," another voice called out from the line of men.

"What Tom means," Jim Brown cut in smoothly, "is that the people Back East don't think we need that right now. After all," he smiled, "we never miss the big stories."

"And there's something else," Carter jumped on the silence Brown's statement created. "About these flash flood warnings or alerts. What the hell are they, Art?"

Art Novak took a step forward.

"Flash flood warnings, Tom. That's different from flash flood watches," he said happily.

"Don't tell me. Tell them," Carter ordered.

"Well, you see we live in a desert and with heavy rain desert areas are prone to flash floods."

"They know that," Carter snapped. "What about the warnings?"

"So," Art Novak continued without losing his smile, "the National Weather Bureau sends out a watch when this sort of thing could happen. It comes across the wire and we are supposed to get the message to the audience."

"Which we didn't do on Saturday," Carter said with a sneer. "If you recall."

Weekend producer Nancy Patterson flinched.

"You've got to get that on the air," Jim Brown added.

"It's a regulation or something," Carter said.

"What do we do, Tom?" Chuck shouted from behind his eye-high wall. "Do we interrupt programming or run a crawl or what?"

"You get it on the air," Carter yelled.

"What you do, Chuck," Jim Brown's voice soothed, "is run a crawl as soon as you can. When you get a chance, you can cut some audio, but that's not the real problem, is it?" He nodded to the weatherman. "The problem is the flash flood warning."

"You bet your ass," Carter cut it. "On Saturday we had a flash flood warning and everybody else had it on the air before we did. If you see that thing come across the wire you break your ass to get it on."

Nancy Patterson stared at the floor. She had already heard the speech.

"That has to go on the air almost immediately after we get it," Jim Brown continued as though he had not been interrupted.

Ellen watched the faces around her for signs of her own boredom. Once again, she caught Chuck's wink.

He called out, "So, what you mean, Tom, is that we get it on as a crawl and then, as soon as we can, we interrupt programming with somebody on-set with the info?"

"That's what I mean," Carter said. "And you sure as hell do it fast. I don't want the goddamn FCC crawling down my neck on this one. We're talking about saving lives here, boy, lives."

He paused for the effect and smiled the smile the viewers so loved.

"A few minutes could mean somebody's life. We could and should be saving lives. That's our job. Right, Jim?"

Jim Brown nodded.

"What if there is a commercial on, Tom?" came Chuck's happy voice. "Should we interrupt a commercial, Tom?"

"Well…well…," Carter hesitated. He didn't know the answer. "No," he said firmly. "We don't interrupt a commercial. I mean, a minute or two isn't going to make that much different. Right, Jim?"

Ellen sighed and stared across the room. Beside her Debbie stiffened. Day One.

5

"I was in Albuquerque before this and before that I was in Jacksonville, Florida," Ellen told Debbie that night over drinks at a bar near the station. "I also spent a year in Paris after college which has nothing to do with anything," she added with a laugh.

"Wow, I would love to go to Paris, to Europe, anywhere," Debbie said.

"It was a good time," Ellen said. "Learned some French, among other things."

"The farthest I've ever been beside Canada, and I was once in Alaska when I was little, but the farthest I've ever been was Baja and that's not really so far." Debbie sighed.

"Baja? Huh. Vacation?"

"Ah, no, well," Debbie stammered. "I lived down there for about six months."

It was more like two months but that now seemed a sadly short period of time, not enough for someone like Ellen.

"We went down there to see some friends," she said.

"Who we?"

"Ah," Debbie laughed nervously, "me and this guy. He was okay. Michael, his name was Michael. We went together for a couple of years."

"What happened to him?" Ellen's hazel eyes looked almost golden in the flare of the table's yellow candle.

"Oh, I don't know. I haven't heard from him in a long time. We split up after Baja. I don't know where he went."

She reached for Ellen's cigarettes.

"May I?"

"Sure."

"I haven't smoked in a while," she said and her hands trembled slightly as she lit the cigarette.

"I did hear from him for a while after I left Baja, but not much." She tried to smile. It still wasn't easy.

"I guess I really didn't want this," she said as she put out the cigarette.

"Good," commented Ellen. "They'll kill you."

"It was really interesting in Baja," Debbie continued, wanting to give this woman a bigger, better story. "We had these friends who lived there, college friends from Oregon and they were renting this house right in Ensenada. They let us have a room. You know, for a few dollars a week. It was a great vacation."

"What were they doing down there, your friends?" Ellen asked. She figured it probably had something to do with drugs but it could be anything.

"Well, Eric, that was the guy, he was sort of building this boat, a ferro-cement boat."

"A cement boat? You're kidding?" Ellen laughed.

"No, really. It's not new but a lot of people don't know about it. Ferro-cement boats last forever and Eric was building one and Michael was really interested in building one too, so he was helping out."

"What did you do while everyone was busy building boats?"

"Oh, I went to the beach and read a lot. There wasn't much else to do." She stared at her empty glass. It did sound stupid.

Ellen pulled back with an exaggerated look of surprise. "For six months?"

"Well, maybe it was more like four. Anyway, I shopped and did a lot of the cooking. Eric's girlfriend Diana was a painter. That's what she was doing down there. She was painting these Mexican kids with the big eyes. You know? A lot of people buy her paintings."

Ellen shook her head.

"This guy would come down from LA and pick up some for his gallery. After he left, we'd rent a sailboat and sail down the coast. It was wonderful." She smiled with the memory.

"She also had this loom."

The words were falling around her, happy, good words.

"It was amazing, all these strings and things and at night, when she wasn't painting, she would weave blankets."

There had really been only one blanket. Debbie watched her weave it with amazement and a sadness at her own inability to create anything.

"I guess she was sort of like a hippy," she said.

"A hippy? Why a hippy?"

"I don't know. She was free, happy, like a hippy." Debbie smiled softly.

"Huh."

"The house was great," Debbie went on. "They painted all the walls these strange colors. The living room was this deep forest green and their bedroom was lavender. It was very cool."

Maybe someday she would tell Ellen that Michael had been her creative writing teacher, that he was thirty to her eighteen when they first met and that he was divorced and the father of a boy he never saw. She could tell her that Diana and Eric had been Michael's friends, not hers. But, not tonight.

"Who was making a living?" Ellen asked. "I can understand the painter, but what about everyone else?"

Debbie lowered her gaze.

"That's what happened. We didn't know how strict the laws were about working in Mexico. Michael thought he could make money by chartering fishing boats and taking people out. He thought Eric was doing that. We found out Eric only did that a couple of times. He met some Americans at Hussong's who wanted someone who spoke English to go with them."

"What's Hussong's?"

"It's this bar that's famous for something. Some writer drank there or a movie star. A lot of Americans go there."

"What finally happened?"

"We left."

They sat in silence.

"Did he ever build the boat?" Ellen asked.

"What?"

"Did this Michael ever build his cement boat?"

"I don't know," Debbie shrugged. "I don't know."

*

Baja had been a nightmare. She still wondered why she didn't get into the van much sooner and drive back home. Two or three days and she could have been safe in the house in Eugene. If she had done that perhaps there would have been no breakdown. But, by the time she locked her hands around the steering wheel, it was too late.

"Let's not worry about money or time or anything," Michael said as they drove to Baja. "Let's have a good time in old Mexico."

She agreed. A good time in old Mexico.

"A few months," he said. "Relax, sit on the beach."

"And help Eric build the boat," she reminded him.

"God," he said to Eric when they first walked along the murky bay, "what a life. Buy a boat, take the tourists out, that's what I want to do."

They met the Captain and his blond lady that first night.

"Dope," Eric whispered. "Watch what you say."

They sat on the deck of the Captain's trawler as the Mexican crew worked around them and they all, except for the crew, smoked marijuana.

The Captain and Eric and Michael sat together, rolling joints and laughing as they smoked. Michael told her that you had to trust a guy after he shared his dope and smoked with you. That's the way it was in the Sixties.

Diana painted in the mornings, Eric and Michael stayed out of the house, and Debbie read and waited for the night. In the evenings they would drink rum-and-Cokes and eat the dinner Debbie prepared. Sometimes the men smoked marijuana and chose cookies and candy over her salads and casseroles.

They would sit on the screened-in porch and Diana's two Siamese cats, Tuptim and Yul, would stroll around them, touching, purring, slapping at them. Eric would sometimes reach for Diana's hand as she sat drumming her long fingers on the wicker side table.

"He's fucking around," Michael told her in the dark of their bedroom. He laughed.

"He couldn't be," she argued.

"Sure as hell is. Didn't you ever wonder why he never gets very far on the boat?"

She said nothing. Eric was still working on the wooden frame.

"He's got this little Mexican chickie who goes down there every day. He's balling her eyes out." He snickered.

"Jesus, she's about fourteen."

Debbie lay in the darkness.

"So," he poked at her, "what do you think?"

She thought at that moment that she didn't love him and from that moment the thought never left her. She had been with him for two years, had followed him, sat waiting for him to come back from whatever dream he was on – forest ranger, farmer, any dream of a good, easy, close-to-the-land life. The way it should be, he said.

This trip was supposed to be the end of all that, the last vacation. That's what she told herself as they drove down the coast to Ensenada.

When the few hundred dollars they had was gone, they would begin their life.

Now, in the darkness, she knew they were in another useless dream and there would be another one after this one. And, so it began. It started with the shaking.

When she came back from the market the next day, Diana and Eric and Michael were gone, down at Hussong's or on the never to be finished boat or at the wharf with the Captain. She cooked the meal, smoked a joint, and waited for their return.

The panic began with the cockroach that reached for her from the food. Filled with disgust, she ran to the porch. She sat with her knees drawn to her chest, her arms wrapped around her legs. Even in the heat, she was cold.

She knew all she had to do was come down and she would feel better. It was only the marijuana and this shabby, empty house. She would come down and go find them and everything would be all right.

She could hear the roach scratching back in the kitchen, somewhere in the garbage, in the food. The disgust turned to fear. She was not coming down.

In the bathroom, another roach swam in the toilet, reaching for her with thin brown antennae. She gagged and vomited as the water moved around in a sluggish flush.

"Debbie," said the voice. "Debbie."

She turned to it, jerking her head.

"Debbie," came the echo.

It was her own voice. The fear was in her.

"What's the matter, Debbie?" it taunted. "What's the matter with you?"

Bad dope, angel dust dope. It would all go away soon. It would. It didn't.

By the time the others came in drunk and laughing, she was deep in the bed in the raspberry-walled room, shaking with the fear.

"Hi, baby." Michael crawled in next to her. "Why didn't you come down to Hussong's? Didn't you know we were there?"

"Please don't touch me," she cried. "Don't touch me."

"What's the matter?"

"I'm sick, really sick. I think it was the grass. Michael, I have to go to the hospital. Please." She was curled far from him.

"No, honey, it's okay," he reached for her. "What's the matter?"

"I'm scared, really scared," she whimpered.

From the tunnel of her mind, the voice called to her.

"And you don't even love him. He's all you've got and you don't even love him."

"Please, I need to go back to the border," she begged. "I need to go home."

"Honey," he put his arms around her, "I can't take you back tonight. Come on. Everything will be okay in the morning." He smelled of tequila, his voice heavy and thick.

She said nothing. It didn't matter. He wouldn't protect her, couldn't. She had no one to protect her. She wasn't coming down now, not ever. The panic had moved to terror. She would sleep and wake up like this. Yes, she would.

"Take a Valium," he said, his voice muffled by the approach of sleep. "That will help. It's some bad dope. Happens to everybody once in a while."

Oh, no, he wasn't going to take her back, not now, and tomorrow would be too late. How to keep the terror away and the voice? She didn't want the voice. Count, that was it. She would count. *One, two, three, four*. She concentrated on each number and each number that followed.

Later in the bathroom, she vomited until she was empty and the dry heaves started. At least, and she was thankful for this, she felt sane enough to be sick. It wasn't the dope. She knew that. This was the way she was going to be tomorrow and every day after and she hadn't the strength to fight it for long.

Back in bed, she began counting again. *One, two, three, four, five.* She held onto each number, not letting another thought slip in, because if she did the tunnel would open up and the voice would start.

The fear tasted like a copper penny.

"Wait until tomorrow. It'll be okay," Michael mumbled to her from his sleep. "Don't worry."

She took a second Valium and began to count again.

Over the toilet she dug her nails into the inside of her thighs. The pain felt good. It was better than listening to her mind.

Wait till tomorrow, that's what Michael said. It will be okay, he said.

It was better but not good. She could hold back the fear but she knew it was in her eyes. She was terrified they, anybody, would see it, see what she had become.

"God, sometimes I get so nervous," the Captain's blond lady said as they sat in the sun.

"I mean, I worry about him and what's going to happen to him." The bikini top barely covered the large, long breasts.

"I almost panic. I mean, jail in Mexico ain't no kick."

Diana and Debbie nodded over their rum-and-Cokes as they sat in the brown silence that came with any talk of the Captain.

Diana sighed.

"I get so tired of the smoking," she said. "I mean, who needs that much dope?"

"I know, I know," Debbie quickly agreed. "I've stopped. I mean, it is really frightening. I had a bad time a few weeks ago," she said of the experience two nights before.

The other women looked at her.

"Yes. I think it was angel dust or something," she rushed to tell them. There could be so much more if they understood.

"Bad shit," said the Captain's blond lady.

"It's all a waste of time," Diana said angrily. "I prefer a shot of booze anytime."

She and the Captain's lady raised their glasses. Debbie slowly raised hers.

After a small swallow, she tried again.

"I mean, I wouldn't want anyone to go through what I went through that night. It was terrible."

They stared at her, hands above their eyes to block the sun.

"I mean, I was frightened," she tried to explain.

The two women nodded in the sun with eyes closed.

*

"I have to go back," she told Michael. "I have to."

"Okay," he said. There was no need to argue. Whatever she wanted was fine. For her.

"Eric and Diana are talking about going down to Cabo for a while," he told her. "I thought I'd go down with them."

"Cabo? What about the boat?"

"Hell, it would be better to build it up in the States, San Diego or up by Frisco. You know?"

She knew.

"Look, I'll take you up to the border. Make sure you get over all right. We can spend a night at Rosarito. You remember, that pink hotel on the beach? You thought it looked nice."

She shrugged.

""I'll take the bus back from Tijuana and I'll be back up in a couple of months. Okay?"

Staying at the pink hotel meant an extra night but she wouldn't argue with him. She needed him to take her to the border. Once across she'd be all right but she couldn't do it alone. She would have to hold on another night.

"I knew things weren't going that well," Diana said and dabbed at the canvas. "Michael can be difficult." She squinted at the face of the Mexican doll-child.

"We're going to Cabo for a change. This place gets old," she said, never looking at Debbie. "I'm only here because it's close to Los Angeles and that asshole's gallery. The stuff sells." Her brush searched the palette for a new bright color.

"Kids, they do sell."

*

"Gonna build me that boat," Michael said as they drove up the wild coast.

"And sail away," she said.

"With you?" he questioned.

She nodded. The Valium had softened the shaking.

He smiled at her. "I'll be back up in a few months," he said and squeezed her thigh.

At the Rosarito, they drank rounds of margaritas by the pool. Near them, an American shouted and pounded on the table for his waiter who ran between the many other tables.

"Boyo, boyo!" he yelled. "Hey, get over here!" As the day went on, the voice became louder and the words more insulting.

"Bring me another one of these and hurry up. Pronto. You got that? Christ, they are stupid," he said to all the others who tried not to hear him.

He watched the women on the patio with narrowed eyes, sure of himself, his bare hair-speckled chest, the big rubbery nipples. The woman with him was young, quiet, and plain. Skinny white legs reached from below her knee-long cover-up.

The waiter ran to his shouts.

"Hey, fella, over here. No tip for you," he laughed loudly.

"They expect a big tip," he told the woman and everyone else, "for nothing."

"What a shit," Michael muttered. "That's what you are going back to. That bastard will be here all day screaming for a waiter and he won't leave a cent. You watch."

They waited until the day had moved into the evening chill. Beyond them the surf pounded the beach.

"Look, what did I tell you." He pointed to the table where the American no longer sat. No money had been left for the waiter.

He reached into his pocket and pulled out a five-dollar bill. He moved as though to put it on the table, then stopped. His eyes sought out the waiter.

"For you," he said with a sympathetic smile. "For that bastard," he motioned toward the American's table. "You understand?"

"Si, si, thank you, señor," the waiter bowed. His white shirt was stained with the drinks of the afternoon.

Debbie watched. He had to make sure, didn't he, that the waiter knew who left the tip. She turned away.

"We could get married, you know," he said to her that night in bed. "We could get married in a few months. You want to?"

She shook her head.

"Christ, Debbie, I thought that's what you wanted. Wasn't that what you've been saying for two years?"

"I guess not," she said. "I guess I really don't want to."

"Well, think about it," he said. "Think about it."

She nodded and curled into a tight ball of fear.

The next morning, as they paid the bill, the American from the day before ran through the lobby clutching his stomach. He crashed through the bathroom door and, as the dollar bills were being traded at the front desk, his moaning and retching rang out from the tiled walls and down the high-ceiling halls. It was gut-scrapping vomiting, agony. Michael smiled.

"Serves him right."

And, while she did not see their smiles, she could feel them as the Mexican workers moved quietly, passing the slammed open door of the bathroom.

*

"Did you ever apply for another job in California?" Ellen asked.

"No," said Debbie.

"I did. Almost got one, in San Diego," Ellen told her. "That is one great town, the ocean, the weather."

Debbie was remembering the day she left Ensenada, saying good-bye to Diana on the tiny porch where she dabbed at her canvas.

"The kids sell. That's what sells," she was saying to the painting.

Debbie stared across the tiny lawn of dust to the parked van. Suddenly she saw them, hundreds of tiny flowers, all colors, on thin stalks, reaching out of the dust.

"Look, look," she cried. She was filled with joy.

"What?"

"Look at all those flowers. Where did they come from?"

"I don't know," Diana said. "Isn't it unbelievable? They started coming up a few days ago."

"I never saw them," Debbie said and laughed.

Diana smiled at her and at her painting.

"Read it," Chuck Farrell ordered. "Read it out loud."

Tears filled her large brown eyes.

"Read it, Maria," he demanded.

"A body was found on the Gila Indian Reservation last night. According to a spokesperson for the Department of Public Safety, the body found near the reservation was that of a male Caucasian, approximately ..."

"Stop, stop there," he ordered. "What does that mean?"

"What?" She turned the large eyes to him.

He grabbed the script page.

"First you say the body was found on the reservation and then you say it was found near it. Which one is it?"

"I don't know," she cried. "I took it off the wires. That's what it said."

Chuck exhaled in loud exasperation.

"Look, Maria, sometimes the wires are wrong. You have to read them first. But, anyway, this doesn't make any sense."

"Why?" She was moving into a hurt pout. "That's what they said. First it said the body was found on the reservation, then later they said it was found near it. What's the problem?"

"What's the problem? It doesn't make any sense, Maria," he yelled. "It has to be one or the other. You have to read these things out loud to see if they make sense. I keep telling you that. Read them out loud. And, if it doesn't make sense you are going to have to make some calls and find out what it should say."

"Okay, okay," she sniffed, "if that's what you want."

"It isn't what I want," he said through a clenched jaw. "It is what is right. Don't you understand that?"

Debbie and Ellen leaned out of their cubicles and looked at each other.

"Doesn't matter," Ellen said in a low voice. "Somebody will soon be writing all her stuff. She'll read it and make a hundred thousand a year in LA. You watch."

"She is beautiful," Debbie said of the olive-skinned woman with the big eyes and the silky black hair.

"Yeah, as she's got the right name too."

Each of the stations in town had their Hispanic or two and each had their blacks, fewer blacks than Hispanics.

"So does Tommy Rodriguez," Debbie said of the evening and weekend reporter. "Have the right name, if that's what you mean."

Ellen laughed. "That's not his real name."

"You're kidding?"

"Nope. I asked him once where he got the Rodriguez, who in the family. He said he didn't know, something about his grandmother or someone. Come on. He doesn't know?"

Debbie giggled.

"He's from New York, right? So, I said, 'Are you Puerto Rican?' and he said no, he didn't think so. Do you believe it?" She laughed again.

"Of course, he made it up. I knew that from the beginning. I asked Sandi in Accounting and she said he had a different name on his Social Security, some Anglo name. He's about as Hispanic as I am. It's easier to get a job as Tommy Rodriguez, that's all."

"Did you ever think about changing your name?" Debbie asked.

"No. I think I'd feel different with another name. Names make people. Think of all the Bruces you've ever known or the, um, Berthas." She rolled her eyes. "All alike, huh? Names make you who you are, the way you are. I believe that."

"What's Jean Ann's real name?" Debbie asked.

"Cracker Sue," Ellen said and laughed.

*

Debbie easily slipped into the talk and the work of the newsroom. She was on five days a week with one stretching into the night. No weekends but that could come. There were never any guarantees about what you might have to do for the good of The Best.

The first few weeks she got none of the run-and-gun stores, the spot news, the accidents, shootings, fires. It was slow, the end of the tourist season, not too hot yet, and the floods had passed them by this year. She had a month or so of city council meetings, county supervisors, new programs at the university. Standard, everyday, everyman's newsroom kind of stories.

"I like it here," she told anyone listening. "I really do."

"Sure you do," seemed to be the unspoken response.

She filled her small apartment with all she had carried, hauled, and shipped from Bakersfield and from the house in Oregon. That made the apartment sidestepping crowded. Still, she moved easily through the rooms, touching at her things as she did so. The apartment and all within it seemed a part of her, an invisible cape that swirled around her.

Someone once told her she was a homebody, a nester. She was also a good basic cook. It was the way she first opened herself to them, the others in the newsroom. Although shy, she pushed herself to say, "I am making some spaghetti tonight if anybody wants to take a chance."

"Sure," came the answer. Why the hell not.

She offered a free meal and they didn't get many of those. Free meals came with a story attached, some luncheon or breakfast. Why not stop by the new reporter's place? You didn't have to pay with work. Some of them thought that way.

Debbie's, "I'll have lots, so come by," may have sounded like a casual invitation but it wasn't. She worried about whether or not they would come. They might dislike her just for asking. She was nobody, the new girl. They didn't need her.

At first, the few who did come acted embarrassed if alone, or boisterous if with others.

"Here for a free meal," they would yell and push past her. "Nice place. When do we eat?"

Those were the married men. They came at least once. Both Jack Benton and Frank Kowalski shared the unspoken feeling that there might be something going on over at the new reporter's place. They weren't exactly sure what but they both had the feeling that whatever it was, they should know about it.

"Fresh meat," is what Benton said when Debbie first walked into the newsroom."Right off the farm," said Ferguson.

All they saw at her apartment was a blushing serving of lasagna and a few glasses of jug wine. It was dumb, too dumb and too tame to go back.

The unmarried photographers felt better about it, the ones who went. They made it a few times. Steve Kramer stopped by when he was drunk or needed someone to drink with him. He was forty-five but, as hung over and miserable as he might be every morning, he could still out-hump all of them. No amount of drinking could blur that fine eye he had for a story. He told Debbie about his third story theory.

"See, first you get the story you see as a reporter. Then the photographer brings back the story he's seen through his camera. You put them together and sometimes you end up with this third story, something neither of you saw. You may never see it but the people watching do." He sighed.

"It's really wild when that happens. Ask Ellen," he said and reached for his drink. "She knows."

The young editor Mark Cunningham also tapped on her door.

"Hey, hi, do you mind? I mean, you said anyone could come."

He wasn't sure he was allowed to be there. He had only been at the station for a few months and he seldom left the editing room. He was hoping he'd get a chance to shoot, maybe with Debbie. She was nice to him. She was nice to everybody.

Paige Allen came. She lived in the same massive complex of balconies and pools and bending palms. Kim Palmeri and Maria Lopez also became regulars of a sort.

The one person Debbie wanted to see never came. After the first few tries of asking Ellen to drop by, Debbie stopped. Ellen filled the newsroom with laughter and excitement and a good static, loud and demanding, but the camaraderie ended when the newscast did or after a few drinks at the nearby bar. With Ellen, there seemed to be a strict, almost frightening sense of privacy.

"I keep my own weekends," Ellen told her.

By the second month, some of The Best made it a habit to go to Debbie's for dinner on Sunday night. Even the television critic from the afternoon paper gave her a call followed by a knock on her door, often with a date standing behind him.

"I don't watch much television," he told one Sunday night group in Debbie's living room. "I mean, not really."

He knocked his pipe on the side of the ashtray.

"I was in radio, you know."

*

Besides filling the apartment with herself and a few people from the station, Debbie managed to create a garden on the tiny patio with its thin strip of dirt bordering the concrete slab.

"Tomatoes," she told Paige Allen one bright Saturday afternoon in

May. "I can grow tomatoes in this corner."

"You can't grow many."

"Sure, I can. In the summer, I can." Debbie stood on the patio holding a trowel and surveying her patch of land.

"I like tomatoes," Paige said.

"And here I can put in some carrots or strawberries," Debbie continued.

Paige smiled and dimpled. Those dimples would take her to a weekend anchoring job somewhere in the Midwest. Those same dimples would keep her out of the top ten markets.

Debbie already had the plants, more than she would ever need. Perhaps she should buy pots and fill them with the plants and give them away, little presents. She knelt down and began turning the hard soil with the green-handled trowel.

"I could give you a couple," she said to Paige. "Some little plants." She smiled.

Paige smiled back. "I don't think so, but you could give me a couple of tomatoes when they get big."

"Okay, but, you might like a plant," she tried again.

"I've got a date tonight," Paige responded, looking at her nails. They were perfect and painted a soft gold color.

SEGMENT TWO

"There's a new plan to bring help to the homeless in our valley. It was introduced at a press conference this afternoon."

Carter's voice was clipped, to the point. This afternoon. Period. Pause.

Jean Ann watched him and, as her camera jockeyed for position, looked down at her script.

"Reporter Frank Kowalski was there," Carter continued, "and has this story for us." The tape was on.

She licked her lips. She would need the spit gloss for the next intro. She waited for the story to end and hers to begin.

7

"You know what I'd like to do?" Debbie looked up from the memo. "I'd like to do stories on Indians."

"Indians," she said again. "You know. I think they are really interesting people."

"What's that?" Ellen asked with a nod to the paper Debbie held.

"The memo about beats, what beats we want. It's not beats though, areas of interest is what it says. What are you going to put down?"

"Nothing. It doesn't do any good. You only end up going out and doing what George says."

"Well, I'd like to do Indians."

Ellen shrugged. The less they knew about what she wanted to do, the better off she was.

George Harding sat at his desk, one shoulder hooked to the phone, one hand reaching for a second phone. His job was simple, feed the news animal, feed it three times a day, twice a day on weekends. Find the stories and the people to cover them. Work twelve to fifteen hours a day, be on twenty-four hour call.

Have fire and police scanners set up in your bedroom so you can be making assignments at four o'clock in the morning for reporters who refused to answer their phones. Be the most hated man in the newsroom and the most pitied. Make thirty thousand a year and hear the word fuck in almost every sentence spoken to you. Be the first one there in the morning, the last one to leave at night and someone somewhere will have the feeling that what you do is interesting.

He had no idea why he did it. He hadn't the time to think of one. He had never been a reporter or a photographer. That was one of the things the newsroom disliked most about him.

"He's got no fucking idea what it takes to do this," photographer and reporter would whine to each other on the way to a story.

"Shit, if he ever carried a camera, he'd know this is ridiculous."

"Hell, he couldn't write a story if his life depend on it."

George Harding thought he could write a story. He had ideas about how stories could be done. He wrote suggestions on the assignment sheets. More often than not, they were met with either silence or a shout.

"What the hell is this, George?" the shout would come.

The morning paper provided his main source for the endless stream of assignments that flew on white sheets to reporters' desks. By eight-thirty, when reporters were moving into their cubicles with coffee cups and their own papers in hand, he had already cut his to shreds. He clipped the stories to the assignment sheets along with his suggestions of whom to call or, if he already made the calls, whom to interview on camera. He set the times, lined up the people, posed the questions, if he had the time.

The newspaper stories that ran on to other pages, and most of them did, were cut in strange geometrical shapes, circumventing, bordering the backs of other stories which also must be cut. That took time, the cutting. If it was impossible to save the stories with scissors, he made copies of their second page continuation and cut the copies instead.

Under his system, the evening newscasts were filled with stories at least twenty-four hours old and already fed numerous times to the public by radio news. Oh, there might be some variation, a national story made local. There might be some updating, press conferences held after the newsmakers realized television was interested.

Sometimes the news was even older, days, weeks, months old. He had a hold list that some claimed had run for years. He wanted it long, this list of stories already completed and waiting for that perfect hole in some future newscast. Bad quality video or audio, problems long ago solved or forgotten, he didn't care. Any story worked when you had a space to fill.

Sometimes, when the panic high to get more stories didn't override everything else, he could feel the satisfaction that another newscast had been filled. It was a satisfaction not shared by others.

"Man, you don't understand," Steve Kramer told him. "It's only time. It'll get filled no matter how many stories you pump out. It'll get filled somehow. It has to."

No, he didn't understand that, not at all. He wanted more than enough stores. He wanted too many stories because too many was never enough.

"Debbie, what have I got you on?" he called out.

"That abortion thing and something about mentally retarded people getting married."

"Interesting combination, George," Ellen's voice reached over the cubicles.

He smiled to himself.

8

"She hears voices."

That is how her father first brought her into his office. He held this big girl by the hand and, as though presenting his daughter at the altar, handed her over to him.

He saw how the man took stock of him, head to toe, how he judged and hoped all in that one look.

"I really don't know what's going on," he said. "I hope you can help. Doctor Cohen told me you were the man to call."

Cohen made his own call. "Known the girl since she was a baby. Hanson is a good man, a good friend. She says she needs a doctor. From what he tells me, I think she's right."

*

Debbie stopped only once in her drive from the border and that was to fall onto a motel bed in a room frozen with air conditioning. Six hours later she was back in her van and counting hard. She could almost reach one hundred and seventy before losing track of the count. The fear would fill in the void and the voice would begin again.

"You didn't even love him and now there is no one," she called to herself from the end of the tunnel.

"And I didn't go away, did I? I'll never go away, never," the voice promised.

Her father was not home when she finally reached the house. She didn't bother to unload the few things from the van. She took a bath and began to cook an evening meal.

"I'm glad you're back," he said after his first surprised hug.

"Michael stayed down there," she told him.

He said nothing. He had not seen her for six months and that visit lasted only a few days.

"You're a little too close to your father," Michael told her. "Try breaking away for a while, be on your own."

"Are you okay?" her father asked.

"Yes, Dad. Why?"

"You look a little drawn or something." His blue eyes searched shyly for hers.

"I think I need a doctor, Dad. I think I need a doctor bad. Hey," she tried to laugh, "it rhymes. Dad, bad."

The tears poured from her eyes.

*

"I really don't hear voices. It is my voice I hear," she told him after the father left her with the assurance that he would be back for her.

"It's like talking to myself. You know?"

"What are you saying to yourself?"

"I don't know." She shook her head. "That I don't love Michael, I guess. He's the man I was living with and we went to Baja. I left him there and came home."

"Is that when this voice started, after you left him?"

"No, before, a little before."

"And what did it say?"

"That I didn't love him."

"Is that what frightened you, that you didn't love him?"

She nodded.

"Why?"

"Because," she said as her eyes filled and her mouth crumbled, "because I don't love anybody else. And," she raised her brimming eyes to his, "nobody loves me."

"What about your father, Debbie? Doesn't he love you?'

"Yes," she said, "but he has to, doesn't he? And something else."

"What is that?'

"Sometimes I don't know who I am."

He leaned toward her, hands clasped together.

"What do you mean?"

"I mean," she licked her lips, "I know who I am, my name and where I live and all that. But, I don't know what else I am. Does that sound crazy?"

"No, Debbie," he leaned back again. "It sounds like something we can talk about, but it doesn't sound crazy."

"Good," she said, her face relaxing. "I don't want to be crazy."

She tried to smile and he realized how pretty she was.

*

She was different from so many of the others he saw, the middle-aged women with their flustering and endless words that said only, "What do I do now that I am worthless, now that the children are gone, now that my husband has gotten young and hard and plays tennis?"

She was different from the girls the parents sent, not understating the glib mouths and mean eyes, the dope and the drinking. Those girls were filled with disdain toward the parents who sent them. Well placed, he often thought.

When he sat trying to concentrate on the women who came with their frightened faces and the men considering face lifts and the children who laughed at him and almost everyone else, he often thought about Debbie and when she would be back sitting in the chair across from him.

"I want the fear to go away," she told him each visit. "I want it to go away and not come back."

"It will," he promised.

"When?"

"When you no longer need it."

The next question came slowly, after thought.

"Why do I need it?"

"I think it's a way of warning yourself, of telling yourself what you're doing is wrong for you and you need to change or move away from it. It's like your instinct talking and when you don't listen, it starts yelling."

She watched him.

"It could be that you needed to come home and this was the only way you would let yourself. Is that possible?"

Her eyes were wide on his.

"When will the fear go away?" That was the answer she wanted, the only answer.

It took her three months to find a job, the beginning of the self-worth he wanted for her. He watched as she faced the rejection from the jobs she didn't get and as she exercised the instinct against the jobs that were not right for her. Finally, she made the connection, at a radio station and everything seemed to change.

"It's great," she laughed with excitement. "Really great. I guess it's something I wanted to do, this news, you know?"

He nodded.

"I mean, I can write. I love to write. I did in college and they said I might get a chance at the station, to write news. That's something, isn't it?"

"It's more than something," he told her.

"I know I'll only be typing for them and answering phones but I could get a chance to do other things, you know? Couldn't I?"

"Of course. Why not? And you really like this news idea?"

"Yes, I do," she said, sitting straight up. It's honest, that's what it is. All you're supposed to do is find the truth and report it. That's what the news is, the truth. It's the only place you get paid for telling the truth."

She fell back in the chair.

"Gosh, I am happy." She laughed.

"I didn't know you liked to write, Debbie. You've never said anything about it. Do you write a lot?"

"Not now, but I worked on my high school paper and on the college paper my first year. The second year I didn't and then I left. With Michael."

She picked up the tiny blue glass bird on the table next to the chair. It was something she did every session.

"I like this bird," she said.

"Tell me more about the writing."

"Oh, it's not so much. I wrote some short stories and poems. I think you have to be real sad to write poems."

He nodded. "Ever try to get your poems or the stories published?"

"No." She put the bird back on the table.

"Why not?"

"They aren't very good."

"How do you know?"

"I know," she sighed. The sadness was back. "I know."

Finding a job was the task he set for her. Finding out what led her to a psychotic episode was the one he set for himself.

*

"Tell me about your mother. What do you remember about her?"

"I don't remember too much. I was only five when she died. I do remember lots of people in the house and Dad hugging me. That's all, really."

Her mother died on her way to the grocery store, hit at a stoplight. The death seemed to have been handled as well as it could be. There had been housekeepers, not too many over the years, to care for the girl when her father was at work. He was a lawyer and able to come home almost every day for lunch. Later, when he became a judge, he still made time for his daughter.

"She is better." It was almost a question asked by the tall man with the tired blue eyes who made a few of his own visits to the office.

"Is she much like her mother?"

Kurt Hanson smiled, apparently without fear or suspicion of what the question might mean or what the answer could expose.

"No. Her mother was out-going, gregarious. She had something going on all the time." He smiled with the memory.

"Debbie was a happy child, but she was different from her mother, not that same exuberance, passion." He paused.

"I think she's more like me," he said. "We're both rather low-keyed." He covered the glass bird with one hand.

"My feeling is that this thing, this thing going on now, started with that man."

"Michael?"

"Yes. He was too damn old for her. Not a bad fellow. I didn't dislike him. I didn't know him. I did know he wasn't right for her. My God, he was more my contemporary than hers." He shook his head.

"I talked to her about it, about the age difference. She didn't have much experience with men or boys and I was worried about her. Then she drops out of school and takes off with him. He was her adviser or teacher, maybe both. I'm not quite sure but it wasn't right. I know that. He was in a position of authority."

The doctor gave a non-committal nod.

"He was going to be a lumberjack or fisherman. That type, you know. In the end, never doing much of anything. I am surprised he was able to teach, if that's what he did. I got to the point where I stopped talking to her about it, about him. But, she knew how I felt.

"It isn't easy," the tall man concluded, "raising a child without a mother. Never is, I would suppose."

*

"Do you think of her often?"

"No," she said and bit at her lower lip.

"Does that make you sad?"

"Yes." She reached for the box of tissues.

"Tell me."

"She was so wonderful. She was little and beautiful. I look like my Dad, big like him."

He chuckled.

"I have this picture of her when she was about my age now and she is smiling or laughing, I guess. Laughing. You can see how happy she was. Gosh," she cried and put the tissue over her eyes. "Gosh, that is sad."

"What?" he asked softly.

"She was so happy."

"And she died," he finished for her.

"Yup. And she died," she said and loudly blew her nose.

*

He wasn't sure he should get her back to the fear that brought her to him. It was anxiety, panic beyond it, the dope, the highs, the strange place with nothing to do and being with this man who apparently planned to do nothing. No sense of safety. Anxiety finally pushed to terror.

Still, she had been strong and rational enough to get out and to ask for help. And, the job was definitely making a difference.

"I think I really can do it," she told him.

She told the station manager the same thing when the call came in and the reporter was out.

"I can do it. Let me go," she begged.

She brought back a story, one short throwaway story but she put it together and it aired. Management now had a fill-in reporter for the price of an office girl who retyped the wire copy for the morning man, answered the phones, and did the filing.

"I love it," she told him.

"It seems like the type of work where you could go far, if you wanted to," he told her.

Why wouldn't she go far? Most of the reporters he saw on the evening news didn't have the brightness, the glow of this girl.

"What about television?" he asked. "I would think there is a lot of opportunity there."

"Oh gosh," she blushed, "getting into television is a whole different thing. I hear them talking about it at the station. I think everybody wants to go into television, even if they don't say so."

"I think they would be interested in someone like you."

She gave a small nod.

"Maybe," she said. "I don't know if I'm good enough."

The voices or that voice that called to her from the end of her tunnel was gone. She told him that, gone.

*

"Are you ever afraid anymore?"

"No voice," she said.

"I know, but the fear, the counting?"

"No. Sometimes I'm scared but not like before. It stopped when I started coming here."

"Do you know why?"

"Why it stopped?"

He nodded.

"Because I was frightened and now I'm not. Everything is so much better now. I feel good about everything."

He wanted another six months with her, at least, six months without the fear and panic. They had been together less than a year.

*

"How will you feel about leaving?"

"Okay." She smiled. "I mean, I'll miss you but ..."

"But?"

"Well, you're not cheap." She laughed.

"Come on, Debbie. How will you feel?"

"I will miss you," she said. "You are my friend."

*

He did get his six months before the opening came in Bakersfield and it was television.

"It's a great place, I mean, the station," she rushed to tell him when she returned from the interview trip. "It's nice, the country. I mean, it's flat and dry but I like it, lots of farms."

Her joy radiated. The office filled with her light.

"I could rent a little house or something. It doesn't pay much but it's a start." She stopped abruptly.

"I'm glad for you," he told her. He also told the father he thought she would be fine.

"And all of that about the voices and being frightened, why did it happen?" the father asked.

"Youth, strange circumstances, no one reasonable to turn to. She left herself in a position of having no one to trust except this man and he was more of a child than she was. And, she saw that. What Debbie needs is stability, work, a plan. Most of us do. To be honest, I would like her to stay for a few more months, but she wants this job badly and I don't think it would be productive for me to suggest she put it on hold."

Oh. he would miss this tall, sweet girl with her legs long in the chair, her eyes peering up at him in confusion or laughter.

"Don't fear the fear," she sang it.

"Yes, and trust yourself and your instincts. Your instincts are good, Debbie. Use them. If something inside you says this person or this situation is not right for you, back off and take another look. Listen to that voice."

"Not the bad voice?" she asked quickly, almost too quickly.

"No, no. Just that sense of what is good for you. And start seeing people. Men too." He smiled.

"Remember," he added, "you can always call me if you need to, for a kind of a tune-up. I'm always here."

The blue eyes filled and, like a shy child, she turned her face away.

"I love you," she said. "You know that."

He felt his own sadness. "I know, Debbie. I know."

*

Her father helped her pack the van he gave her the year she left for college.

"An old van?" he had asked her. "Are you sure?"

"Like a hippy," she said. "A VW hippy van. That's what I want."

When they found the van, her hippy van, she laughed with joy as she got in the driver's seat.

"It's all I've ever wanted," she told him. "I will never want anything else ever again."

9

When the television van drove into sight, the cries went up.

"Abortion is murder! Abortion is murder!"

Six women made up the parade, one pushing a stroller while holding a sign. The baby in the stroller slept, his head rolling from side to side.

"No more abortions! No more abortions!"

Until they saw the news van, their chanting had been half-hearted, growing only when other women approached and entered the clinic.

A carefully coiffed woman broke away from the circling line.

"Hi. I'm Betty Craft, the one who called the station, and you are?"

"Debbie Hanson." She offered her hand. "We're going to get a few pictures and we'd like to talk to you on camera."

"Of course." The woman gave a pink-lipsticked smile.

Cappy, the photographer, set up his tripod on the sidewalk. New smiles and vigor swept across the women. A happy chattering broke out and the smiles broadened each time their march took them past the camera.

"How long do you plan to picket the clinic?" Debbie asked.

"As long as it takes," the woman told her. "It is murder, thousands and thousands of babies are being murdered. We have the pictures."

Debbie nodded.

The temperature was already in the high nineties. It promised to hit one hundred and three.

"You better get over there now," George Harding told her. "They're not going to be doing much marching after noon."

"There wouldn't be marching at all, George, if we weren't going to be there," Ellen commented.

"No, they've been marching for quite a while," he said. He knew that because Betty Craft called, demanding to know why no television station covered their protest.

"We are going to march until they close and we'll go to another abortion clinic and another until they are all closed or until our legislators do something about this murder," Betty Craft told Debbie Hanson.

"Keep it up, girls," she called out. "No more murder. No more murder."

They picked up the chant and the camera followed.

The interview took only a few minutes. The answers to Debbie's questions were short and complete. She and the photographer went into the clinic before the polished woman could say anything else.

"You know," said the woman in the white coat, "we don't do abortions here. They don't seem to understand. This is a family planning clinic. That's what we do. Look," she motioned to a table display of diaphragms, condoms and plastic packets of birth control pills.

"We show women how to prevent pregnancy, if that's their choice. We tell them about birth control, the different types, the benefits or problems with each."

Cappy knew the rules. He shot the diaphragm case, the pill packets and the wrapped condoms, not the unwrapped one. In the examination room, he avoided shooting the metal stirrups. They would give Carter an opportunity to made one of his jokes.

"And don't show our clients," said the woman who led them through the spotless rooms. They have a right to privacy. We guarantee them that. Although, it is almost impossible with those women out there."

"Only the back of their heads, shadows," Debbie assured her and gave a nod to Cappy which he didn't bother to acknowledge.

"The point is we don't do abortions and we're serving a poor section of the city. If our clients choose to terminate pregnancy, we direct them to other support organizations. We don't advise them. That's their choice." There was a haunted look in her eyes.

Debbie gave a reporter's nod, showing neither agreement nor judgment.

"What those women are doing out there is scaring away frightened young women, children themselves. That's our biggest problem, the teenage girls who need our help. Tens of thousands of teenage girls get pregnant every year in this country. That's the problem, not abortion. Tell them that."

It was going to be an easy piece to put together. A quote from each side, a few shots from inside and out. Debbie cut a transition stand-up in the clinic and moved back outside for the close.

"Got the marchers?" she asked Cappy.

He nodded, one eye glued to the camera. If the shot held, it would be Debbie slightly left of center screen with the marchers moving behind her.

She began practicing her stand-up as he fiddled.

"With what some view to be almost an epidemic of teen-age pregnancies this country, the people who run this clinic believe …"

"Ah, Miss?" came the voice. "Miss?"

She turned. Betty Craft stood there, a tight-lipped worried mouth having replaced the thin pink smile.

"Yes?"

"That thing, that thing you were saying about an epidemic."

"Almost an epidemic is what I said."

"Yes, well, but what does that mean?" The smile was back and it was small.

"It means a lot of young girls get pregnant who may not be able to handle it."

"So what? Does that mean abortion is okay? Is that what it means?

Because it isn't. Abortion is never okay."

"If you would let me finish," Debbie said. She was anticipating the pain of holding her eyes open in the sun's glare. There could be no squinting as she spoke to the camera, no lowering her gaze and never any sunglasses. She could feel the sweat under her arms.

Cappy waited, annoyed. It was hot and they had another story before he could break for his brown bag lunch in the photographers' room.

Debbie gave a nod, lowered her gaze and then raised her eyes painfully wide to the camera.

"Three, two, one. The people who run this clinic believe they are offering an important service for women in this community. But other women say they want this clinic closed and plan to march until it is.

"This is Debbie Hanson for ..."

Suddenly the cry went up. "Abortion is murder! Abortion is murder!"

As each woman in the short parade passed, she looked directly into the camera. Betty Craft had given the signal, a tight, clinched fist held at face level.

Cappy straightened up and gave Debbie a quick nod. Betty Craft smiled.

"Want to do another one?" Cappy asked.

Debbie shook her head. What was the use? It was the best she could do, considering the sun and Betty Craft.

"I sort of wonder something," she said to her as she wound the microphone cord.

"Yes?" It was a smile of condescension.

"Do you have any adopted children?"

Now it was a smirk.

"Why, yes, I do. Thank you for asking."

Ellen told her to ask that question. She said they all marched and shouted about abortion and murder and little baby fetuses with fingers and toes, but how many actually adopted any of the babies other people didn't want?

"Not unless," she added, "they have blond hair and blue eyes."

Debbie knew she couldn't ask Betty Craft if her baby had blond hair and blue eyes but she bet Ellen would have.

"What's next?" Cappy asked when they were back in the van.

"This doctor is teaching these mentally retarded people about sex. Or, they're getting married and he gives them this course about sex in marriage."

He stared at her.

"What the hell are we going to cover it with?" he demanded.

"I don't know." She was reading the assignment sheet. "It says it's an interview and to ask him if he knows any couple we can talk to."

"Retards?"

She nodded.

"Oh, great," he moaned. "Who thought this one up?"

She shrugged. It sounded okay back at the station.

"How the hell you gonna get releases on them?" Cappy demanded. "You can't shoot these people. You have to have a release. Man, this is impossible."

He shook his head.

"Harding is an idiot. He knows we have to have releases. He knows that."

He could already see it would be another two hours before he hit the brown bag.

A few miles away the counselor waited. He was not a doctor nor had he given George Harding that misinformation. In front of him were the teaching materials he used in his sessions with the young men and women who believed they were in love and wanted to marry. They were black and white line drawings of naked couples in sexual positions. He doubted the cameraman would use them.

He bet the reporter would ask him about his feelings about these people having children. He grimaced with the thought. Funny, what they considered news.

*

"Take Indian School all the way," Ellen told the handsome black man drving the van. "We should probably get there sometime tomorrow."

Photographer Clifford Williams gave a short laugh.

"Why do they call it Indian School?" he asked.

"It's where the Indians go to school. They used to bring them in off the reservations after we took over their land. Haven't you ever seen those pictures with all the little Indian kids dressed up like they were white?"

He shook his head.

"We wanted them to look and act white. Now they come to the school because there aren't a lot of schools on the reservations. Maybe it's a way to get away."

She wasn't surprised Debbie wanted to cover Indians. She wanted that as well back in New Mexico. She wasn't fascinated with the Indians in the city who sold their jewelry along the plaza in Old Town or in Santa Fe. She saw a sullen meanness about them that was changing, not for the better, with the look of a new merchant class, attractive young women with glasses and too fast smiles.

What fascinated her were the Indians she did not see, the ones who lived far off the freeway on the sand and hard earth that ran for hours between Grants and Window Rock.

"It's a bitch trying to do a story on Indians," she told Clifford.

"Why's that?"

"You have to get special approval for anything you want to do. It's a real pain."

She came up against it a few times in Albuquerque when she tried to cover some story on a reservation.

"We'll bring it up before the council," would be the standard response.

"Okay." She would keep her voice calm and low. "When will that be?"

"Next meeting is in a month. We'll talk about it then."

She once traveled to a council meeting, hoping to be allowed to film afterwards. They told her to wait outside. She napped in the car while her photographer sat in the meeting. They never got permission to do the story.

"Damn," Clifford swore and hit the steering wheel. "I am hot."

The van's air conditioner had been broken for two weeks but George said he couldn't spare it for a day or two of repair work. The heat from the massive engine filled the front of the van. Searing hot air blew on them from the open windows.

"You got any money?" Clifford asked.

She fumbled through her big purse stuffed with notebook, cigarettes, pens, wallet, mirror, and lipstick for the stand-up she would have to do.

"Nothing. Not a dime. I didn't get a chance to get to a bank," she said.

"I am going to die if I don't get something cold to drink. I am so fucking hot," he moaned.

She laughed. The sweat dripped down her neck.

He leaned back in the seat. "Man, I should be driving a goddamn Bekins van. My goddamn back is gone, shuckin' and jivin' this shit all over town. And we don't even have a fucking quarter for a fucking soda."

He sighed deeply and peeked over at her.

They both exploded in laughter. They still had a story to shoot west of town and an hour's drive back to the station. The sweat dripped down her back. She shook her head and turned to her window.

The first time she saw an Indian was in a grocery story in Albuquerque. She watched as the Navajo woman passed in her long black skirt, her bright blue velvet blouse and her turquoise jewelry big and heavy on her chest.

"Interesting," she commented to the cashier as she reached for her change.

The girl followed her eyes. "Yeah, well," she said between quick chews on her gum. "I grew up with them. They ain't so interesting when you know them."

She watched them, the women with their long dark skirts and their wide silver belts and rivers of necklaces. She studied the tiny serious-eyed children. At stoplights, she stared into the windows of the pickup trucks at the young male drivers with their cowboy hats decorated with a single feather. She watched but neither she nor they ever let their eyes meet, except for the children. They would stare solemnly back at her.

"Man," Clifford Williams sighed again as they continued their way west, "not one fucking quarter."

10

Back at the station, they told Debbie about the release problem. First it was Tony Santella, the weeknight producer handpicked and trained by Jim Brown.

"You get releases on a story like that or we'll all be sued from here to hell," he told her.

"You know, somebody's grandmother or uncle or something sees the story and starts saying you defamed their kid and we get sued for thousands. Brown will tell you," he nodded. "It happens."

It did happen. They knew the stories.

"That bozo Fred Painter did some story on a drooly old grandmother," Jack Benton said, "in some rest home for the criminally insane or something."

Her eyes widened.

"Nah, nah," he sneered. "It was only some nursing home, but the next thing you know this grandson of hers who hadn't seen the old lady in five hundred years is on the phone screaming that we embarrassed the family and what the hell were we going to do about it and who the hell said we could take a picture of the old babe anyhow?"

"They paid 'em off," somebody offered from another cubicle. "A couple of thousand."

"Yeah, but they think they're going to get millions," Jack Benton said. "So now they make us get a release for every moron. Hey," he shouted, "you hear that, Kowalski? That's good. For every moron and she's out doing retards. I am good," he cackled.

"You're the moron," Frank Kowalski yelled.

Chuck Farrell explained it to her.

"You see, they can't sign a release because they aren't supposed to be able to handle their own legal affairs. And, sometimes their parents can't sign a release because the state is sort of a guardian and the state won't sign because they want the kids' permission or the parents' or somebody's that we can't get because they keep telling us to get them from the state. Most of the time we get nothing so we don't do the stories. Nobody wants to do them anyway."

"What the hell am I supposed to shoot, George?" photographers would demand in front of his desk.

"Am I supposed to shoot shadows, George? How the hell are we going to do a story about shadows, George? Why the hell are we doing this story anyway, George?"

Reporters didn't want to deal with any of it. And, even the tough ones had trouble laughing their way through some of those stories. Chuck Farrell saw their faces when they came back and he listened to them.

"You know it's this program where they bring dogs into this nursing home for a few hours and all the people play with them. You know? We got some good stuff and we got releases," Frank Kowalski told him.

"But, I mean, you wonder," his voice grew hoarse, "why can't they have pets? It makes them happy. You could see that. I don't understand. They get to be with a dog for a couple of hours and then they take them away. That doesn't make any sense. Give 'em a fucking dog."

"They do it with children too," said Harold Lewis, moving into the conversation.

"What?"

"They have these programs where they bring in children like a grandma, grandpa thing. They hold them and play with them and then the kids go home."

His soft, gentle face with the black-rimmed glasses looked over the partition. "It's strange."

"I'll bet," shouted Jack Benton. "All those old guys holding all those little girls. You want to sit in my lap, girlie?" he rasped.

Chuck Farrell had to laugh. Benton would never change.

Ellen had been to her share of nursing homes. She wanted to get out fast. The patients would reach for her, grab her hand. It was as though they were begging her to get them out of those airless, horrible places.

She had seen it all. She had seen the old ladies in the gray rooms lying on white beds, already corpses, already with the nose pulled into a beak, cheeks sunken, dying.

"No one has come to see her in years," some nurse would tell her. "Isn't that terrible, and she's such a dear."

The nurse seemed to relish the story, whatever nurse it was.

Ellen told Debbie a few of the stories in the quiet of an early afternoon newsroom. She told her about the old woman who had somehow fallen into the care of the sloppy, grease-speckled woman.

"She's happy, isn't she?" the woman insisted. Her voice was brittle, the mouth mean. "She's a hundred years old."

Ellen stared at the small body that moved with shallow breaths. The heat in the tiny room was stifling. An orange sheet covered the window, turning the light of the day into a haze of shadows and dust.

"Who's going to take care of her if I don't? Who?" The woman moved to the bed. "She can't move. She can't talk. She can't do nothin' but," she bent over the body and shouted into one long, white ear, "we love her, don't we."

The body made a whimper, like a child startled in the night.

"I mean, what would happen to her without me?"

"What is going on there?" Ellen shouted to county authorities who certified nursing homes. "Is she actually getting paid for this? Is anybody checking on this place?"

"Did they check it out?" Debbie asked her.

"Probably, but I don't know. I didn't follow up on it." She sighed. "I did one story at a beautiful nursing home, a big bucks place. This nurse told me about this one old woman who got all dressed up every Christmas morning, gloves, hat, the whole bit. She would sit in the lobby and wait for her children to come. All day she would sit there. She did this on all the holidays. All dressed up."

"And they never came?" Debbie whispered. "That's so sad."

"Nope, never did."

They sat without speaking. Debbie saw a gentleness in Ellen's face.

"You're really a big softie," she said and smiled.

Ellen returned the smile. "No," she said. "I'm not." The smile was gone.

11

When she first arrived in the city, a rental agent showed her an apartment in a complex, gushing on about all the people she could meet there.

"It's incredible," she said. "They have all these pool parties and movie nights. There's lots of people you can meet, lots of things to do."

"That's not important to me," Ellen told her. "I see people all day long. I don't want to see anyone when I get home."

She rented a furnished condo, two bedrooms. She kept the second one dark, using it only once for a visit from her mother.

"You like living like this?" her mother asked, staring around the sterile rooms.

"It's okay."

"Yes, well ..."

That about described it. She did add the two artist-signed posters bought after too many glasses of free art show wine. The framing cost more than the posters. But, they pleased her. Her only concern was how much trouble it was going to be to move them when the time came, and it would.

She had nothing more than a nodding acquaintance with her neighbors. They included an older man from New York who seemed to be bleary-eyed drunk every day by noon, two homosexuals from Indiana, well-dressed and tight-assed, and a middle-aged man who appeared to have money but no job. The people living next to her spent almost all of their time traveling in an RV the size of a small house.

Some nights the clicking sound of high heels running down the concrete paths would bring her out of her bed. She would go to the window to see who ran in such a panicked steps and once caught a glimpse of a brown, red, and gold print dress as it curved out of sight around a corner of the building.

There had also been the incident with a skinny, rodent-faced renter who brought all of them out of their beds one summer night with the shouts of, "I've got a Three-Fifty-Seven in here. I've got a Three-Fifty-Seven, man, a Three-Fifty-Seven."

He screamed it at the police in their light beige uniforms. Screamed it at the tenants who stood in their doorways or behind the dark windows of their condos.

"What the fuck, man. Can't a man do what he wants to his own wife? You got a law against it or something?"

What he wanted to do and did do to his own wife was beat her up at two o'clock in the morning. When she tried to run from him, he caught her and dragged her by the hair across the grass and back into the condo.

The policemen spoke to him in whispers while he taunted them. Then, he saw her, or she thought he saw her, standing, arms crossed, in her doorway. That's when she knew that sooner or later he was going to shoot her with the Three-Fifty-Seven, man, his Three-Fifty-Seven. He disappeared soon after with his wife and, she surmised, with the gun.

For the most part, it was a quiet complex where she only had to acknowledge fellow residents with a short smile and a nod. In the winter, it was dark by the time she got home from the station. In the summer, it was too hot to go outside even at night. For over a year, she came home to sit, read, drink wine, and watch television.

She tried to explain to Paige Allen why she didn't go to parties.

"I can barely stand to work with those people. Why would I want to party with them?"

"Come on," Paige insisted. "You really should. It's a birthday party for Kim and you like Kim, don't you?"

She did like Harding's assistant. Kim was young and funny. She had none of his depression and horror-filled stare at yet one more newscast to fill.

"Okay, okay," she agreed in defeat. "I'll go."

She dressed for the night, tight jeans and a white silk blouse. She knew she looked good. She liked the strong, sexy look of her short hair. That haircut cost her a job in San Diego.

The news director called and told her that, after seeing her tape, he only had one question.

"Is you hair long or short now?" he asked.

"Short," she said. "The way it was in the prison escape story."

"It really looked good long."

"Yeah, when I first got here it was long." She waited, knowing what was coming.

"So, are you growing it?"

"It does grow," she replied.

"Well, yes." He gave a little laugh.

"Are you saying the length of my hair has something to do with the job?" she asked evenly.

"Hey, we're not talking jobs here. I was only wondering. You did look great with long hair."

There had been no second call, no offer of a free flight out for an interview. The tape came back one month later without a note. She kept her hair short.

At the party, they all turned when she came in the front door. Everyone in the room filled with sitting, standing, talking people, glanced over or up. No one missed her entrance, as silent and as uncomfortable as it was.

The new weatherman from Across the Street stood completely still, his six feet two inches giving him enough height to be seen in a perfect pose with a slight smile, his eyes looking over and beyond her. They were all like that, all the other media faces, frozen in the moment. Even their breathing stopped for the few seconds needed for the self-recognition they knew would come.

Then, snap, the movement began again as they realized she was one of them. Only the weatherman from Across the Street held his pose. He could hear the sounds of someone else coming up the front walk.

She elbowed her way to the kitchen and the jugs of cheap white wine. A few people nodded and smiled. The network reporter from New York leaned against the refrigerator. He was in town using the Best's editing equipment for a story on water use in the Southwest.

Even though he had been on story for three days, most of the footage he sent back to the network came from the station's files. He did manage to cut the necessary stand-ups while out in dry fields and along the canals. He gave her a unblinking stare.

"So, what is it you do?" he asked, his dark eyes demanding.

"Report, mainly. Some documentary work." She tried to smile and relax. "I get the mass murders, when we have them," she said and laughed, to show him she understood how he might see that, giving a woman those types of stories. "They give me the good stuff."

As she spoke, his eyes moved from her face to the other faces in the kitchen. She saw the movement, the checking out of the audience, the possibilities. Slowly, reluctantly, the eyes moved back to her.

"Yeah," he said, "but what is it you really do?"

She left.

Back in her apartment, over a glass of scotch neat, she studied the poster on the wall in front of her. It was the drawing of a tough-looking woman wearing a black top hat, a cigarette hanging out of one side of her mouth. Orbs of neon-colored lights fanned out behind her. She knew she bought it because it reminded her of herself when she was younger. The colored lights, she thought, could be the lights of a circus or a stage.

12

By August, Debbie had her Indian story. A phone call from a newsroom friend in Albuquerque gave Ellen the lead and she passed it on.

"Radioactive leak or something up on the Navajo reservation. The thing is nobody is really covering it here. It was in New Mexico, close to the Arizona border. Might be a good story if they let you do it."

"Don't you want it?"

"Hell no. I've got enough to do."

Debbie started making the calls.

"The thing is," she told Ellen, "this dam broke up by this milling operation, something they do with uranium, and all this contaminated water ran into this river. But, this is what's so interesting, the river runs into our state." Her face was flushed with excitement.

"That's your hook," Ellen told her. "Give it to George."

"I can't," George told her. "Everybody is on vacation. Maybe in September." He tried to turn away.

"September? It won't be a story then. Nobody has it yet, George. Nobody. Please. I'll set it up so we can get it in three days. Please. I'll do some interviews here. I'll do it on the weekend. Please, George."

"Three days?"

"Three days, maybe four."

"I don't have anybody to send with you," he kept trying. He couldn't afford to lose a reporter and a photographer and a van for even one day.

"Clifford said he'd go. He said he'd do it on his days off."

She wasn't going to back down on this one. This was a good story and nobody in the state had it or seemed to care about it.

"Well," the government man in Washington told her, "it would be different if somebody lived out there."

"Do you believe that?" she shouted to the newsroom. "He said it would be different if somebody lived out there. I told him they did, Navajos."

"Not the same," someone called back.

It took her three days of phone calls made in the few minutes she had between stories to find out who was monitoring the spill, who was testing the river water, and where the tests were sent. She spoke with people across the country, in Dallas, San Francisco, Santa Fe. Even if they did know something about the spill into the little river, they seemed confused by her questions.

"We've told them not to use the water from the river for drinking or washing."

"What about their sheep, their livestock?" Ellen asked Debbie.

"What about their livestock?" Debbie asked the people.

"They shouldn't drink from the river either," they told her.

"God," said Ellen, "those bastards."

*

"Man, I am glad to be getting out of town," Clifford told Debbie as they drove the long hours it took to get to the reservation.

"We are really going to have to move fast," Debbie told him. "We only have three days."

Ellen had laughed at the timetable.

"You'll be lucky if any of them show up for interviews. I mean, Indian time is different. It's a whole different animal."

Debbie passed on the warning to Clifford.

He nodded. Outside of movies, the only thing he knew about Indians was that somebody used to make them go to school in the city. He did see people he thought were Indians walking downtown, tall, thin, hawk-faced men. The women he saw were short and fat with long black hair and tight dark pants. Could be Mexicans.

"Ellen says they're good people," he told Debbie.

"Yeah," she agreed. "The Navajos were real fighters, warriors, but now they are more farmers than anything else, or they have cattle, sheep, you know."

"Still live in tents or what?" He was only half-joking.

"Never did. That was the Plains Indians. All that war bonnet stuff and teepees, that was on the prairie. Ellen was telling me that."

"Yeah? I didn't know that." He sighed with pleasure.

This is what he liked about television, being able to get out, to see the land, to meet new people. Best of all, he liked leaving George and his whiny ass behind. And, he liked Debbie. She was easy to be around.

He shifted uncomfortably in his seat. They were sure to get some looks when they checked into the motel up in Gallup. This was cracker country, the whole state. He knew that. He wondered if Debbie did.

At the motel, the only thing they cared about was that Debbie and Clifford were from a television station.

"You need some help?" the desk clerk asked him.

"Nope."

The next morning the sky was crystal blue, the land dry and brown.

"Man, it's empty," Clifford said as he drove the van down miles of dirt road.

"Yes, but isn't it beautiful," said Debbie.

"We'll have somebody out there to meet you," the tribal officials told her. They were waiting, a young woman and a boy.

They followed the woman, the small boy tagging behind Clifford.

"I will help you," he said softly. "I will carry that." He pointed to the recorder.

"Watch the dial," Clifford told him. "Tell me if it doesn't move or if that needle goes into the red. Okay?"

"Yes," promised the boy solemnly, "I will."

The woman led them down along the little river.

"We have to haul in our water from Gallup," she told Debbie. "For our water and our animals. Many can't do it. It is too expensive."

"It is bad," a shepherding Navajo told them. "It is bad, very bad," he sang.

"We sometimes wonder, you know, if anyone cares," the young woman said.

"They will after we put this story on the news," Debbie promised.

"Hmm." The woman nodded. She left the reservation years before for Albuquerque and the university, but not for lack of love of her land. The Chairman's office asked her to make the trip back to work with the television people. She understood both white man's time and white women.

"You know I think I might be frightened living here," Debbie said as they sat together by the side of the slow-moving stream.

"Why?"

"I don't know. All the radiation. All that. I might be afraid." She blushed with the words.

"It's really something," Clifford said and shook his head. He meant the land and the few people they had seen, but mostly he meant the great stretch of land and the cloudless sky with the red rocks jutting out suddenly from the brown earth and cutting jagged holes in the horizon. He'd never seen anything like it.

That night they filmed the lights of Gallup from the Santa Fe rail yard. They worked as a team, Clifford shooting while Debbie handled the tapes and monitored the audio levels on the recorder.

"Tape," Clifford would order.

"No sound. You're not getting any sound," she would caution.

Both nodded to their work.

In the morning they went to tribal headquarters. Now the softness of the people and the land was gone. Now it was business.

"You tell me if anyone cares," the man from the Chairman's office demanded. "You tell me where the authorities are. You tell me if we are going to die from cancer. Do you know? Does anyone know?"

They had what they needed, the anger at the federal government and the company that mined the uranium, the fury at the questions no one was answering. Millions of gallons of uranium-contaminated water had flowed into a river that was the lifeblood of their land and their animals and no one seemed to care.

One young Navajo flung at her, "We are last on the white man's totem pole. Always have been. Always will be."

They talked about the story during the six-hour trip back to the station. Three parts, probably, done and on the air in a few days. She drove while Clifford lay in the back surrounded by his equipment.

He was exhausted, every muscle ached, and once back at the station they had at least another hour unloading and spot-checking every tape for bad audio and poor video. Better to know now.

"I want to edit this baby," he told her. "I don't want nobody else touching this."

"I don't want anybody touching it either. It's yours and I don't want to work with anybody else putting it together," she assured him.

He felt some relief but not enough. There was no guarantee a photographer would get to edit his own work. He mentally traced his shots, the land, the red rocks. He could see them, see them the way he shot them.

"Start with the river," he said. "That's where you should start."

"How? How would you do that?"

"Open with a tight shot on the river, the one where I pull back to a wide shot. That's where you start talking about the river and the spill, during that pull back."

"Okay, okay, that's good," she agreed.

"Sure was a great kid," he said of the boy who had helped him.

"Hauled that recorder all over the place. Wouldn't let it go."

He laughed at the memory.

"The thing weighed more than he did. I finally had to tell him it was more important to carry the tapes."

She laughed and Clifford closed his eyes.

*

She took the tapes to Brown on Monday morning.

"Good work, really good," he pronounced from his seat in front of the monitor. "You've got yourself an award winner here."

She smiled. It was as good as she thought.

"Clifford did a great job," she said.

Brown nodded. On the screen, the sheep moved along the river.

"He really wants to edit this."

Brown said nothing, his eyes on the screen.

"And we can get it together in a couple of days."

He fiddled with the sound, bringing up the tinkling of the bells around the necks of the sheep.

"Okay?"

He reached out and punched the stop button on the tape deck.

"No." His lips pushed out the word. "No, I don't think so." He shook his head and turned to face her.

"I don't think that's who you want on this one," he said and stood up. He walked back to his desk.

"Yes, yes, I do," she said quickly. "I do."

"Not this one," Brown said. "No, no." He shook his head again as he sat in his chair.

"But why not?"

"He isn't good enough or fast enough."

"He is good enough."

"No, he's not, Debbie," Brown's voice was firm. "He's shot some fine things for you but, ah, I want Tim to work on this one. He's the pro," he said of the chief editor, Tim Johnson. "You'll see."

"You don't understand. This means a lot to him. It's his story too. Please," she begged. "He knows where all the shots are. He knows what he wants to do."

"Tim will do a great job." Brown smiled. "You'll see. You'll get an award on this one."

*

"But why?" Clifford demanded.

"He said he wanted Tim to do it."

"That's crazy. This is mine. I know what I shot."

"I know, Clifford. I told him that. Maybe if you talk to him?"

"Fuck that shit."

His body stiff with anger, he marched away from her and into the photographers' room where he paced and swore. The other photographers stayed away from the room. Later they could give him a pat on the back and tell him about the stories that were taken from them and edited by some idiot who knew nothing. Finally, Tim Johnson himself would search him out and tell him he was sorry and he would do the best job he could.

Even the reporters would shake their heads and tell him it was a tough break. Not that it meant anything to them, not really. It was good for some talk though, a line or two back in the cubicles or on their way to their next story. Dumb decision, they would sneer, per usual.

The only person who wouldn't be talking to Clifford was Jim Brown and Clifford wasn't going to be talking to him. He didn't like Brown, never did. He called him the Fat Boy, like the Fat Man in the *Maltese Falcon*. That's how he saw Brown, only smaller, much smaller.

"He took my fucking story," he chanted. "He took my fucking story."

Now, it hurt, the memory of the trip, the whole golden, dusty light of that day on the land and the people they met. He felt raw.

"They want Tim to edit it," Debbie told Ellen. "I don't want that but Brown says he's better than Clifford."

"Who the hell knows? He is good, though." Ellen reached for her purse and her notebook. She never fought over who edited her pieces unless it was one hell of a story and then she would insist someone like Tim Johnson did it.

"Gosh," Debbie moaned, "I wish I could do it myself."

"Tim will do a good job," Ellen said, "and sometimes it helps to have a third person on the story. He sees things you didn't see. He can make it a better story."

"Brown said it could win an award." Debbie looked at her hopefully. "You think so?"

"Indian story? You bet your ass, if Indians are in this year." She left the newsroom for her first story of the day.

13

Debbie's series hit the air the following week on the six o'clock news Tuesday, Wednesday and Thursday, again at ten, and ran again on the following day's noon newscast. Each segment was allowed to stand at a ponderous two minutes plus.

"Two-five? Where the hell am I going to put that?" Tony Santella yelled. "You have got to cut it down. Cut it or I will."

Each day brought the same threat and each day Debbie steeled herself and shook her head. She and Tim worked long hours making each piece so tight that nothing could or should be eliminated, not one shot, not one word. Each day Brown looked over the finished piece.

"Great piece," he said each day. "Good work, guys."

The pieces stood even with Tony throwing up his hands, pulling other stories from the lineup, and arguing with muffled shouts from behind the closed door of Brown's office.

Every night Clifford watched the pieces as he sat in the photographers' room. He didn't focus on them. He glanced at them.

"Goddamn, incredible shots of that old Indian man." Steve slammed into the room.

"Man, that's some nice stuff." Cappy came in with his last cup of coffee for the day. "Nice."

"You got to get that on a résumé tape," Jason Osner told him. "That'll get you out of this place."

"Did you call the network?" Debbie asked George.

He shook his head in annoyance as he tried to hear the caller promising him a good story.

"Well, could you?"

He shook his head harder.

"Darn it." She flipped through two of his Rolodexes before finding the scribbled name and number of the man who could buy her story.

"I think I might have something for you," she said on the call to New York. "It's about a radioactive spill on the Navajo reservation."

He told her to send it out.

"We'll make some extra money if they use it," she told Clifford. "We'll split it. That'll be good, right?"

He nodded.

"Johnson, too," he said.

It was a flat statement without sarcasm or self-pity. The man edited it. He deserved his piece of the action.

That night, after the last part aired, Tim Johnson stood in the doorway of the editing room, watching and waiting.

"Night, Cliff," he said as Clifford passed on his way out of the station.

"Night," Clifford echoed and left the building.

*

The nights the stories on a radioactive spill ran the front-desk operator was kept busy with phone calls from viewers. The first night fifteen people called about the slight change Jean Ann Maypin had made in her hairstyle. There were ten calls about her hair the next night. On the third night, when her hair was back to normal, twelve people called to say they were glad. Two people called to say they liked the new style and wanted to know why she had changed it back again.

14

Brown leaned over Debbie, his hand on her shoulder.

"Told you, didn't I?" he grinned. "Johnson did one heck of a job."

"Clifford would have been good too," she said.

"Not as good as Johnson," he said, giving her shoulder a final pat. He made a short tug at the top of his slackes and went into his office to sit in the high-back vinyl chair.

God, sometimes he loved it so much he almost cried. He loved this business. He loved his people, loved them. He was forty-two years old and they were like his kids.

He grew up in the station, came in right out of his second year of college. He never finished, never had to. This place was his education, his school, his home. He knew he spent more hours caring about it and how it ran than he had ever spent wondering or caring about his family. He knew his work led to the divorce but he loved it.

He loved how they came to him, like Debbie, all excited and talking a mile a minute.

"They called," she told him. "They're going to use it. They want me to cut it down, but they're going to use it. Next week, that's what they said. It will be national."

"That's wonderful, Debbie. Have you told your father?"

He knew about her father. It was his business to know about their families, the people of his people.

"I'm going to call him. It will be on next week, that's what they said."

"You deserve it," he told her.

He cared about them and they knew it. They were all so young and happy and in love with the business. They still got excited when they beat somebody else to a story. They shouted and laughed when the network gave a nod in their direction. And, when they got their first offer from a bigger market, they came to him. Sometimes the men shuffled their feet, almost embarrassed but also proud.

He knew why. Like children, they were growing up and proud of it but also worried they might be punished. They weren't. Not by him. He only wanted the best for them.

If someone in his newsroom seemed unhappy or frustrated, he'd tell them, "Hey, if you want, I'll make some calls for you." He wanted them all to be happy even if it meant helping them find another job.

Only the most frustrated and the angriest of them asked him to make those calls. That only happened a half a dozen times in as many years.

"I want you to be happy," he would tell them before they left the station. "Be happy. That's all that counts. Right, guy?" If only they could all be happy.

He believed most of them were, these kids, these great hardworking kids. He laughed when he thought about them.

Sometimes you did have to pull them up, tell them the way it was. Sometimes, like with Clifford, you had to do what was best for all of them. Clifford was a slow editor, not too much imagination. And, there was something about Clifford that made him uncomfortable. He wasn't sure why but he did have the feeling Clifford didn't like him.

Clifford was his second black photographer. The first went on to another job. They did have a black woman reporter, Cynthia Reid. She had been there two years, their only on-air black.

He liked her and he liked Clifford. He really did. He liked and cared deeply for all his people. They would fight and swear and stomp around outside his office. Some would come in, all of them at least once, and yell about things they thought were wrong. But, have an emergency, a flood, a prison break, and they would come together like a machine and he would run it all. They were his army, an army that might be sloppy or slow in peace but boy, could they come together to fight the war. That's how he saw it, a band of soldiers.

He even liked Ellen Peters. The thought brought a small smile to his face. Sure, she was mouthy and loud but she was one heck of a reporter and she was going to stay. He knew that. You had to have one pushy woman, he supposed.

He nodded thoughtfully. There was some outstanding photography in Debbie's story. He'd have to tell Clifford that and he would. Sometime in the next couple of days he would say to him, "Nice work on the Indian story, fella." If he saw him, that is, if he actually passed him in the hall.

15

He checked the clock again, resisting the urge to stand and pace his office. He was looking forward to this call.

The phone rang exactly on the hour.

"Hi," came her soft voice.

"How are you, Debbie?"

"Great. I'm great."

"That's good to hear. And, thanks for the letters. It's sounds like you are making a good life for yourself out there."

"Yes, yes, things are good," she said, her voice stronger.

"So, why did you decide you needed a session?"

"You know, like you said, for a tune-up, a check-up."

"Nothing else?"

"No, no, everything is fine," she said brightly. "There are a lot of nice people at the station and I have a nice apartment. I had this little garden too, but it was too hot to grow anything. I didn't think it was going to be so hot."

"Hotter than Bakersfield?"

"Hotter than anywhere."

He chuckled.

"It's a city," she said and he could almost see the small lifting of her shoulders.

"Is there something on your mind, something we should talk about?"

Seconds passed.

"Sometimes I don't think I'm very happy," she said finally. "It sounds stupid, I guess. And, it isn't all the time, only sometimes."

"That sounds normal, doesn't it? No one is happy all the time."

"I know. You're right, but sometimes I don't know how much I like television, the job, the whole idea of it." There was a slight tremble in her voice.

"I mean, it's good most of the time and I like the people I work with but, well, I don't think it's all that great. It sounds so silly."

"You wrote me about that story you did on the radioactive spill," he said. "You enjoyed doing that."

"Yes, but …"

"But?"

"You see that's not what you do all the time. That was special and even that didn't turn out right. Not really. And, that is not what you do all the time."

"But, it is part of it, right?"

"Yes, I guess." There was a slight hesitation before she began again.

'You see, most of the time you are doing these nothing stories everyday and people come up and say, 'Oh, your job must be so interesting,' but it isn't, not all the time."

"Almost all jobs have a day-to-day routine, Debbie."

"Yes, I know, but a lot of the things we do aren't much fun. They're boring or awful and the people, the ones we report on, they can be awful too." She gave a startled laugh.

"What that's about? You laughed."

"I didn't know," she almost sang. "I didn't know that I felt that way, that it can be awful."

"What? Tell me what is so awful."

"Well, there are a lot of stories about accidents and women getting raped or about abortion clinics." The words tumbled after each other. "Or about kids nobody wants. Or we go to these meetings like city council meetings and we sit there for hours and nobody says anything and we have to make a story out of it."

"Every job has its boring parts, Debbie. But, it seems to me that television can also be exciting. You get to use your mind, your talents. You can be with people, meet new people. That's important, especially for you."

"I know."

"And, you have done well there, haven't you?"

He heard the sigh.

"Debbie?"

"What I mean about being awful is like what Ellen told me. She's one of the reporters and she's great. She did this story about a little boy dying after somebody stabbed him. She was right there with the paramedics and she was watching the little boy bleed to death. She said she was taking notes and when she got back to the station all she worried about was getting it done in time for the news, this story about a little boy dying."

He could hear the tears building in her voice.

"And you know what happens? This guy Jim Brown, the news director, tells her that he didn't think it wasn't emotional enough, her story. Can you believe that? He's the guy who's in charge and he didn't think a story about a little boy dying was emotional enough. How could it not be emotional enough?"

"Okay, I agree. That does sound rather callous, but what does it have to do with you and what you're doing? You're not telling me about you."

"I know it all sounds silly."

"No, I didn't say it sounded silly. I said you haven't told me anything about what is going on in your life. Are you making time for friends, getting out, that sort of thing?"

"Sometimes, and I have people over. I cook for them, dinner. But, then it got so hot. Nobody wants to do anything here when it's so hot."

There was a whine in her voice he hadn't heard before.

"Any special friends at the station?"

"There is Ellen, that reporter I told you about. I really admire her. She is the best reporter there." Her voice lifted.

"Oh, I have a feeling you are right up there."

"No," she said. "I'm pretty good, but not as good as her. But everything is fine," she said strongly. "Really, it is."

He had no reason to doubt her. He also had no reason to believe there was anything wrong but a vague discontent with the job and a city known for its oppressive summer heat. Probably nothing more than the usual boredom that comes when a job is learned. Still, was she telling him everything? He was beginning to think phone sessions were almost useless.

"You know, Debbie, you might consider seeing someone there, if you feel the need." He said it casually, as though it didn't matter, and perhaps it didn't.

"Why?" There was a note of fear in her voice.

"I think it helps to know you have that option. Don't you think so?"

"No," she said, her voice tight. "I don't think I need to see anyone. Everything is okay. I'm a little tired, that's all."

"I'm only saying it's good to have the option."

"You think there is something wrong?" Again, the fear.

"No, no. You sound fine. And, it doesn't hurt to check in once in a while with me or someone out there. Just think about it, will you, Debbie?"

"Okay," she said. "I will think about it."

She lay back on her bed, the phone in her lap. Why would he say that about another doctor? It made her feel shaky, him saying that. She was tired, that was all. Maybe she didn't explain it the right way. That was it. She needed to call him back and explain how she was working hard and sometimes she got blue. That's all. Everything else was good. It was.

This was nothing like what happened in Baja and that only

happened because she lied to herself about Michael and he had lied to her. This was completely different. She could tell him she knew that but if she called him back now, so soon, it would sound crazy.

Besides, who wouldn't be tired and sad with all this heat. Like Ellen said, humans weren't supposed to live in the desert.

*

Ellen didn't tell Debbie the story about the dying boy the same way Debbie told it to the doctor. Ellen was neither shocked nor angry by Jim Brown's reaction to the piece. In fact, as she told Debbie, it made her laugh.

"Didn't think it was emotional enough." She rolled her eyes at Debbie. "What an idiot."

What bothered Ellen was her own reaction to the story.

"There I am watching the paramedics trying to stop all this bleeding and I am standing there trying to figure out if I can get back to the station in time to get this on the air.

"Then, I get back to the station and I am trying to confirm whether the kid died. I had to get that one piece of information before the piece went on. I am yelling at someone at the hospital to confirm death. That's all I wanted. That's all I cared about." She sighed and shook her head. "Then, I go home and sit on the couch at stare at the wall. I realize I have no feelings at all about the boy, no feelings at all."

She looked at Debbie then, to see her reaction. There was none.

WEATHER

"Art, when are we going to start having some of that weather that makes everyone want to move here?" Jean Ann beamed.

"Very soon, Jean Ann," Art Novak beamed back from his standing position at the end of the anchor desk.

Tom Carter gave a hint of a smile. No words now but he'd have his say later. Sports was his baby.

This is what the audience loved, ate up, the anchors relaxing, talking. The consultants Back East told them that.

"Relax, chat," they said. "This is the place for it. Right before weather or sports. Weather is a big draw, you know. You know, some people watch the whole newscast just to get the weather."

Carter couldn't care less. He used the three minutes of weather time to straighten his tie or check his script for incomplete sentences or grammatical errors.

"What the hell is this?" he would demand during a story or a commercial break. He would yell it into the anchor-desk phone, sending his words to the director's booth and the producer.

"What the hell is this supposed to mean on page twelve?"

Jean Ann used her three minutes of weather to check her face in the small hand mirror and to lick her lips. She made her own grammatical corrections as she read from the TelePrompTer. That's what made her so good on-air. She saw the mistakes coming and made some sense out of them.

Even when she couldn't make that fast mental to verbal copy change, she would keep on reading as though it was perfectly clear and those watching and listening would only think they had somehow misunderstood. How could what Jean Ann Maypin said be gibberish? They both sat, lost in their thoughts, as Art Novak chattered on.

16

"I can't stand that song," said the young woman who worked in accounting.

"What's wrong with it?" Ellen asked.

"That stuff about dust blowing in the wind. I don't think I'm dust in the wind," she sniffed angrily. "I think I am way more than that."

Ellen looked at the thick legs, the sturdy shoes, the short curled hair that should have been on the head of a middle-aged woman, not this twenty-two year old. But then, she had met the mother.

She came to see where her daughter worked. She carried a brown plastic handbag in the crook of her arm. Her hair was steel gray and tightly permed. She wore a bright blue polyester dress with a matching jacket and a thin, white, plastic belt. She wore dark pantyhose and white, thick-healed sandals. She was from Wisconsin.

Ellen watched as the woman's eyes darted from the lights of the television monitors to the sounds of the scanners to the beige carpeting to the figures moving through the newsroom. She felt sorry for the woman who was so excited by her trip to the station.

"Hey, let me give you a tour," she offered.

The tour included an introduction to Tom Carter who was curt and to Jean Ann who grasped her hand with both of her own.

"Thank you so much," the mother murmured over and over again as they walked through the station.

"It's nothing," Ellen told her.

"That's all we are in the end, isn't it, dust?" Ellen now said to the daughter. "I mean, dust to dust and all that."

"I think I'm more than that." Her face was red with indignation.

"Much more."

She turned abruptly and walked away.

Ellen shrugged and looked over at Debbie.

"I don't know," she said. "I sorta like the idea."

"What are you going to do for your series?" Debbie asked without looking up from her typewriter.

Chuck Farrell had warned them that if they didn't come up with their series for the fall rating book, he would assign them ones of his own choice.

"I think I want to do something on that hospice down south," Debbie said.

"Oh, that sounds like fun."

"I think it could be good."

"I'm going with the Klan," Ellen said of the group that had recently started to make its presence known in the area.

"They're recruiting," she told Tony Santella, handing him a flyer she found posted on a light pole.

"Can you get all the visuals you need?" was his only concern.

"Like it," said Brown.

He did like it. Good subject, lots of interest, four or five parts. Talk to black leaders. One part shot at a Klan meeting, another with shadowed interviews with Klansmen. It would work.

Debbie's first idea for a series had been one on bikers.

"Are you crazy?" roared Tony.

"What do you want to do, pull a train or something?" Jack Benton sneered.

"No way," stated Brown.

"Why not?"

"They are scum," Tony said.

"No," she said, "that's the story. Some of them raise money for charity. They do things for handicapped children. They do a lot of things besides wearing black leather jackets."

It didn't matter. Brown shuddered at the thought of long-haired men in black jackets roaring up to the front door, parking their bikes on the sidewalk, walking around his newsroom. No way. He didn't want it and neither did the audience.

They might go for crashes and bodies, carefully shot, on the freeway. That was natural. They were curious about that sort of thing. But, they didn't like sleaze and bikers were sleaze.

The Klan story, that was something else. They needed to know about it, that it was out there in their neighborhoods. Ellen would do it right. He could already picture the night shot of white-hooded men standing by some bonfire. Did they still do that? he wondered.

Do series during ratings, that's what they said Back East. Series helped the ratings, gave them something to promote. The Klan was good, he nodded. But, what they really needed this rating book was some sort of uplifting, happy, hopeful series, something that would make them feel good. They could run it on the ten o'clock, the last story, the kicker, and again on the noon.

"You have any ideas for a light series?" he asked Debbie Hanson. "Something uplifting, you know, happy?"

All she could offer was the hospice and a title.

"I thought I'd call it 'A Good Place to Die.'"

Brown stared at her, his hands folded on his stomach.

"Well, I suppose so," he sighed. "But what we really need is something light."

"Somebody Across the Street is doing a series on incest," Chuck announced to anyone within hearing distance.

"Why don't we get Kowalski to do one on rape?" Ellen called out.

"It's been done," Kowalski yelled back. "Won an award last year for some station in Colorado."

George was listening. Any mention of a story cut through the clatter of the scanners and the constantly ringing phones.

"We could find a new angle," he offered.

Chuck rolled his eyes.

"Right, George," Ellen laughed, "a new angle on rape."

"Well," he said, "there's always more than one angle, isn't there?"

17

Chuck Farrell prepared his speech on all the reasons he deserved more money. He had been at the station four years. He pulled the early morning producer shift that nobody else wanted. He filled in on the assignment desk. He worked through the day and part of the night when there was a big story or when somebody called in sick. What would the argument be? He didn't do his job? He did his job and a few others too.

"You should tell them how valuable you are," Mary Jo told him. "Tell them you deserve more money."

God knows they were going to need it with a new baby coming. They had a right, didn't they, to two children and their two-bedroom house on the west side of town.

"We don't have it," Jim Brown said as they faced each other across the dark wood desk. "I'd do it if I could, but we don't have it."

"Ah, come on, Jim," Chuck snorted. "You know I'm worth more and I'm only talking about thirty or forty dollars a week. If I was working by the hour, I'd be making more than that in overtime."

"We don't have it," Brown said again, and shook his head slowly. "You know we get this budget from Back East and we have to stick to it. You're already at the top for your job."

"I'm doing other things," Chuck argued. "I've been working with the series."

Brown shrugged.

"Is there something else I can do to make more?" Chuck asked. "Give me something. I've got a baby coming."

"You know I would if I could, but it's not up to me."

"Then who? Carter? Who? I'll go talk to them."

Brown smiled. "The guys Back East. You know that. It's their station."

He mimicked the hopelessness of the situation by opening his arms wide, palms up.

"Tell them not to buy another microphone and give me the money instead," Chuck said.

"Wish it were that simple. I really wish it were."

Chuck sat back. Jim was telling him the truth. He didn't have control over the money. He would give him a raise if he could. He was a fair man. You could see he cared. It was written all over his face.

"We'll figure out something, guy. We will," Brown promised.

"I guess Mary Jo and I have made it before," Chuck tried to reassure him. "Like you say, Jim, piece of cake."

Brown smiled. He did say that.

"Piece of cake," he would tell the guys Back East who called with a suggestion, a request, a demand. He said it with a smile in his voice.

"Sure, piece of cake."

They loved hearing it. They would carry that "piece of cake" to the men above them and on it would move, through the planning meetings and the luncheons and the after-work drinks.

"Brown said it's a piece of cake," they would say. The others would smile. It was good knowing Brown would come through.

He also said, "No problem," and he meant it. He had no problems in his newsroom, no changes that could not be made, no advice that would not be taken.

Brown offered the guys Back East no opinion other than the one he thought they wanted to hear. He never offered information that did not support their beliefs. He never disagreed with them unless he knew that's what they wanted. After all, as he told himself and his people, they owned the candy store.

"They want us to do what?" the cry would go up at the weekly newsroom meetings.

He'd shrug and shake his head. It was a silent statement of, "Hey, that's the way it is. What can you do?"

"You've got to be kidding," they would shout. "Are they nuts?"

The people Back East were a combination of other stations and newspapers and charcoal gray suits carrying attaché cases filled with consultants' reports and rating books.

"Who are they?" Debbie asked the other heads that languidly turned toward the gray parade on one of their sporadic visits.

A pursed mouth, a lifted eyebrow would be her answer. "Who cares?" the movements said.

"Who exactly do we work for?" she asked Chuck Farrell.

"Some guys in Philadelphia who'll probably sell the place in two years."

Those people Back East did not think long and hard about the station as long as it worked. The ratings were high, the budget tight. As long as everything but the budget numbers stayed high, everything was fine. As the number two station in the twenty-fifth market, it made the obscene profit that kept even those Back East moderately content until someone felt the need to make his mark by making the station even more profitable.

"Does the local news make money?" Debbie asked Brown.

He smiled and then laughed. It was an open, full, deep laugh. Strange for Brown.

"We are the station," he said. "We make the money."

"But we spend it too."

"Doesn't matter." he said. "We make money."

Which, of course, meant he had been lying to Chuck Farrell. They had plenty of money. They had money for a helicopter, for trips covering stories around the state, for Jean Ann's hairdresser and wardrobe. They had money for state-of-the-art equipment and a fleet of vans and company cars. They definitely had money for that.

Farrell would get his bonus at Christmas. They all would. The bonuses came in a block and Brown and Carter would divvy it up. Most of them would get about the same amount. Someone would get a little more. One person might only get a token. The message was clear. Time to move on. A good a way as any, Brown thought, for letting them know.

Like he said, no problem. No problem but one. He had wrestled with it for ten years. Carter was the one problem he couldn't knock loose and he wasn't sure he should. Carter made his people unhappy but he was also the perfect fall guy. He could be blamed for everything that went wrong in the newsroom.

"What can you do?" Brown's soft smile would say. "What can any of us do?"

No matter how insipid his comments, how ridiculous his demands, Carter pulled in the ratings and kept them in that solid contender spot. Sometimes he even took them into first place. Happened a few times and it would happen again.

Tom Carter was top dog even if his title of news manager put him one rung below Brown in the chain of command. Of course, the minute those ratings started their downward slide, and they would, he was a dead man.

In his fat vinyl chair, Jim Brown dreamed of how he would handle the day when it happened. He pondered it, sent the thought meandering pleasantly through his brain, tasting it, feeling it, the day when it finally happened.

"Well, Tom," he would say when the moment came. "Well, Tom, what can I say?" And, likely as not, Carter would spit back at him.

"Eat my ass," he'd say or something like that. Brown smiled with the thought. Carter would look like a mean, ugly dog and he'd say, "Eat my ass."

Now, if he did his Well-Tom-what-can-I-say? standing at the door of Carter's office so everyone could see and stretch to hear, there would be a different response. They would shake hands and pat at each other's shoulders.

"Yeah, I know," Carter would say. "Not your fault."

Carter would leave right away, no matter how it was done. He'd be out the door, coming back later for his boxes. There would be no good-bye to the newsroom and certainly not one to the audience. You didn't do it that way. You disappeared. By the next day, the television critic for the morning paper might have the story and he might run with it for a few days, adding quotes, opinions. It didn't matter. Neither would the phone calls.

Oh, they'd come, hundreds that first week. Some would be shrill with indignation, the How-could-you-do-this-terrible-thing-I'll-never-watch-your-station-again calls. Letters would be written to the newspapers. A radio show would open the phone lines to listeners.

"We've watched that man for years," they would say. "We're never going to watch that station again."

The callers would be women, usually, in their fifties and sixties. The important men, the men who sat with Tom Carter at the front tables, might try to get through to the men Back East, thinking they would listen and rethink the decision.

Even the old hands in the newsroom, the ones who had been through this at other stations, would stoop to the temptation of wondering when they would give in to the pressure. Even Carter, as well as he knew the business, would be there waiting, relishing the dream of that moment when he got the call with the Hey-guy-look-we-want-you-back.

There would be no phone call, no gloating return. There would be no sneering glance across the newsroom before going into the glass office and slamming the door. There would be no more three-camera nights and knowing snickers to the audience. It didn't happen, anywhere.

Station powers and their minions knew you waited it out. The phone calls eventually stopped and the audience would forget the men and women they loved every night. Months later there would be that stray call from someone who had moved away and come back.

"I was wondering where he was," they would say. "On vacation or something?"

There would be short laughs in the newsroom as the words were passed around. That was all.

Brown could taste every second of it. Carter would disappear one night and that would be it. When you disappear from television, you are almost immediately forgotten.

Poor Carter, Brown nodded to himself, he wasn't such a bad guy. He'd say goodbye to him when the day came and he'd make Carter say goodbye. It would be done in the glass office with an open door. They would both shake hands and put their free hand on the other man's shoulder. Brown knew there would be a tear in that old guy's eyes. Yeah, there would be. His too, probably. When all was said and done, they had been through it together. They were men of The Best.

18

Ellen parked her car in the middle of the empty library parking lot as she had been told to by her phone contact, a Klan leader named Harry.

"That way we will be able to tell if we're being followed," he explained.

She shook her head at his stupidity. If she wanted, if Brown insisted, it would have been easy to follow the car that picked her up, too easy.

The big green Buick pulled into the lot.

"You Ellen Peters?" the driver asked, leaning out of the window.

"Hi." She tried to keep her voice friendly and young.

"I'm Ken. That's Bruce," he said, nodding to the shadows of the backseat.

"Hi," she said again.

His eyes darted from her face to the parking lot to the few cars passing on the street.

"Did Harry warn you about anybody following us?"

"Yes, and nobody is," she told him. She walked around the car and got into the front seat.

"Yeah, well, we'll see," he said and threw the car into gear.

"It's a nice night," she tried. "Not too hot."

He said nothing. There was no movement in the back.

"Where are you from?" she finally asked.

"A lot of places," he snapped.

"I'm from Boston," she said and smiled again.

"Lots of nigger trouble up there. Lots of it everywhere," he said and laughed over his shoulder to the man in the dark. A snicker came back.

The driver's hair was cut short to the skull. He wore a white T-shirt and jeans.

"Take this down, hurry," he ordered, passing a small pad and pencil across the seat. A hand reached for it.

"BGT," he read out. "Zero, zero, six."

"What are you doing?" she asked.

"Taking down that guy's license." He pointed to the car in front of them. "He's been acting strange. First he was in front of us. Then he was behind us and now he's in front of us again."

"It's nobody from the station."

"That's what you say."

The car in front of them made a right turn.

"It's okay for now," Ken said to the backseat. "We'll check it out later."

He sighed in disgust.

"Probably one of those fucking Jews, those JDL kikes. They blew up a Klan office down in Mississippi. Christ. Could be the FBI too. You know?" He looked at her.

"They're really with us," he went on, "but they give us problems. We had a G-man in our klavern once."

"Really?"

"Yeah, he told us. You know most of the big problems came with the Kennedys," he spat out the name. "He got what he asked for. So did his brother. Right, Bruce?"

There seemed to be a grunt of agreement.

"Bruce here is joining us," he told her. "Right, Bruce?"

"Oh?" She looked back and nodded to the man in the shadows.

They left the wide avenues of the city and drove west.

"What's this story you're doing?" Ken asked.

"I don't know yet. I want to see what happens at a meeting first."

"You gonna write about a bunch of dumb hillbillies?" he jeered. "You gonna write about how dumb we are?"

"No." She gave a small laugh.

"I joined about two years ago," he said. "I was living in Tennessee. I work, uh, construction. There wasn't any work there and there were too many niggers. Right, Bruce?"

"Yeah," came the muffled voice.

They rode the next miles in silence, passing out of the city and into the beginnings of the desert. Suddenly, he pulled onto the shoulder of the road and stopped.

"Harry tell you about this?" he asked and moved toward her. Now she saw the gun tucked in the waistband of his jeans

She felt the burning stab of fear in her stomach and gave a quick shake of her head. Damn, this was stupid. She had let it happen to her.

"It's only for a little while," he said, his voice husky. In his hands he held a yellow-print bandana.

There was nothing she could do, nothing. She couldn't show fear, couldn't babble at him, not if she wanted this story. She had no choice but to take the chance. She lowered her head and he tied the bandana over her eyes.

"Can you see anything?" he asked.

She wondered at his lack of smell as he fumbled at the knot at the back of her head. She expected the smell of sweat, a stale smell. He had no smell at all.

"No, I can't see," she told him.

She could sense the man in the backseat moving forward. She fought to control the fear. They would pull her out of the car, rape her in the desert and shoot her. Who would know? How long before anyone found her? Goddamn it, she didn't want to die like this.

The car pulled back on the road. She took a deep breath.

Okay, okay, she told herself. Do the James Bond bit. How many beats of time were passing? Feel the road, the land around you. Was the road bumpy? Were there cattle guards? Were there strange noises? On the right? On the left?

"Check the map." Ken ordered as the car slowed.

"It says Quail Road. This isn't Quail Road," came the confused backseat voice.

"Shut up, goddamn it," Ken shouted.

She coughed and cleared her throat to show she didn't care, didn't realize the importance of the slip. Had it been a slip? Were they making motions to each other, signaling each other to make her think they were near or on Quail Road when it didn't exist?

After a few minutes the car stopped and her door was opened. Someone placed a hand under her arm, helping her out. It was Ken who untied the now musty smelling yellow cloth. Over his shoulder, she saw the small stucco house with the wooden porch.

"Cover her face, damn it," ordered the big man who walked toward them. "Cover her eyes. Ah, forget it, it's too late."

"I'm Harry," he said. "Don't look left or right. Look down."

"Okay," she said as he led her to the house.

A few people sat in the tiny living room. He pushed her through and into the cramped kitchen where a heavy woman in a nurse's uniform stood talking to a thin man in loose blue jeans. A young boy sat at the kitchen table.

"What's the number?" Harry demanded.

She gave him Brown's office number. He punched it out on the wall phone and handed her the receiver.

"Okay," she said to Brown. "Everything is okay."

"Let me talk to him," Brown said.

"He wants to talk to you," she said, handing the receiver to Harry.

"No problem," he said to Brown's words. "You keep your side of the deal and we'll keep ours."

In the living room, he introduced her as "the television reporter I told you about who's going to do a documentary show about the new

Klan."

They stared at her.

"Let's get started," he said. "I know some of you are thinking about joining us. So, we've got this tape of what we believe in and what we think is going wrong in this country of ours. The guy who's talking is one of our national leaders and he is a great man. I've met him."

He turned in a small circle, including each of them in his head nodding. He wore a light blue sports coat, open over the start of a wide belly. His shirt was white, open at the neck. There was no trace of a beard on his fleshy face. His small eyes narrowed with the power and the importance of the moment.

"He's a man who cares more about America than any of those politicians in Washington. Listen to this tape. Listen to what he has to say. I think you are going to be shocked."

Ellen leaned forward, her notebook in her lap. Across from her a young woman with long straight hair sat on the couch next to the man from the kitchen, an obvious couple. The woman nodded with the drone of the tape while the man smoked.

A bearded man in the easy chair next to the couch puffed on his pipe. When Harry introduced her, he seemed to do a double take as though stunned. The nurse sat in a folding chair next to him. A big man in a denim shirt sat in another chair. An older woman with short gray hair sat on Ellen's left. She assumed Bruce from the backseat was the man in the folding chair on her right. He had pulled the chair slightly behind their circle. She still couldn't see his face.

Ken stood across the room guarding the front door with his arms crossed high on his chest. Harry moved as the tape played, pushing his large body between the chairs, around the tables, smiling and nodding.

It was a condemnation of Jews, nothing else. There was no talk of blacks or other minorities, no plea for a pure white America. There was, instead, a steady stream of talk about the Jews, how they owned the media, ran the country, were filled with evil. Rabbis slept with little girls, the voice said. Part of the Torah, it said.

The young woman gave a yip of shock, her frightened eyes searching the room for other reactions. Ellen wondered if her husband beat her, he looked like the type. So did she.

"God, that is horrible," said the older woman, her face folding in lines of disgust.

The nurse grunted with satisfaction. She heard it all before. The bearded man puffed quickly.

"It was like Nazi Germany," Ellen would tell them later in the newsroom. "I didn't know people still believed this crap."

They did. She could see that. They believed all of it.

Harry waited almost a full minute after the tape ended. He waited for the emotion, the tension to build. Then, he spoke.

"You see what I mean. That man knows what he's talking about. He's been to college. He knows."

They nodded.

"Now, I want to show you something you aren't going to believe. This will prove to you what's really going on in this country. This will show you who's trying to run this country." He left the room.

She shifted uncomfortably in the hard metal folding chair. She ached with the long sitting. She tried to give them all a friendly, safe smile.

Harry was back, his arms full of boxes and cans of food.

Thank God, she thought, he's going to give us something to eat.

"I want you all to look at these. Look. Right here." His large forefinger stabbed at one of the boxes. "This is how the Jews run this country. Do you see?"

He flashed the offending box with his finger now cemented on one spot.

"Take it." He thrust the box at the young woman. "Pass it around.

Everybody look at it."

The woman stared at the box. She turned it, examining all the sides.

"No, no," he snapped. "Here." He grabbed the box, pointing again. "See?"

Ellen leaned forward.

"Oh yes," said the woman, smiling with relief. It was a test and she passed.

"I see it. I do."

All of them were leaning forward now.

"It's on everything. Everything," Harry shouted. "Go home and check your own cabinets. You'll find it. Kosher," he crowed. "It says kosher."

The faces in the room did not respond to the horror of his pronouncement.

"The Jews force companies to put that on their food. They make them do it. And, if they don't do it, the Jews won't buy it. Do you believe that? This is one of the ways they are running this country. We say ruining." He gave a sickly smile.

They were obviously confused by this kosher thing. What did it mean? It was bad, they knew that, because it had something to do with those Jews, those filthy Jews.

They began to slowly nod and to reach for the boxes and cans being passed around the circle. Yes, they could see that, another filthy Jew thing, those filthy, big-nose Jews running the country, those rich Jews. Ellen kept her head down. She had not opened her notebook, not written one word.

The blindfold went on at the door. She felt no fear of Ken or Bruce. Twice on the ride back to the city Ken shouted out a license plate number. Twice they were copied down in the backseat.

When they reached the parking lot, she saw her one mistake. She walked stiff-legged to her car, trying to stand between it and them.

They would see her license plate. They would add that to their list. On Monday, they could easily get her address along with all the others from the Motor Vehicle Department.

*

"It's right about here," she said, pointing to a spot on the map. "I'm sure it is."

Frank Kowalski looked over her shoulder.

"I am sure that guy with the beard was a cop or a newspaper reporter," she said. She now remembered his reaction to her as the fear of being recognized.

What an idiot she had been to go out there with those morons. No protection, nothing. And, for what, she asked herself. For what?

"I ain't the photographer on this one," Clifford told them. Frank and Ellen laughed but she wasn't so sure she wanted it either.

Two days later Harry called.

"So, you told them," he hissed. "You told them, squealer."

"What are you talking about?"

"You did have us followed, didn't you, and you told them all about us. You know how we feel about squealers?"

"I don't know what you are talking about," she said strongly. "I wasn't followed and I haven't talked to anybody outside this newsroom about anything."

She looked around the room, trying to catch someone's eye, to signal someone to pick up another phone and listen.

"Then how do that cops know? How?"

"What cops?"

"The ones sitting outside the house all the time, the ones following me. How did they find out?"

"It wasn't me, Harry. I gave you my word." She filled her voice with indignation.

"Yeah, well, maybe not." Now he sounded unsure. "It better not be you. We'll find out," he said, his voice strong again. "And we don't like squealers."

She could feel the sweat starting under her arms. She was almost panting.

"And I'm not big on threats," she snapped back. "I didn't tell anybody and no one followed me."

"Yeah," he said. "We'll see." He hung up.

She went straight to Brown's office. She wanted out, she told him, out of the series.

"What good will it do?" she asked him. "The ones who think the same way they do aren't going to change. I don't think it's worth a series. And frankly, I don't think we're going to tell anybody anything they don't already know."

He shrugged. There hadn't been any wasted time, no camera tied up for weeks. The idea sounded okay when she first brought it to him but he could see the problems now. Did he really want to give those guys airtime on his news? He could hear the phone calls. He frowned. Was it worth it?

Of course, he didn't like setting a precedent, letting a reporter pull out of anything, but her news judgment was usually good and she'd never done this before.

"Sure," he said, "if that's the way you see it. You'll have to come up with something else and fast."

The sudden wave of relief made her feel faint and guilty.

"I wouldn't drop it unless I really thought it was worthless," she rushed to assure him. "I just don't think it will work."

He nodded.

"I feel bad about this," she said.

"God," she told Frank Kowalski, "they scared me in a way. All that stuff was such garbage. It was awful."

He chuckled.

"No, no, I'm serious. It made me sick. And, about half of the guys there were either cops or reporters."

She knew the bearded man with the pipe was and thought the man in the work shirt probably was as well.

She shuddered. "And I thought they were bringing me something to eat. Do you believe that? I thought all those cans and boxes of food were for a snack."

Frank Kowalski laughed.

"What does Brown want you to do?" he asked her.

"Something happy," she said. "A happy series. What the hell is happy?"

19

"I would have been scared to death," Debbie told her.

"I was when they put that blindfold on, but after that it was all right," Ellen said. "It wasn't anywhere near as bad as that time I was on the manhunt."

"What manhunt?"

"It happened before you got here. Three kids helped their father and some other guy break out of prison. They went on a rampage, killing babies, everything. And guess who was following them."

"You?"

"Of course." Ellen laughed. "Now, that was frightening."

They sat at the edge of the pool, their legs dangling in the water.

"I'm out there in a van with that fool Rappaport, right in the middle of the Tonto National Forest, two hundred thousand acres or something. We were there all night. There were these two state cops in their car who were about sixteen years old and jumpy as hell. We couldn't even get out to go to the bathroom because they got scared when they heard the door open. I sat up all night and Rappaport slept. He was sure his wife was going to get pissed that he was up there with me."

She kicked at the water. It was October and the water was warm.

"You know what I figured out that night?" she said.

"What?"

"That I didn't want to die that way, out in some forest for some nothing story. Still, we did the story and it won an award. The funny thing is they weren't even there that night. They were someplace else killing somebody."

She hadn't talked to someone like this in a long time, not since Dale in Albuquerque. They used to share their station stories over Tecates with lime at Al Monte's bar.

"My father once told me what he was afraid of," she told Debbie. "Here is this guy who fought hand-to-hand combat in Europe in World War II and he had this wild fear."

"What was it?"

"It was about New York. That's where he worked after the divorce."

"What did he do?"

"His company handled international insurance, like Lloyds, you know? Insurance for things like revolutions, wars. He would go to these countries, meet the top guys and figure out what could go wrong and when. His company would insure companies and their people who were going to do business there."

"I didn't know people did that." Debbie said.

"He loved it and when we were young we used to travel with him all over the world."

"You have brothers and sisters?"

"Two brothers, one younger and one older. We spent holidays and summers in Hong Kong, Madrid, London."

"I've never even been to New York," Debbie sighed.

"My father liked New York but he couldn't understand how the blacks put up with it. He thought that one day they were going to get mad enough to come out of Harlem and seal up the whole city."

They looked at each other.

"You know," Ellen continued, "it's an island and he said if they got mad enough and organized they could cut off the bridges and seal off the tunnels and let everybody fry in the city." She laughed.

"I think he wanted them to do it. He said he didn't understand how they could stand it, living there in Harlem and watching the trains taking all these fat cat businessmen in their Brooks Brothers suits back to Connecticut." She leaned back, stretched her neck.

"All the commuter trains to Connecticut go through Harlem. These guys, and I've seen this, are sitting there in this air-conditioned train, reading their newspapers, and playing these ridiculous card games that have been going on for years. They are going past the tenements where the people are hanging out of the windows, T-shirts, housedresses, hot as hell. They're watching the trains go by. My father wondered why they didn't kill all those bastards on the train. And," she laughed again, "he was one of them."

"Is that what he was afraid of, that the blacks would do that?" Debbie asked.

"No, he wasn't afraid of that. He was afraid he would have a heart attack or something and fall down on the street and people would step over him, thinking he was some old drunk. That's the way they are in New York. That's what scared him, but it didn't happen. He died four years ago of cancer. Real fast. Nobody stepped over him except the doctors." She kicked the water.

"My mother died when I was five," Debbie said, putting the same strength in her voice she heard in Ellen's.

"I hardly remember her at all. Some man hit her car. He was drunk. Dad told me that the man had never done anything wrong in his whole life, except hit my mother."

"That's a bitch," Ellen said.

They both sat without speaking, moving their legs in the water.

"You know what I'd really like to do?" Ellen broke the silence.

"What?"

"I'd like to go sit on a pier and stare at the ocean and drink piña coladas until I fell over dead."

Debbie giggled and kicked a soft splashy beat.

"And, that's why I'm here," Ellen sighed, "as far from the ocean as I can get. Sitting in the middle of a fucking desert."

Debbie laughed.

"I know what I want to do," she stated. "I want to be this great reporter, pounding out stories on an old typewriter, smoking a cigarette, my hair all messed up. You know?"

Ellen reached for her cigarettes. "You could be," she said, "if that's what you want."

"What do you really want, Ellen?"

Ellen pulled her legs from the pool. The water and the night felt cold to her now.

"I want to go someplace where they don't know what the *Today Show* is," she said.

"What do you mean?"

"I mean a couple of years ago I went to Cape Cod with my mother. We were staying in this small inn right on the ocean. The first morning I woke up and I could smell the ocean and I heard the sea gulls. It was fantastic. A few days before I had been in New Mexico and now I was in a completely different world. Then, you know what I hear?"

Debbie shook her head.

"I hear the *Today Show*. That's exactly what I heard every morning in Albuquerque when I was getting ready for work, the *Today Show*. There is no place you can go anymore. Everything is the same everywhere." Now she was cold.

"Let's go in and have some wine," she said.

"Ellen, how old are you?" Debbie asked as she got to her feet. "You don't have to tell me."

"Doesn't matter," Ellen said. "I'm thirty-two. That makes me the oldest reporter in the newsroom. Any newsroom." She gave her snort of a laugh.

"Yeah, but you're the best," Debbie said and smiled. She had found a friend.

20

Jason Osner thought the hospice was damn creepy. That wasn't the way Debbie saw it at all.

"It's all happy and bright and everyone is so positive," she said. "They give them all the drugs they want so they don't have to die in pain."

Fine, but nodding patients weren't his idea of great pictures and the only thing he wanted to do the two days they were at the hospice was to leave. And, there she was, talking about how happy the whole thing was, dying the way you wanted to die, dying with dignity. He wasn't getting that on tape. He wasn't seeing that at all.

To top it off, in every interview they did, somebody had to say that one thing about how their work at the hospice helped them accept their own death. And, after they said it, they all gave this open-mouthed grin. Fucking creepy.

"What about living?" he demanded on the drive back to the station. "I'd rather think about living than dying. That's going to come no matter what I do, so why spent the rest of my life thinking about it?"

"That isn't the way it was," she argued. "They're helping people."

"You'll see the tapes," he told her. "You'll see. All those patients were gray. They weren't happy. And those other people weren't that happy either. You'll see."

She watched him as he drove, the strong profile, the strong hands on the steering wheel, the muscular arms and the long lean thighs tight in blue jeans. He was wrong, she thought. It was a happy place.

She stopped at a drugstore before going home. She saw an old man moving slowly along the aisles. He reached for each rack, not so much to steady himself but to touch. He wore a light-blue golf sweater, fawn-colored slacks and a white baseball cap.

She watched as he bent close to the rack of thick, gold-wrapped candy bars and let his small, white hand touch them. She could see his blue eyes searching from behind the thick glasses. His fingers ran lightly across the gold foil. The tears caught in her throat.

It was that way all weekend. She was filled with tears and she knew what Ellen would say. She would say it was the hospice.

"What did you expect, Debbie?" she'd say. "I told you it was a depressing story."

"And don't tell me it was the hospice," she begged when she finally did make the call.

"All right, so it wasn't but it was," Ellen said with a laugh. "Who wouldn't come back depressed as hell, and then you go chasing some old guy around in a drugstore who probably has more money than God. Why do you have to worry about stuff like that?"

"I don't know," she sniffed back the tears.

"Listen to this, if you want depressing," Ellen said. "I decided to take Brown at his word and do something light and happy for my series. That's what he said he wanted, light and happy. I decided to do a series on local comedians. Last night I went to a comedy club to set it up.

"Talk about depressing, you don't know the meaning of the word until you talk to comedians. Those guys are miserable. Now, what can I do, circus clowns? Talk about depressing."

"I thought I might see a doctor," Debbie said. "A therapist."

"For what?"

"Well, I used to see one and sometimes it helps to have sort of a tune-up. What do you think?"

"Some of the guys I met last night could certainly use a few visits but I don't see it for you. It was that story, Debbie. That's all."

"Maybe you're right," she agreed quickly.

"Why did you see one before?"

"I had some problems. No big deal. I saw one for a couple of months, that's all."

*

"A shrink? No way," Jason told her. "You're fine."

They sat in the editing booth putting together the second part of the hospice series. He switched off the machines when she started telling him how she had been feeling.

"And when I was coming to work today I saw this little boy and he was all dirty and he was sitting on the curb and he had this scruffy little dog with him and he looked so unhappy and I started to cry. I started to cry all over the place."

She bowed her head and clasped her hands tightly together in her lap. "It's stupid, I know."

"Christ, come on," he rushed to say. "We'll finish this and go for a drink. Okay? Two drinks, twelve drinks." He patted her knee. "Okay?"

Jason was moved by the sound of tears in her voice. Until this moment he saw her as too cheery, too full of smiles. He had no problems working with women but he had never been entirely comfortable around any woman who matched him in height. This one was a big one, he smiled as he turned back to his machines, but there was definitely something about her.

"I'm sorry about breaking down," she told him.

"Don't worry about it."

"I cry all the time," she said and laughed. "I do, really. I cry when I see some old lady using food stamps. I cry when I read the newspaper."

"You are what is known as a blubbering fool," he said.

"I guess so."

"Hard to be a reporter crying over everything."

"I do okay. Don't I? Well, most of the time."

"Yeah, you do."

"Yes, well, I wish I could be more like Ellen. She wouldn't get all weepy about anything."

"She's a pain in the ass," he commented as he shuffled through the box of tapes.

"Not Ellen," Debbie said firmly.

"Oh, yeah? Nobody likes working with her."

"That's not true," she argued. "She's great."

"Okay," Jason said, pulling a tape out of the box. "If you say so."

He didn't have much to say about Ellen Peters, not much at all. She was too much in charge, too much knowing what she wanted and how she wanted it. Christ, the thing she had about earphones.

"Don't forget your earphones," she said every time he started taking his equipment out of the van. Earphones? Who the hell wanted to carry those damn things around with everything else you had carry? So what if a couple of times you came back with some Mexican radio station jabbering all over your interview? It never happened on the big stories or the spot news.

No, he didn't like Ellen. He heard her yelling at George one of those times when the audio wasn't up to her standards. Who the hell knew why? Maybe it was his fault. Maybe not. Who knew?

"You tell that son of a bitch to use his earphones, George. He does this to me all the tine," she was yelling.

It was easier working with the guys. You felt more like a team, the two of you against George. You could joke around, turn off the car radio. Harold Lewis was the funny one with those radios. He'd do the static bit.

"This is Unit Seven," he'd start to answer one of George's nagging calls. He'd roughen his voice and run his fingers across the microphone. At George's end it sounded as though the connection was breaking up. Along with the scratching and some finger tapping, Harold would start dropping words.

" This is … to .. mayor's … "

George would keep calling and demanding and Harold would say, "George? George?" while he scratched his nails across the mike.

"I don't know what happened," he'd tell George when they got back. "Something must be wrong with it. Better get it looked at."

His eyes would be all innocent with that little boy face of his. What could George do? Harold was great and those art stories of his weren't bad.

"Want to get something to eat?" he asked her.

She hesitated. "Why don't we buy something and I'll cook."

"You don't want to do that."

"Sure I do. I love cooking and I don't have anyone to cook for."

"Okay," he said. Why argue. He liked the idea. He liked her. She was a big 'un but she was cute.

21

"How long has this been going on?" Ellen asked her.

"Oh," Debbie started to blush, "a couple of weeks, but don't say anything." She glanced toward the other cubicles. "I don't want it to get around."

"It will. Everything does," Ellen said.

"I don't want people talking about it," Debbie insisted.

"I won't say anything," Ellen assured her.

Debbie nodded and smiled.

"He's really nice, Ellen."

"Not a doubt in my mind," Ellen said.

Debbie hadn't filled up with tears in the three weeks she and Jason had been together. She was too happy. Jason was happy as well, a contented laid-back happiness that would, at strange hours during the day, grow into a reaching, demanding passion. Jesus, why hadn't he seen her before?

She was easy to be with and so relaxed about herself. Right after the first time, she was as comfortable as hell sitting cross-legged on the bed, naked. She walked around the room naked, the apartment. She didn't grab for a towel or his shirt or the corner of the sheet to cover herself. She got up and paraded away. Boy, he liked that ass, that big apple butt. The breasts were small, yeah, and that made this strange for Jason. He was a breast man but with this girl it didn't matter.

Sometimes she'd put on one of those nightgowns you could see through and he would watch her from the couch. She'd stand there, the curtain filtering the light from the window behind her and he would see her body beneath the gown. That would be enough to take him right off the couch.

The sex was good and he hadn't been with anybody since Ashley and her big tits left for Washington. Damn her. He had planned on making the move too, but it didn't work out. She was going to keep her eyes open and he was sending tapes, but nothing came through.

"What's wrong with my stuff?" he shouted on their weekly phone call.

"I don't think anything is wrong with it, Jason. I can't tell them to hire you. I only got here myself and there isn't an opening right now. Not now."

"Maybe I should fly out there and look for a job."

"Give it some time," she suggested. "Give it a few months."

"You'd be crazy, man," Frank Kowalski told him.

"Don't go following some bitch anywhere," Jack Benton said.

"Whatever," said Steve Kramer.

Ashley used to say, "We make magic together." Back then he thought she was right, Now, he wondered. Who had done most of the work? He had. He worked hard on her stories and series, fighting to edit them. He showed her how she could tighten her writing to let his video tell the story. He worked with her in the audio booth. And who gets the big job? Not him. Had he been used? Could be.

He told Debbie about her. If he didn't, somebody else in the station would.

"Right now I am damn glad I didn't get a job in D.C.," he told her.

Yeah, he liked this one, this big girl, right there to be grabbed. Right there for him.

He hinted to George that he liked working with her. Couldn't hurt. That didn't mean George would schedule them together. It might mean when there was a problem with another crew, some other photographer or reporter yelling that they wanted to work with anyone but the bastard assigned, George would remember that Jason and Debbie never gave him trouble. He might send them out together more often.

Everyone in the newsroom knew they were sleeping together, or thought they knew. Jason told Charles Adkins he was seeing Debbie. Adkins passed it on, not thinking much more abut it. Ellen told no one but when the story got back to her she said, "Yeah, I know."

Nobody cared. What Debbie and Jason were doing didn't affect their jobs or their stories. Still, they filed it away. You never knew when something like this might come in handy. Now it was worth only a few words, a nod, but later it could be important, grown to something that could affect someone. They might need it someday. Everything was worth knowing.

*

"So what do you think about this Debbie and Jason thing?" Clifford asked Ellen as they sat in the noonday traffic.

"I don't know," she said. "He's not my favorite."

"He's a good photographer."

"Sure, if you don't want to actually hear your story."

Clifford chuckled. Things had been going well for him, real well. He was doing less and less of the grunt shooting and more medical shooting with Richard Ferguson.

"Specializing is where it's at," he told Ellen. "Ferguson says I'm a natural."

Even when they warned him to look away at the first incision during the kidney transplant, that thin red slice when first timers hit the floor, he held steady. He pointed that camera right down at the place where the knife was going and he held steady.

"Good work," Ferguson told him later. "You're a natural. I threw up at my first operation."

"Ferguson is going to tell George to keep putting me on the

medical stories," he told Ellen.

She could hear the pride in his voice.

"You're right," she said. "If you get to be a pro in one area, you can write your own ticket in the big markets."

"That's what I'm thinking. But, I don't know if there's a big call for medical stories."

"Medical stories? Are you crazy? Everybody is doing it. You'll be able to go anywhere you want. You'll have the expertise plus the balance. You can do sports, spot news, anything, plus the medical."

"Yeah," he agreed happily. "You are right. Hey, look at that."

He pointed to her window. A man stood on the sidewalk babbling to himself. He wore a long, tattered, gray coat. His eyes and arms moved wildly as his lips kept up their constant, one-sided conversation.

"Now, that is something nasty," Clifford moaned and shook his head.

The man's trousers stopped well short of his ankles. On his feet he wore high-topped black sneakers without laces, the tongues hanging out, flapping as he shuffled and gossiped with the air.

"That's what happens to old assignment editors," Ellen said.

"Hell no, baby," Clifford said. "That's what happens to old photographers."

They both gave snorts of laugher mixed with pity for the man and for themselves.

22

The diaphragm turned into a fiasco.

"You'll like this lady," Paige Allen told her. "She's not a doctor but some sort of nurse or midwife. She fits you and shows you how to use it."

She hadn't used anything the first few times with Jason but she had been at the beginning of her cycle so she considered herself safe. She wouldn't use birth control pills. She used them with Michael and they made her gain weight. She also believed, half-believed, they might have had something to do with her breakdown.

The woman who measured Debbie chatted as she worked.

"You see, most doctors, most male doctors anyway, don't take the time to measure correctly. That's why there are so many pregnancies with diaphragms, but if they are fitted correctly …" Her voice trailed off as her fingers poked and probed Debbie's vagina.

"I haven't had one unplanned pregnancy and I have been fitting diaphragms for three years.

"Here, you want to look?" she asked, her fingers still inside Debbie.

"No, not really," Debbie said. She was sweating with embarrassment.

"You should, you know," the woman said. "And remember to examine the diaphragm for thin spots or breaks before you use it."

Arranged by size, a line of diaphragms was displayed on the counter. Debbie giggled at the largest one.

"No, it has nothing to do with that," the woman said with annoyance. She picked up the diaphragm from the middle of the line.

"Now, this is the way you put it in. You pinch it together and insert. Many women do it while sitting on the toilet or with one leg up on the toilet seat. See this?"

She led Debbie to the large clear plastic model of the vagina and uterus. She wiggled one long thin finger up the plastic opening.

"This is where you put it, open it, so it lays flat across here. Do you see?"

Debbie nodded. The model fascinated her. The parts appeared to be removable.

"Now, you take this in there." The woman handed her the rubber disc and pointed her to the bathroom. "You wash it off and put it in. You don't leave here until you get it right. When you think you have it in right, I'll check it."

In the tiny bathroom, Debbie tried, carefully folding the disc as the woman had but when she started to insert it the disc sprang out of her fingers and bounced off a wall. She rushed to retrieve it from behind the toilet.

On the second try, it exploded again and bounced away. Good grief, she asked herself, what kind of woman was she? She couldn't even do this simple womanly thing.

Quietly, cautiously, she opened the door and peeked into the examination room. She took the smallest diaphragm from the display. She folded it and started to insert it into the plastic vagina. If only she could see how it should work, how it should fit.

Suddenly, the diaphragm snapped open, blowing the model apart. The clear plastic stomach cover flew to the floor, the pink ovaries bounced, the two red fallopian tubes jumped in opposite directions.

She cried out and fell to her knees, scrambling for the pieces. She was wet with sweat. How could she tell this woman she couldn't do this, didn't want to do it. She put the pieces she found on the counter.

Back in the bathroom, sweating and shaking, she tried again and this time the diaphragm stayed inside her.

"Perfect," announced the woman. "Perfect. Feel it."

Debbie reluctantly inserted a finger.

"Feel that? Do you? Do you remember how you put it in?"

Debbie nodded quickly.

"Remember how it feels once it's in there. It's important that it lays flat."

Debbie nodded again. She had no idea how it felt or how it was supposed to feel. She doubted she would ever put it in the right way again.

"I sort of broke your thing," she said before she left the room. She nodded toward the counter.

The woman said nothing.

At the pharmacy, while the druggist was finding her size, Debbie did feel some relief. At least she didn't have to ask for the big one.

"For an elephant," she whispered to Paige Allen. "I would rather die."

*

Jason didn't ask her those first weeks if she was using anything. She knew what she was doing and it was soon obvious she had a diaphragm. He didn't care what she used. It all felt good to him.

Debbie didn't want to use the diaphragm. She didn't like touching it, folding it, putting it in. She felt embarrassed by her trips to the bathroom. She did it for Jason. He was good for her. He held her back from the worry and the tears.

"Stop thinking about it," he would order when he saw her start to react to a story on the national news.

"Think about something else. Think about how great everything else is. Come on, big 'un." He'd pull her close. "You worry too much. What are you going to do, feed all the starving kids? Save all the elephants?"

"It's not that, Jason. It's ..."

"It's all hype, Debbie. We call it news but it isn't. You know that."

He made sure the movies they saw were funny, that the television they watched, with the exception of national news on the weekends, didn't include PBS documentaries on war or concentration camps or anything about animals. They watched, when they watched, situation comedies and old movies.

He could watch the documentaries in his own apartment. That was his business, photography and editing. He had to watch, wanted to, but she didn't. And, he liked being able to keep her from the bad crap. He liked making her happy, making her laugh. He liked everything about these days except for the time he spent wondering when he would be able to make his move to a bigger market.

Debbie knew Jason was taking care of her, keeping her safe. He was smart in a way Michael had never been smart. He had a good job. He had a future. This wasn't another Michael. No way. She was, Debbie knew, very, very lucky.

"He's so great," she told Ellen.

"Right," was Ellen's response before she changed the subject.

*

"Afraid there's no Grand Canyon trip in our immediate future," Jason told her.

"Oh, no. Why not?" She was looking forward to leaving the city and seeing the Grand Canyon for the first time.

"I'm going to work with Ferguson on the breast cancer series. It's going to take two weeks of shooting. We may end up going to California or New York, maybe both."

"I thought Clifford was working with Richard."

"Not on this one." He reached to stroke her arm. "I guess we'll have to put the Canyon on hold for a while."

"Okay," she sighed deeply.

"Hey, it's no big deal. It ain't going anywhere. Come on, give us a smile." He chucked her under the chin.

She laughed in spite of herself. They would still be together most of the time.

Brown made the decision that paired Jason and Ferguson.

"I think you should do this one with Jason," he told the medical reporter.

"Well, okay, but Clifford has been doing some good work with me."

"He's a good man, but let's go with Jason on this one. I think it would be better." He nodded as though they both agreed on the choice.

Ferguson said nothing until he was back in his cubicle. He leaned out to talk to Jack Benton.

"Says he wants Jason on the breast thing instead of Clifford."

"Why?"

"I don't know. It doesn't matter to me."

"Maybe it's because he's black," said Benton. "You know, white women's titties and all that."

"Come on," laughed Ferguson.

"You never know," said Benton.

Charles Adkins was in the photographers' room drinking a can of soda and talking with Steve when Clifford slammed in.

"I hear Jason's doing the series with Ferguson," he told them. "Does anybody here have something against me?"

Charles Adkins shook his head. He honestly didn't know.

"Happens all the time," he offered. "Probably Harding's fault."

"Shit, I don't know," Clifford said, shaking his head in frustration. "I don't even know who to talk to about it. Ferguson said it wasn't his decision."

"Ah, let it go," Charles Adkins advised.

Steve nodded a vague agreement from his seat at the equipment bench. He had taken apart his old CP16 to clean it. Brown gave him the film camera when they changed over to videotape.

"You deserve it," Brown said.

He could tell Clifford how it felt to be one of the best in the business and have the business change around you and some mealy-mouth punk hands you an old camera and says, "You deserve it."

He could tell him how it felt to be working with kids who didn't know the beauty of film, didn't know the feel of it, the weight of it, who didn't know how to open a camera and see in a second what was wrong. Now they brought the equipment back to the station and called an engineer to fix it.

"I'm sure it's nothing personal," Charles Adkins was saying to Clifford.

"Well, fuck, man," Clifford shouted, "sometimes I think this nigger is too black for the Fat Boy. Is that it? Is this nigger too black?" he drawled.

Charles Adkins gave a short laugh.

"No, man, that's it and it ain't making me laugh." Clifford gave a hard shake of his head as he picked up his equipment. "No, I ain't laughing," he said, and left the room.

"You know," Charles Adkins said to Steve after a slight pause, "Across the Street they give out ice-cream cones when somebody leaves." He took one last slug of soda. "Isn't that strange?

"Good old George is leaving," he chanted, "and here's an ice cream cone. I think that is perverse."

"More than we get," Steve said, his head bowed to his work.

He cleaned the old camera at least once a month and kept it in the back of his van. Sometimes he would say he was going to take it out and shoot a few hundred feet but he never did. Why bother? Who was going to develop it? The processor hadn't been used in two years. Sooner or later they would get around to tossing it.

"It's not the same. The quality is all wrong," he had argued about videotape. "Film has a texture to it, a depth. Videotape is flat."

They didn't know what he was talking about. The only ones who were into film wanted to go to Hollywood to make movies. Of course, they didn't want to shoot the camera. They wanted to direct.

He also had a sweet little DR. Best little camera every made. They covered the war in Korea carrying that camera. Hell, they were using them for news right up until about five years ago. Sometimes he'd bring it in. Some of the guys liked to look at it. It was so damn simple. Fit right into your hand. Made for it. Cappy knew. Cappy started with a DR. Neatest, tightest little camera ever made.

Well, he'd keep his CP16 in the back of the van, ready to go. There might be that one time when he would need it, reach for it and it would be there, taking those beautiful film pictures. He sighed and Charles Adkins made a clean shot into the trashcan with his empty red soda can.

23

They came to the city by the thousands, a ragtag army. They stretched across the parks, piles of rags and tatters pushing grocery carts filled with their lives. The newer arrivals tried to wash themselves and their clothes in the few working fountains and under the spigots city janitors had neglected to cap. The others, the ones who had found themselves here for years, accepted their filth. They were young men with woolly beards and wild eyes. They were middle-aged men with frightened eyes and missing teeth.

They had a schedule to keep, given to them by those who cared and those who made money by caring. They began at the plasma center, selling their blood for the few dollars that bought booze at the corner convenience store. The booze brought friends and conversations and finally, at night, brought the laughing or stench-sick cops who dragged them into the detox center. A few days later they began the cycle again.

In the mornings they lay on the grass in their parks or played cards at the picnic tables. Then, when the time came, they rose to the march, a gray Confederate shuffle in the dust and sun and across the cement. They became a slow-moving line feeding into the charity dining hall

Twice a year the Best went there as well. They showed up in a van, a grim reporter and a sullen photographer, to show the audience how charity was dispensed on Thanksgiving and Christmas. Behind them or in front of them were other crews from other stations. Each had been given or had requested a specific time slot for the story. It was the one story Ellen swore she would not do. It was that horrible.

The reporter would wander up the aisles, mike in hand, past the tables filled with the poor and the crazy. The photographer was told by those in charge not to embarrass these people and to ignore any anger they might show.

They had enough dignity, these people, to resent the reporter and his camera and his words. Even the craziest, the never-ending mumblers, the worst of the shufflers, the rag-layered worst of them, had enough dignity to be ashamed and angry that they were being used as a story. On the other hand, the holidays were slow news days and this was a sure thing.

The managers of the dining hall allowed the television people in because they felt it might help donations.

"We're usually okay during the holidays," they'd say, "but we operate all year round. We need more help after the holidays. Could you say that?"

They went live with the story even if the dinner was served in the afternoon. They would run the tape of the meal and the poor and the crazed beneficiaries. Sometimes they got lucky when so many showed up that a line still stretched outside as it had since ten in the morning.

The story made viewers feel full and contented and happy not to be bundled in filth and desperation. Yet, it was tear-touched as well. All those poor people, ah well. Yes, a perfect holiday story.

As a rule, George Harding gave the story to a male reporter. No one asked why, although Charles Adkins did ask why it had to be him and pointed out he got these types of stories more than anyone else. It was true he was divorced, something Carter was still pissed about, and had no family dinner to go to, but didn't he deserve a break?

He did handle the story with a certain gentleness. He would walk through the dining hall talking about how many meals had been served and how the city and the business community came through once again to make this dinner possible. Behind him, inevitably, an old whiskered face would stare into the camera.

"Why me, George?" Adkins would demand.

"Because you are so good at it," George Harding would give his infrequent grin.

*

When Jack Benton did the story, he made it seem as dingy as it was, and as reeking and ugly. His report would make George Harding frown before returning to his phones.

"Back to you, Tom," Jack Benton would say with a slight smile. Carter would nod and give his thanks and that alone would indicate that he, too, felt sorry for those folks down at the charity kitchen, and he, too, felt glad to be sitting warm and cozy in the newsroom on Thanksgiving Day.

Carter worked the Thanksgiving newscasts. It came on a Thursday and Tom Carter always worked a full week.

*

"Turn that thing off," Clifford ordered from his seat on Debbie's couch. "Man, I don't want to look at that nastiness."

Paige Allen switched the channel to another newscast.

"Man, that is awful. Why do we have to go down there with all those sorry people?" Clifford asked before going back to his high-piled plate.

Charles Adkins stood at the dining room table, stabbing another piece of turkey.

"Thank God I didn't have to do it," he said. "Why do I get those stories?"

Debbie cooked the Thanksgiving dinner for those who had no family in the city and no time to make it home to another state. Clifford, Charles Adkins, Tommy Rodriguez, and Paige Allen accepted the invitation.

"I might live," Tommy groaned from his seat next to Clifford. "But only if there is pie. You better have pie."

Jason couldn't make it. Instead of flying straight back from shooting in New York with Richard Ferguson, he took a flight to Chicago to be with his parents.

"Sorry, babe," he told her. "I'll see you Sunday night."

They hadn't seen much of each other in the past few weeks. Jason was either out of the station or in the editing booth. Ferguson decided to work on another medical story at the same time they were doing the breast cancer series. Jason was shooting both. There were those few hours of sex and sleep before he left by six or seven to get back to the station.

"Richard has him tied up fifteen hours a day," Debbie explained to Ellen. "And this breast cancer thing is important to him."

"Let me check for breast cancer," he said on one of those late nights. "No, seriously."

He grabbed for her and she laughed.

"Come on, big fella. It shouldn't be so hard to find." He placed his hand on one small breast.

She missed him.

"November is always busy," Ellen said, "with ratings and everything. It should slow down soon."

Debbie wasn't sure. Jason seemed to have so much to do and to be so excited by it.

"Ferguson thinks he already has this thing sold to the network," he told her when he called from New York. "We got some some new info on the reconstruction surgery they're doing here."

"Come home soon," she told him. "And, don't you go fooling around with those big-city women." She kept her voice light.

"Not me, babe. I'm straight-arrow," he told her.

Ellen had to work Thanksgiving.

"What are you going to do for dinner?" Debbie asked. "At least you could come by for a sandwich or something." She could see Ellen eating a turkey TV dinner in front of her television.

"No, thanks. I'll give you a call later," Ellen said.

Debbie knew she would call late in the night and they would talk, as was becoming their habit.

24

"Why bother?" Richard Ferguson asked when Jason told him what he planned to do.

"It's only fair," Jason said.

It was only fair to tell Debbie he saw Ashley in New York, that he had called her and asked her to take a commuter flight up from Washington. When she walked into the hotel bar, every head turned.

Richard stayed only long enough to say, "Looking good, Ashley." That made Jason smile. When did she not look good?

"I think you should start applying in DC again," she said that night while his hands made an inventory of all the places they knew of her body. They stopped to cup the large full breasts.

"And what would that mean for us?" he asked.

"I think we might want to spend some time together," she said softly. "I think about you a lot."

He told her he had been seeing a woman but, he added quickly, "It's nothing serious." He felt her body stiffen before relaxing again with a sigh of acceptance.

"That's all right," she said. "Be warned, though, things will change once we start working together again."

He laughed. He did like this woman and he wouldn't mind being with her again. No, he wouldn't mind at all.

On Sunday, Debbie cleaned the apartment for him, changed the sheets. She made a casserole. They would eat a late dinner and sit on the couch and laugh. They would go into the bedroom and make love and he would stay the night.

He came at ten and stayed only long enough to tell her what he thought she had a right to know.

She grew pale with his words.

"But what about me?" she wondered aloud, still confused by his confession.

"Nothing has changed," he assured her. "I may be here for another five years. I thought you should know that I saw her. I thought it was only fair."

"I don't understand why you came here." she cried, glancing around the room.

"Because I like you, Debbie. Because we're friends." He reached for her. She pulled back.

"No," she said. "Friends don't hurt each other and I thought we were more than friends."

"Hey, Debbie, don't get so serious about this. I care about you. You know that. There's no reason for us to stop seeing each other. It was only one night. Come on." He opened his arms. "Come on, big 'un, give us a hug."

"One night? You spent the night with her? Is that what you mean?" She was stunned.

He shrugged.

"Get out of here," she ordered, jumping to her feet. "I don't want you here."

"Debbie, don't be ridiculous," he argued. "It wasn't anything. It just happened. We can talk about it."

"No. You get out of here now."

"Debbie, this is silly. I don't want to leave you like this."

"You go now, right now," she demanded. "Now."

"Okay, then." He shrugged. "If that's what you want, but it doesn't have to be this way. It doesn't."

So much for telling the truth. He'd talk to her later, when she calmed down. Everything would be fine.

She told Ellen on Monday morning.

"I cried all night. I couldn't even talk. But, I am okay now."

"He's a bastard," Ellen stated loudly.

She looked around to see if Jason was near. She'd give him a look if she saw him.

"I mean, I don't even understand," Debbie was saying as she wiped at her eyes with a tissue. "He's with me and goes to her? And then he comes back to me? That doesn't make any sense, does it?"

"Yeah, well."

"And then he says it is nothing. How can that be? How can it be nothing to sleep with someone? Is she really all that wonderful?" she asked.

"Who, Ashley?"

"Yes, Ashley," Debbie snapped.

"She was okay. Blond. She was pretty in a loose sort of way. You know, the sweater girl."

"Was she a good reporter?"

"Not bad."

"Oh. Well, maybe he won't get a job in Washington." Debbie pulled a tissue from her purse.

"Who cares?" Ellen shouted it out. "He's not important, Debbie. He obviously doesn't worry about your feelings."

"Maybe I should see somebody."

"Who?"

"A doctor, like I told you before."

"Because of this?"

"No, not this, lots of things."

"I suppose," Ellen said. "If you think so. What could it hurt?"

*

He smoked and drank coffee while Debbie tried to read the degrees hanging on the wall behind him.

"How did you find me?" he asked.

"The phone book," she said and smiled. "I liked it because you called me back yourself."

He reached for another cigarette.

"Do you mind?"

She shook her head.

"Is there something in particular you want to talk about?"

"The crying," she said and smiled shyly. "I cry a lot and I don't think it's the job anymore or because this man I was dating slept with an old girlfriend. I think it's because I'm not happy about a lot of things and I want to change that."

"You said there was this other doctor who told you to find someone here?"

"That was a few months ago. He was my doctor for a while in Oregon and he said I might need a tune-up. I guess this is it."

She tried to see the time on the watch he had placed on the small table beside his chair.

"Anyway, I feel okay now so I thought this might be a good time to start changing."

"Tell me about this crying."

"It's nothing. I get sad, that's all. I see things and people that make me sad and I don't know why."

"Have you ever been on medication for depression?"

"No!" She yelled out the word. "I don't believe in medication."

"I'm not suggesting it," he told her quickly. "However, sometimes we find medication useful."

"Not for me," she stated firmly. "Nothing is that wrong."

He may have seen her on the news. He couldn't remember. He knew at least one doctor who was seeing a few of these television people. Once the word got around, others came, he supposed. He'd have to call him, mention this reporter and ask about her melancholy. Possibly part of the business.

He put out his cigarette. Ridiculous that he couldn't hold off for fifty minutes.

"I want to do this fast," she said. "I don't have lots of time, but I've been reading that there is some therapy that goes really fast."

"It all depends on the problem and how committed the patient is. Would you like to come twice a week to begin with, for speed?" he said with a smile.

"Yes, yes," she agreed. "That would be good, at first."

It wouldn't be two times a week for long. Soon she would be coming to this office once a week and soon, she told herself, not at all.

Clifford waited in the van. He looked around the parking lot while he ate his fast-food lunch. The cars were no big deal. No Mercedes, no BMWs, and that's what these guys drove. Her doctor could be parked around back. Still, he didn't like it. If you were good, you had a Mercedes or a Jag, not some old junky Toyota or Ford.

"Everything okay?" he asked when she got back to the van.

"Great." She smiled.

That night she told Ellen about the visit."He is nice."

"What's his name?"

"Waddell. Stanley Waddell."

"What's that? I mean, isn't Stanley Polish? What's the Waddell?"

"English?"

"Or German. Man, what a combination."

"There was one thing, though," Debbie said.

"What?"

"He wanted to know if I wanted pills, you know, medication."

"That's the last thing you need," Ellen pronounced.

"I told him that. I told him I didn't want anything. I never took pills, even the first time. I went through therapy without pills and I was worse then, not like now. Why did he bring that up?"

"It's all part of the quick fix philosophy. Got a problem, take a pill. The whole fucking country is taking pills."

"I got scared when he asked me that, Ellen, like something was really wrong."

"Nothing's wrong. You told him you didn't want pills. That's the end of it."

"I know. I know."

"Maybe he's testing you, seeing if you went to him to get pills. People do."

"That could be," Debbie said hopefully. "That was probably it."

"You have to trust him," Ellen told her. "If you don't, don't go back."

"I have to go back," she cried out. "That's the point. I won't be better until I figure out why I feel so sad all the time."

"Debbie, there is nothing wrong with you."

"I know. I know. You're right."

Ellen was right. She was always right.

"And thank you, thank you, for being my friend."

"Right," Ellen said, with a long exhale.

She was lucky to have Ellen, Debbie thought as she put the phone back on the nightstand, so lucky. She pulled up the quilt her grandmother made for her own wedding night, and lay with her hands atop it.

What would happen if Ellen got tired of her the way Jason did? she wondered. What if Ellen stopped believing in her? She stared into the darkness, folding her hands in prayer. Was it there? Yes, it was, the hint of it, the taste of the copper penny of fear.

"One," she whispered silently to her mind. "Two," came a pace behind.

25

"I'm going to Albuquerque for Christmas," Ellen announced. "They actually have Christmas there. Snow, the whole bit. It's more like it is on the East Coast. Parties, people getting together to celebrate. I like that."

"The worst news in the world comes out of Albuquerque," Harold Lewis said, leaning out of his cubicle. "Good art, terrible news."

"I don't think so. I learned more there than anywhere I've ever worked. You had to do your own shooting sometimes, editing, setting up the lights. That's the way to learn television."

"I think it would be a good place to end up," Chuck Farrell commented. "Some little station in New Mexico."

"No money," she said. "That's the problem. The whole state is dirt poor. In a way, I like that too. Nobody there seems to care that much about money."

It was safe, this love for another place. She knew that. She didn't have to live there again. She didn't have to wonder how she would buy a new dress or a winter coat on a miserably low salary. She didn't have to turn her eyes from the ugliness, the dirt, the poverty. Albuquerque was only a place she could call upon when she needed to leave town. Still, it wasn't a bad place. She actually might go back to Albuquerque, someday, when all of this finally got to her.

All of what? Television was the same everywhere. Like she told them, same people, different faces. To get away, you had to get out.

"And do what? What would you do?" Chuck Farrell asked her more than once.

"Good God, Chuck, there is life after television."

"Sure there is, but what would you do?"

She didn't know. What she did now was relatively easy, a formula. Once you figured out the formula, you could turn out stories all day long.

"You're wrong about something," Jack Benton shouted out.

"Yeah, like what?"

"Everybody cares about money. Everybody."

Debbie listened to the banter. She wouldn't be leaving town for Christmas. She wouldn't even be able to spend the day in her apartment. She had Thanksgiving off. That's the way it worked. She wouldn't bother cooking for herself or anybody else. She didn't feel that well.

Jason had called her a few times and she kept the conversations short and cold. She saw no sense in speaking to him. He left on another trip with Richard Ferguson.

The doctor tried talking to her between puffs of cigarettes and sips of coffee. When he tried talking about her mother and her father, she shook her head and told him there wasn't time for that. She said that would be like starting all over again and she didn't have the time. Instead, she told him about how Christmas carols made her cry and how the Santa Claus in the mall made her sad.

"It's a hard season for many people," he assured her. "The holidays are never what we expect them to be."

She stared at him.

"Is there something else bothering you?" he asked.

"I'm not sure yet," she said. "I will talk about it when I am sure."

"How soon?"

"Soon," she said.

She told him one week later. She was pregnant.

"Was that why you came to me?"

"No. I didn't know. I found out for sure yesterday."

She sat deathly still, her feet flat on the floor, her knees pressed together, hands clasped tightly in her lap.

He rubbed his forehead with the tip of his middle finger.

"Debbie, I don't know what to say."

"There is nothing you can say. I've already made my decision."

"What decision?"

"Well," she gave a sour laugh, "I obviously can't have a baby. I can't go out and do stories and be unmarried and pregnant."

"Perhaps you could."

She shook her head angrily. "Please."

"What about the father? Does he know?"

"No, and I'm not telling anyone else." She opened her hands and stared at them. "This is for me to do. I don't want anyone to know."

"Debbie, I don't think dealing with this by yourself is wise. What about your family?" He leaned forward from his chair, his palms rubbing on his thighs. "Isn't there anyone else you can talk to?"

"No," she said firmly. "This is for me to do. I don't have any problems with having an abortion. People do it all the time, don't they?"

She looked at him, her face now full of pain.

"Besides," she tried to smile, "I have you to talk to."

*

One other person did know. Clifford Williams. She made the doctor's appointment for the time of their usual lunch break between stories. She believed, whatever the news, she could handle it without letting Clifford know. Anyway, as she kept telling herself, everything was probably fine. She had missed periods before.

"Six to eight weeks," the doctor said. "Any decision has to be made soon. Termination is more difficult after the first trimester."

"How soon will I need to do it?"

"Within the next two weeks. On the other hand, you are healthy and young and would probably carry a healthy baby to term."

"Do you do it here?" she asked the man with the kind eyes.

"No. We'll give you the information you need if that's what you decide."

"But, not you?"

"No, not me. Not me," he said, shaking his head.

"Okay, Debbie?" Clifford asked when she came back. She said nothing and he threw the van into reverse. When he finally spoke again it was to ask if she wanted to stop.

"You want lunch or a soda?" he asked, the worry etched on his face.

She shook her head and quietly began to cry.

"I am so sorry, sorry," she wept, "you shouldn't have to go through this."

"It don't bother me," he said quickly, afraid of her tears.

"It's so stupid," she sniffed. "I can't do anything right anymore, nothing."

Leave it alone, he told himself, but had to ask, "You need some help or something?"

"I'm pregnant," she cried. "Pregnant."

Ah, man.

"What a mess," she said, the tears falling. "What a stupid mess."

"I hear that," he nodded. It was a mess, her mess, and he sure wasn't going to ask her anything about it. It had to be Jason. Sure, except Jason was talking a lot about DC and that girl he used to date. If it wasn't Jason, then who?

He shook his head. With his luck, they'd think it was him and there he was, his big black self, driving her to the doctor. Wouldn't Brown like that.

"It's okay, Clifford," she said and touched his arm. "I don't want to put you through this. Please don't say anything. I'll be okay. Promise me you won't tell anyone, promise."

"Don't worry," he told her. "Ain't none of my business."

*

"You'll be in Christmas?" George checked with her. "That's what my schedule says." He steeled himself for an argument.

"I'll be here."

"You might have to do the Christmas dinner story," he said. "It has to be you or Adkins and he does it all the time. That's what he says, anyway. You'll be on with Cappy."

"Ah, George, come on," Cappy whined as he walked to the desk. He knew he was working Christmas. The schedule had been hanging in the photographers' room for a month, but it was worth a try.

"I got kids, George. Don't you ever give it a rest?"

"That's okay," Clifford moved in behind him. "I'll take it. I got no plans."

"You mean it?" Cappy asked in surprise. "Really? You don't have to."

"You can cover for me New Year's."

"You got a deal," Cappy laughed.

George frowned. He didn't like them changing the schedule, making their own plans. He didn't understand why they fought him all the time. It was their job, damn it.

"Too bad," said Ellen when Debbie came down the cubicle row. "I think this is the first Christmas I haven't worked in five years."

"When are you leaving for New Mexico?" Debbie asked.

"Tomorrow at the crack of dawn."

"Do you have friends there?"

"Debbie, I lived there for three years. Of course I have friends there."

"I'm sorry," Debbie said. "You don't talk much about things like that."

"Things like what?" There was a warning note in her voice.

"Personal things, like what you do and who you see when you aren't here."

"Maybe I think some things are my business." Now her voice was tight.

"Yeah, you're probably right," Debbie nodded.

"Debbie, do you have something on your mind?"

"No," she said, sitting down at her desk. "I was only thinking that you know so much about everyone but nobody knows much about you."

"And what is it you want to know?" Ellen asked, leaning back in her chair.

"Nothing, I guess," said Debbie. "Sorry, I'm just in a funny mood."

"So it seems," Ellen agreed and went back to writing her story.

SPORTS

He tapped the script twice on the desk and laid it down. It was a signal that the next part of this newscast would be relaxed and he was the one that made that choice. He swiveled slightly in his chair to face John Devlin.

"So, John, the hometown team looks like the one to go with this year."

He smiled. Tom Carter was a sportsman, a jock, and the audience knew it. And boy, there wasn't any question about his loyalties. Hometown teams all the way.

Jean Ann leaned forward as though to make a comment, to join in with them. Carter, sensing the movement, cut her off.

"So, how do they look for tomorrow's game, John?"

They told him he had to work with her, make it look all honky-dory and friendly, but that sure as hell didn't mean she was going to sit in on his newscast and talk about sports. He made that his rule when they first brought her on. God, he hated her.

26

She loved the drive to Albuquerque, the texture of it. For the first few hours, it was the deep reds and blues and purples of desert buttes and mountains stretching across all horizons. Then, there were those miles when the whole world went flat before the desert finally fell away and the roll to the forest began.

Somewhere between that flat stretch and the pines, she gave up a deep sigh and sat back ready to enjoy the rhythm of the wheels and the forward movement. By Flagstaff, that place of green and white, she would be totally relaxed.

There would be snow by Flagstaff, on the ground, and the smell of it in the air. She always turned on the radio when she got close to the town and listened to the station where the drumbeat of Navajo was strangely punctuated with white man's words. The suck-breath, push-breath Navajo would suddenly spit out "hamburger" or "Chevrolet." Money words. Once out of town, she turned off the radio and let her mind stretch out as did the miles before her.

From Winslow to Holbrook she watched the horizon, imagining how it would feel when she first sighted a massive head and the following rise of the immense body and the city-block length of tail, one of Tommy Rodriguez's dinosaurs.

"Every time I drive that stretch, I get the feeling that some sort of prehistoric animal is going to start coming at me from over the horizon," he told her. "You know what I mean?"

Looking at the flat land all around her, she knew exactly what he meant.

After Holbrook and into Gallup were the advertising reminders that this was the *Wild West*. A few stores painted bright orange and yellow beckoned tourists to leave the freeway. One, cut into the side of a rusty butte, offered the passing cars a wooden fort and teepees.

Signs alongside the freeway promised cheap cigarettes and moccasins and the last and best of all sales from *Real Indians*. The signs were landmarks. Their sales had been the last and best for decades. Each one made her smile.

By Gallup, her back was stiff. She spent the ten miles before the town with her left leg pulled up on the seat. She had no need to move her feet on the pedals, only the gas. Truckers would pass and glance back to see if she was worth a few blinks of their taillights and a few static-cut CB words to fellow truckers.

Sometimes, when she would flick her highbeams to show them where she was as they moved in front of her, they would blink those taillights slowly, seductively, like the knowing wink of a big-hipped woman.

The Navajos would pass her in their white and dark blue pickups, the women tight to their men, the children at the side window and an old woman blanket-bundled in the open back.

The fast-food hamburger in Gallup was dry and tasteless, the bathroom clean. She was in and out of that straight-road town in twenty minutes. Now the anxiety began and the excitement, waiting for Grants, waiting for it and passing it.

Wasn't it Grants where the train derailed and because of it she had to tell Ronnie McBain they couldn't have their first dinner together?

Didn't she do a story on some small college in Grants or was that further south? And, where was the turn-off for the mountain scratched with the graffiti of three hundred years of travelers? The conquistadors carved their words on it, followed by the settlers who added their names before heading on and, before any of them, the Indians made their drawings.

The mountain was there, somewhere between Grants and

Albuquerque or perhaps it was before Grants. She could never remember.

The lava land, the choppy badlands, that was out there too. She remembered the freezing day when she and photographer Pete Romero spent twelve hours doing three stories somewhere between Grants and Albuquerque. Pete turned the film, all of it, purple when he ran the processor. Three stories, twelve hours of driving and marching over the shoe-slashing lava rocks and freezing, all purple.

"Geez, Ellen, I am so sorry. I don't know how it happened."

"That's okay," she told him. It was his film as well.

"All purple?" she had to ask.

"Well, I guess a foot or two is okay," he said and started to laugh. She joined him, laughing together until they were almost hysterical.

Acoma was out there as well. Acoma, the sky city, the place of adobe brown walls high on the butte. She thought of it as a cold mud city offering little reason to drive up the narrow road. She found the village's adobe church as bleak and cheerless as the handful of worshipers.

The first hill before Albuquerque always promised that the city came next. The second hill, the third, all stretched equally long and high but once atop, the lie was seen. The city was not there, only the hint of the Sandias, the watermelon mountains, before the car went down again.

The air was different now, the sky different as well. Puffs of white clouds punctuated the blue. She inhaled deeply.

Finally, at the top of that one last hill, the city appeared like a jewel framed by the mountains that had begun their late afternoon change to deep pink. At that moment, she turned on the radio, loud, and hit the city singing.

27

Kim Palmeri's blond head poked around the partition of Ellen's cubicle.

"I've got you on that new factory tomorrow, on the west side," she told her.

Ellen looked up in frustration. Two hours until the six o'clock and she didn't have her stories written.

"Fine."

"You gotta be out of here by eight."

"Yeah, I got that."

Kim leaned close. "What's going on with Debbie?"

Ellen looked over at Debbie who was flipping through her notebook.

"There is something wrong," Kim decided. "I caught her crying in the ladies' room."

Ellen shrugged. She had been back a few days and hadn't had a chance to talk with Debbie. She tried calling her but got no answer. And, Debbie hadn't called her.

She watched as Kim stopped at Debbie's cubicle, speaking softly to her. Debbie looked up with a smile. A few minutes later, Ellen watched as Harold Lewis stopped at the cubicle and gave Debbie a little pinch on her arm.

"Hey, hey, cutie," he sang.

When he passed Ellen's desk, he gave her a short nod.

She felt a strange twinge of anger and something else she couldn't identify. She glanced over at Debbie who was putting paper in her typewriter.

Others in the newsroom made it a point to stop by Debbie's cubicle or they watched her when they had the chance. Something had changed. The excitement and the joy that had been so much a part of her seemed to have disappeared overnight. They didn't see any anger or frustration. That they could understand. They all had that. No, this was different, and they felt the danger of it.

They watched and waited. Eventually they would know what was going on. See someone else change like this and they would know why. Oh, yeah, everything was worth knowing.

Ellen saw them bending over Debbie, talking to her in the hall. She heard the concern in their voices, the joshing they did to make Debbie laugh. She found it increasingly annoying.

Both she and Debbie were in early the next morning.

"Did you have a good time in Albuquerque?" Debbie asked.

"Yeah, did. And your Christmas?"

"Oh, it was okay. I had to work," Debbie said as she sat down at her desk. She pushed a strand of her hair behind her ear.

"I tried calling you, Debbie," Ellen told her.

"I've been going to bed early."

And apparently, Ellen thought, annoyed again, that was all she was going to say.

"I've got the house guest from hell," Sandi from Accounting interrupted her thoughts. "You wouldn't believe this woman."

"How so?"

"She came with my mother. They're staying a week and she is crazy. She's on this special diet, has to eat six times a day. Drives me nuts. There's nothing wrong with her, not really," she explained. "I just hate it, that's all."

Ellen looked over at Debbie. She was reading an assignment sheet.

"She goes crazy if I even suggest a restaurant or going out for a drink. She does it in public too," Sandi was saying. "It's embarrassing. Everything has to stop for her."

"Oh," said Ellen as though she had just made a discovery. "It's all about attention. She wants attention." She looked over again. Debbie was still reading.

"Well, yes, I suppose so," decided Sandi. "The worst thing is this panic she goes into for no reason. She screams, actually screams. I almost drove off the road."

"I once gave a neighbor a ride to pick up her car," Ellen told her. "One of her kids in the backseat starts screaming at the top of his lungs for no reason and she does nothing. I stopped the car and turned around and said, 'Don't you dare scream when I'm driving.'" She gave a loud imitation of the voice she used on the boy.

"Sure, with a child, " Sandi agreed.

"No, you can do it with adults too," Ellen stated.

"Maybe you can. I feel terrible even talking about her. She isn't so awful, not really."

With a hooded glance at Debbie, Ellen got to her feet.

"Sometimes," she said in a stage whisper, "Truth can be a great kindness."

In the van, waiting for Steve, she put her head in her hands. Why had she done that? Why? What was she thinking? Debbie would know she was talking about her. Of course she would.

She hit at her chin with a closed fist. What possessed her? Debbie had only sat down, pushed that blond hair behind her ear. And this is how she reacts?

That vision of the blond hair and the creamy skin and the pretty profile was vividly clear. My God, was she jealous of her? Was that it? She had never been jealous of anyone in her life. She shook the thought off. No, it couldn't be.

Besides—she took a deep breath—Debbie probably didn't hear a thing and, if she did, she wouldn't know she'd been talking about her looking for attention. No.

Still, she told herself, she had to fix this. She had to do something nice because what she had done in there made her feel lousy and stupid.

28

After a week, Ellen decided to break through Debbie's silence, pounding on her door one night while holding a half-gallon jug of white wine and balancing a pizza. The decision to move into the situation made her remember one of the newsroom stories in Albuquerque.

Dale told her how one Christmas they heard about some poor artist starving up in the mountains, a guy who used to be famous. Now he was old, broke and forgotten. A few of the people in the newsroom chipped in for groceries and a Christmas tree and drove to his house, all ready to sing carols and tear up over the good feelings of the night.

The adobe hut in the mountains turned out to be an expensive ranch house. The housekeeper, surprised at their Christmas Eve visit, told them the artist was spending the holidays at his home in Aspen. They backed away, smiling and waving, and jumped into the cars, hoping they hadn't been recognized. They deposited the bags and the tree in front of the first shabby house they saw. She wondered if her trip to Debbie's would be equally misguided.

"It's me. Let me in. I'm dying out here," she shouted at Debbie's door-filtered questions. "Hurry up, Debbie."

"Thought you might want to get drunk and get fat," she said once the door opened, and she pushed past Debbie. "I brought everything we'll need."

"Where are the plates?" she asked, heading for the kitchen, ignoring Debbie's "But, I already ate."

"So, your vacation was good?" Debbie asked after Ellen poured the wine and grabbed a slice of pizza.

"It was," Ellen said between bites. "I saw a lot of people I haven't seen in a while. It snowed, a couple of parties. It was a good time. It usually is up there."

She knew exactly how to do it. You keep the patter bright and happy, filling every second with talk, dumb, quick talk. You did it before a tough interview, one where you were going to have to hang the guy out to dry or when the man was angry or nervous or impatient. You smiled and laughed and chattered on and on, keeping his mind off the photographer setting up the camera and the lights, running the cords, pinning on the microphones.

"And how about you?" she asked. "Christmas can be a bitch. The whole holiday season, if you're working. I know."

Debbie didn't respond.

"Still, the weather is fantastic, isn't it? I mean, this is why we are all here, right?"

"I guess so."

"The first year I was here we had three floods, January through March. What a way to start a job. You started in March, didn't you? April? Almost a year. It went fast." She paused for a sip of wine.

You keep it going, the idiot babble, fast, happy, and meaningless, until the photographer nodded and you started the interview.

"Debbie, what's the matter? You seem so quiet."

"I'm tired, that's all."

Okay, she would wait. You always waited that extra second, that uncomfortable second of silence that cried out to be filled with a sound, a word. Inevitably, the person being interviewed filled that silence, usually by saying something they shouldn't.

"I mean, I don't know. I feel bad," Debbie ended the discomfort.

Ellen paused again, as though in thought.

"What's bothering you?" she asked softly.

"I don't know. Maybe it's the weather."

"The weather is perfect."

"Yes," Debbie agreed without meeting her eyes.

"Don't worry. It will probably rain in February and we'll be flooded out and we'll be working twenty-four-hour shifts and Brown will have us all sleeping on cots in the newsroom. He thinks he's in Viet Nam or something, not that he ever was, God knows. You won't be hoping for rain after that. Can you imagine seeing Brown sleeping next to you on a cot?" She pushed for a smile, a relaxation of the tension.

The small smile came but ended when Debbie lifted her shoulders like a child who knew she was going to stay unhappy, no matter what treats and promises were offered.

Ellen went back to the banter.

"God, I thought the second flood had come. Brown kept staring out the windows, praying it would keep raining. I kept praying somebody would let me go home. Where'd you get that?" She nodded toward the enormous hutch filling one wall of the dining area.

"It was my great-grandmother's," Debbie said. "I couldn't leave it."

Ellen could imagine somebody hauling that damn thing across the plains and the Rockies in a covered wagon. She had seen the paintings of the household goods tossed along the wagon trails.

"Can you imagine bringing that thing across the country in a wagon?"

"I think it came by boat. I think that's what Dad said, or train."

Ellen nodded. They were talking now. One slight push, a nudge, and they would move wherever she wanted them to go.

"Where did they bring this thing from, originally?"

"I know what you were doing," Debbie cut in angrily. "I know what you were doing."

"What? What are you talking about?"

"When you were talking to Sandi."

"What do you mean?"

"I know you were talking about me." Debbie was looking at her now, her eyes wide and questioning.

"What? I don't know what you're talking about," Ellen lied.

"Yes you do," Debbie nodded. "You were talking about me, weren't you? You were saying that I wanted attention. You really think that?"

"Debbie, we were talking about an obnoxious house guest," Ellen tried half-heartedly. She knew she wasn't going to win this one.

"You meant me," Debbie insisted. "I'm not dumb, you know. You may think I am, but I'm not."

"No, I don't think you're dumb," Ellen protested.

"And you meant it. Didn't you? About the attention?"

"Maybe for a minute, but I can be so wrong about things. It was a bitchy thing to say and I am sorry for it. I didn't mean to hurt you."

"Okay," Debbie nodded, the anger gone. "That's okay."

Good, thought Ellen, that was done.

"You were wrong about that other thing too," Debbie said then.

"What other thing?"

"That truth can be a kindness. That's not true," Debbie said, pushing the slice of pizza around her plate with her finger.

Ellen shook her head. "You're the one who feels so strongly about the truth," she said, reminding her of that first-day remark, the one she found so naïve.

"Maybe not anymore."

They both sat with the thought.

"Look," Debbie finally said, "I need to tell you something, but you can't tell anyone."

"I won't," Ellen assured her, willing to do anything to make up for the past few minutes.

"No," Debbie said, leaned over and touched at Ellen's hand. "This is important. You have to promise me you will never tell anyone else."

"I won't say anything, Debbie." Ellen smiled reassuringly. How bad could this really be?

"Because I don't want anyone to know ever," Debbie said in a worried voice.

"And who would I tell?"

"No one!" Debbie shouted it out. "You can't tell anyone!"

"Debbie, it's okay. I won't say anything to anyone." She put both hands up. "You have my word."

She waited.

"How do you feel about abortions?" Debbie asked, looking away.

"You know," Ellen chose her words carefully, "like it is not my business to tell another woman what to do with her body."

"I had one," Debbie said. Her voice was so low Ellen had to lean toward her.

"What?"

"After Christmas. I had an abortion."

Ellen shook her head slowly. Time, she needed time.

"It wasn't bad," Debbie continued. "I thought it might be bad, painful, but it wasn't bad. It only took a few hours. I was only worried that somebody would find out. And poor Clifford." Her face softened with the name. "He was scared to death. He was sure I was going to die."

"Clifford?" Ellen all but screamed the name.

"Yes. He was the only one I told and he said he wanted to come with me," Debbie explained. "He kept acting like everything was okay, but I could tell he was scared about what was going to happen. He kept saying, 'I better come in. I better come in.'"

Ellen could barely breathe. Each word hit her like a slap.

"I'm okay, though." Debbie touched her hand again. "Everything is okay. I promise. I am glad I can tell you. It means so much to me."

"Oh, Debbie," Ellen's breath finally came. "I wish I had known."

She did not wish she had known. She didn't want to know now.

"Was it Jason's?"

"It doesn't matter," stated Debbie.

"Of course it matters, and it was, wasn't it? That son of a bitch bastard."

The anger made Ellen feel strong again.

"No, I'm the one who got pregnant," Debbie insisted.

"And he had nothing to do with it? That man has been getting away with bloody murder for years."

Even as she said the words, she worried about them. Was it bloody murder? Is that how Debbie felt about the abortion. Is that what she would hear, a reminder of what she had done?

"I'm sorry. That didn't come out right. It just makes me so mad."

"You don't have to be mad," Debbie told her. "I don't even have to be mad. I'm just so ashamed." The tears started to fall. "It wasn't right for me to do that. Nope. It wasn't right."

"Ah, Debbie," Ellen reached to touch her. "It's okay. What does your doctor say about this?"

"He thinks I should go into group therapy. I don't know why but I said I would."

"And you and Jason haven't talked to each other about this?"

"No," she said loudly. She stood up and began to pace, her arms crossed over her chest. She stopped to examine a painting on the wall, to look at the silver-framed photographs on the end table. She straightened and paced again.

"About the abortion," Ellen said quickly. "A lot of women have them. It happens."

"You?" Debbie demanded. "Did you ever have one?"

"No," Ellen said. "There were times I had to think about it. Who hasn't? I got lucky. I don't know what I would have done."

"Whatever you did would be right," Debbie pronounced. "Everything you do is right."

"Me?" Ellen laughed. "You must be kidding. I hardly do anything right. I hardly do anything period."

"You are the most together person I have ever known," Debbie stated. "You know what you want. You know where you are going.

You're not afraid of anything. I wish I were like you."

"Debbie, that is crazy. I don't know what I am going to eat for breakfast, much less what I am going to do for the rest of my life."

"Oh, yes, you do." Debbie smacked her right fist into the palm of her left hand. "And, everybody knows it. Everybody looks up to you."

"You are wrong." Ellen laughed again. "Most people can't stand me. They're forming a club."

"Oh yeah? And what about me?" Debbie's face was bright red with emotion, her eyes large and demanding. "I come here, get pregnant and have an abortion. That's really somebody to look up to. That's why nobody can ever know, ever." She collapsed into a chair. "I don't know what I am going to do."

"About what?" Ellen asked, truly confused.

"About anything. I don't know what I am doing here. I keep dragging other people into these things. Poor Clifford. Even Jason and now you."

Ellen wondered when Debbie would reach up and wipe at the tears that were running down her face.

"And my father. What am I supposed to say to him? Hey, Dad, how's everything? Oh, yes, I had an abortion. Something else you can be proud of."

"You're not dragging anybody in," Ellen interrupted. "That's what friends are for. Forget Jason, and Clifford needs a little excitement in his life." She smiled.

Debbie gave up her own small smile and reached for the tears.

"Here, drink," Ellen ordered and lifted the newly filled glass. "What the hell."

It worked. It always worked when Ellen was on a story.

29

The three group members sat in the waiting room and greeted her with short nods.

"Hi," she said and smiled.

The older woman smiled back, the younger woman nodded. The boy in the sunglasses breathed out a quick, "Hey."

Dr. Waddell moved through the room carrying his coffee mug.

"Let's go in," he said. "Bob is going to be late and I don't know where Alan is." He opened the door to the meeting room. "Have you all met Debbie?"

Debbie waited until the others took their seats before choosing one of her own.

"I'm Maynell," said the older woman

"Carol," said the younger one.

"I'm Terry," said the boy with the sunglasses.

A tall black man came into the room.

"Sorry, I'm late. Hi, I'm Bob." He offered his hand.

"Debbie," she said with a shy smile.

"Well," the doctor said to them all.

No one spoke. Debbie could feel her fear growing. They would ask her first. She knew that much.

"Does anyone have anything they want to talk about?" the doctor asked.

"Well," the black man said, "I guess we should find out about Debbie."

The younger woman lit a cigarette, turning away from Debbie as she did so.

"We might as well ask it now," the older woman said. "Why are you here, Debbie?"

"Doctor Waddell felt I should go into a group."

"That's simple," the younger woman said.

"You came because he told you to?" the older woman pressed. "That's all?"

"I guess because I was afraid not to."

"Afraid not to come to group? How's that?" the black man asked.

"Afraid if I didn't, I would get scared again."

The younger woman looked up, a sharp interest in her eyes.

"Scared of what?" she asked.

"I mean sad." Debbie corrected herself. "I cry at silly things."

The boy with the sunglasses nodded sympathetically. Debbie smiled at him.

"You said scared. That's what you said. Scared of what?" the younger woman demanded.

"I don't know. I guess that's why I'm here, to find out." She looked at the doctor who busied himself lighting a cigarette.

"You know, Stan," the older woman said to him, "I really think you should give us more warning when a new patient is coming into the group. I think you should let us know a few weeks ahead of time."

"Why is that, Maynell?"

"I think we should know, that's all." Her arms were folded across her chest.

"What difference does it make?" the younger woman snapped.

"Well, maybe Alan would have come. I mean, he should be here."

"Who cares?" the younger woman snapped again. "He's hardly here anyway."

"I think it would make a lot of difference." The older woman seemed to be holding onto herself, her arms hugging her ribs.

"I don't think it makes any difference at all," said the younger woman, stabbing at the ashtray with her cigarette. "I think this room is too crowded, anyway."

Debbie inhaled deeply as the attention turned away from her. From her chair, she could see the room's one small window high on the wall across from her.

"I'm an addict," the boy on the couch said suddenly.

She felt her stomach clinch. "Yes?"

"I get frightened too."

He took off the glasses. The brown eyes were strangely vacant.

"I've been off it for a month. Heroin, that's what I use. Heroin."

"That's great," she tried to smile. "I mean about being off drugs. It must be hard."

What was she supposed to say?

"Yes, Terry is working hard. That's why he's here. He needs our support," said the doctor.

All the faces in the room now turned to Terry. Debbie nodded at him and tried smiling again. She felt the rush of fear, the wave of it rising in her as everyone else seemed to sigh and reach for a cigarette or cup.

She would have to tell them the truth. Even though the doctor said she didn't have to if she didn't want. No, she did have to tell them. It was part of getting better. She would have to tell them everything, about the abortion and the breakdown and the counting. Yes, she would. She would have to tell them everything, these people who seemed angry she was there, except for Terry the addict.

No, how could that be? They weren't angry. She just didn't understand them yet. They would help her get better, yes. All she had to do was tell them the truth about everything and they would help her.

The younger woman puffed at another cigarette, the older woman sighed deeply, Bob shrugged and Terry put the sunglasses back over his eyes and melted back into the couch.

*

"Are you ever afraid?" she asked Ellen on their late night call.

"Of course, who isn't?"

"You don't ever act like you are."

Ellen took a puff on her cigarette.

"Oh, everyone is at one time or another. They better be. Being afraid keeps you safe. Makes you watch out for what may be coming at you. If you're normal," she exhaled the stream of smoke, "you're afraid of something."

As Ellen talked, Debbie could feel herself becoming safe again.

"Like what?" she asked.

"Circus clowns, absolutely. They are the most terrifying thing I can imagine. Think about it, big red noses, crazy hair, floppy feet, horns honking all the time."

Debbie giggled.

"I went to that group thing today," she told Ellen. "It was interesting. Only a few people but they seemed nice. Someday I'll be tough like you and I won't need doctors and groups."

"Right."

"Tell me why you like New Mexico so much," Debbie asked, not wanting the phone call to end.

"Beautiful land, interesting people."

"That's all?"

"That's enough for starters."

"Maybe I'll go there," Debbie said, "and meet someone and get married and be happy."

"Sure, why not?" Ellen agreed.

"Did you ever want to get married?"

"Oh, there was this guy once, but it didn't work out."

"You going to tell me about him?"

"Nothing to tell," Ellen said. "Believe me, nothing at all."

30

She didn't tell people about Ronnie McBain. She left that story in Albuquerque. She had stories about other men, Sam the reporter in Florida who made her roar with laughter and the surfer she met in Paris. Leave it to her to spend a year in Paris with a blond from California.

She could talk about the public relations man for the electric company in Albuquerque and the photographer who would take her on the shag rug in her apartment before leaving her for the redhead with the Brooklyn accent.

"Isn't it cute? I think it sounds so cute," he gushed about the girl who sat outside in his car.

"Want to come with us? We're going to Rosie's for a drink."

"You and me and her?" she demanded.

From the car came a loud redheaded Brooklyn laugh.

"Are you crazy?" Ellen shouted at him.

"What?"

"You think I'm going to go with you and her? You must be out of your mind."

She suffered her way through that one for about a month. Then, she met Ronnie McBain, the tall, slow-talking cowboy who pulled his boots on with a huff and a sigh.

"Are you sure these are my boots?" he once questioned her with a sheepish grin. "I can't see that these are my boots."

He struggled to pull one on as he sat on the edge of the bed. She burst out laughing.

He once stood naked at the hotel window in San Francisco, staring down at the street.

"Why don't the police come?" he asked. "They've been down there for five minutes. Can you explain this?"

"What?" she called from the bed.

"The accident. Where are the police?"

"Does it look like anyone is hurt?" She joined him at the window.

"Can't tell."

For him it was a few days off in a big city. For her it was a trip to find another job.

"You really are ashamed of living in New Mexico," he said after a visit to an art gallery where she had been quick to tell the gallery owner that she lived in Albuquerque but came from Boston.

"Ah," the owner nodded. That made a difference.

"You leave Albuquerque," her mother told her. "You don't move there."

"It's not for me," she told Ronnie.

"I like it," he said simply.

Not her. She had no ties to the city. She could move at the drop of a hat and she would. Tempting as he might be with all that ah shucks talk, Ronnie McBain wasn't going to change that.

She met him while covering a fundraiser for the city's art museum. His sister Sara was the assistant to the museum director.

"It looks like you've got yourself an interesting job," he said after watching her do a stand-up.

"It has its moments," she said.

She liked his family. Sara was sweet and smart. The oldest brother, Bob Junior, spent most of his time at the family ranch down south. She liked what she had seen of him. Phillip, the youngest, was a student at the university in Las Cruces. They were loved and owned by their mother, Joan McBain.

She lived in the north valley in a house as big and comfortable as the woman who built it. She had short brown hair, beauty-parlor streaked with blond, a hard weathered face, narrow slate-blue eyes, the lashes spiked thick with black mascara. She wore polyester pants over her ample rear and sipped her chilled vodka from a shot glass.

Sara also lived in the house. Ronnie lived in the guesthouse. Bob Junior came up on weekends. Phillip visited every so often.

"I always dreamed about being in business," Joan McBain told Ellen over an early morning cup of coffee.

"Father and Mother spent their whole lives together working the ranch and, I'll grant you, they had a good life but and I never wanted any part of it. I wanted to be in business, to have a clean office and air-conditioning. Not that we knew much about air-conditioning back then, but that's what I wanted. I wanted to go to work every day and have my hair done and have long red nails."

She held up one big hand and examined it. The short manicured nails were a blazing Revlon red.

"That's what I wanted, a business. After two years up north I said, hell, Bobby, let's go to the city and make a living. I had Bob Junior and Ronnie was coming and Bobby had some money put aside and Lord knows we weren't getting fat up there. And really, he never did anything but say yes to me." She laughed.

"So, you came to Albuquerque?"

"Yup." She took a deep pull on her Benson & Hedges. Her red lipsticked mouth left its mark on the filter. In another hour the lipstick she wore would be nothing but a pink blur.

"I had some cousins here and they owned this empty building out on Twelfth Street. We made a deal and worked our behinds off for five years building the store. Bobby went back to his folks' ranch to help bring in more money. Me and the kids lived behind the store, if you could call it that. We sold feed, some saddles, ropes. Not much more to start."

She was warming to her subject. Last night had been a long, good drinking night. Ron's new girl obviously slept in the guesthouse even if everyone made a big deal about her using one of the spare bedrooms. Joan figured this girl slipped out of the big old four-poster a few minutes after the house quieted down and ran the few hundred yards to the guesthouse. She like the girl and where she slept was of no-never-mind to her except it was only natural she would go to Ron's bed.

"I decided I needed to go to school to learn more about running a business and I was pregnant with Sara. It sure was a busy few years."

Her head wasn't bad this morning even with only five hours of sleep and all that vodka.

"Coffee?" she offered.

They were sitting at the long wooden stretch of an eight-person kitchen table that ended at the desk in front of the wide bay window. From the desk, Joan McBain could see her land and her horses.

"I didn't get into the horses, breeding and selling them, until I saw all these folks around here start buying Arabs," she explained.

"I heard there was big money in those Arabs but I wasn't interested in them. I kept thinking about horses, though. I took some courses at the university. I knew some already, growing up on a ranch, but bloodlines and new methods of breeding was something I was short on.

"My first real good quarter horse, well, real good for me, cost me four thousand. Bobby thought I'd lost my mind."

She chuckled.

"Bobby died a few years ago," Joan McBain told her, "fast, the way he would have liked it." She sighed and reached for another cigarette from the small metal box.

"Heart attack. One minute here," she snapped her fingers, "and bang, he's gone. God, I do miss that man." Her eyes sought Ellen's. "There's a lot of him in Ronnie, you know. In all my children."

*

"I can't see raising cuttin' horses," Ronnie said about his mother's business. "I mean, they're the best for working, but how long is somebody gonna pay fifteen or twenty thousand for some cow pony?"

They were almost the same words spoken by his father when Joan McBain told him her idea about raising quarter horses. No matter what he thought about the plan, he found the money for her first horses. He loved his woman as much as he loved life.

She was eighteen when he first took her to the ranch up north. The land was empty, cold and hard, no green valley like those of the surrounding ranches. Still, it was his and paid for with the years of sweat and bloodied hands on his father's place. He started his ranch with thirty head, nowhere near enough to survive but enough to begin their life together.

They lived in a root cellar dug into the side of a hill. The small pane of glass in the door let them watch the snow grow high around their hole in the hill. Joan had her first baby ten months after they married, barely making it into Española and the doctor. She came back to a trailer Bobby hauled in for her and the baby. For the next year, she carried Bob Junior on her hip or on her back and worked the ranch with Bobby McBain.

They took their baths from a bucket. They spent their days riding the land, building fences, barbed wire cutting through tough leather gloves. She said nothing of her fear of the rattlers she knew waited for her between the rocks and under the brush. She set her mouth in a grim line and worked.

At night, even in sleet or rain, she would stand outside cooking the steaks he loved so much on an open fire. She learned to use that same fire for the stews and biscuits that made him smile. And, in the morning, she made his thick black coffee.

"That's good, honey," he'd say about everything she put on his plate or in his mug. "Real good."

After two years, with Ronnie in her belly, she had to go. She could smell the future dribbling away with the cold and the cut hands and the flash floods and the calves they nursed in that dugout where they spent their first winter.

"I gotta have this baby in a big hospital," she told him. "I don't want to take any chances with this one."

He took her to the city. She never left. Within a few months she began stocking the feed-and-tack store using the money from the sale of their cattle. He went back to his father's ranch east of Roswell. He came into the city on weekends, driving the three hours after five days on the back of a horse, fifteen hours a day.

He'd pull in late Friday night and grab his big wife. He never questioned her decision to build the store, never questioned that the money she needed to keep it going would have to come from breaking his back on his dad's place. He would do that for Joan McBain.

Bob Junior, Ronnie, Sara, and Phillip grew up in the sand of the north valley and the dust of the feed store. As their childhood passed, Bobby McBain grew old. The muscle began to turn to fat, two hundred and forty pounds on his six foot two inches. At fifty, he was half-owner, with his brother Joseph, of his father's ranch and half-owner with Joan of the feed store in Albuquerque. He still held on to the ranch up north. The dugout rotted back into the hillside.

For the last five years of his life he had a town woman in Roswell. She was good to talk to, to share a drink with and a home-cooked meal. She didn't matter, though, not the way Joan did. He made that drive over to Albuquerque almost every weekend and now stretched those weekends out to three days, sometimes four.

Right up to the day he died, Joan McBain could still make him moan with those big, firm breasts and hard thighs.

"Joan McBain," he would say, "you are one gorgeous little heifer."

He did warn her about those quarter horses with their big muscles and too short legs.

"Smartest damn horse ever was," he'd say. "But you never gonna make the money on them those Arab people do."

"I wouldn't have none of those pin-headed jackasses on my land," she'd say.

"Talking horses or people?" he'd ask and they would laugh.

He heard the figures, people spending thirty or forty thousand on one of those Arabians, even more. Those stories would bring roars of laughter over beers in a Roswell bar or a confused, frustrated bout of head shaking. Shit, forty thousand for a horse that wasn't winning no races. Shit. And now they were hearing stories of Arabs selling for a hundred thousand and more. The world had definitely gone bug nuts.

Bobby McBain never had a chance that night he left that bar in Roswell. He was pulling that extra fifty pounds and riding the land or the truck twelve hours a day, finishing off with a two-hour ride on a barstool. He was dead by the time he hit the frozen ground of the parking lot. His last thoughts before the red-hot pain were about how cold the night was. It could get awful cold in Roswell, New Mexico.

"Hell, there ain't no money to be made in raising and training these horses," he told Joan McBain. "Not big money."

"No money in feed stores either," she reminded him with a smile of how he felt all those years ago when she told him her idea for a business.

"You watch," she said of both the store and the horses.

He did and then he hit the frozen ground of the bar parking lot.

His half of the family ranch near Roswell went to her. Bob Junior joined his uncle Joseph in working the ranch. Big, like his father, muscled, able to work all day and part of the night, Bob Junior made those same weekend trips his father had, back to Joan. She would find him late on a Friday night sitting in her kitchen, nodding over a cup of coffee.

He was the quiet one. Sara was the runt. That's what the boys called her. Like Joan, she wanted the city life. She loved her job in the clean, bright office at the museum.

Phillip didn't have the height or the power of his father. What he did have that country friendliness. He loved people right down to bear hugs.

Joan McBain loved them all but she knew she favored Ronnie. He took over the feed store and left her free for her horses. He liked the store, the customers and the salesmen. He worked hard but made sure get home home for dinner. Every few months he would take off and head to the ranch up north.

"Bobby used to go up there every so often," she told Ellen. "We leased the land to one of the neighbors but he kept his eyes on things. That ranch is where he got his feet on the ground, proved he could make it through those winters. Good Lord, it was miserable but we made it and it proved something to both of us. It proved to me I wanted a business." She laughed.

"It wasn't all bad," she admitted, her voice softened with the memory of the skinny bed and the long cold nights when lovemaking was the only way to pass the time.

"Ronnie's a lot like him, you know," she said, and used her scarlet nails to pluck up another cigarette.

*

He was tall, like his father, ruggedly handsome but lean, not thick with muscle. He walked with a slow, ambling gait. He wore cowboy boots, jeans, Western shirts. They were working clothes, not shiny, new and fake like the ones Ellen saw on shop owners in Old Town.

Only a few years away from New York, they wore cowboy boots with too high heels and iron-pressed Sergio jeans. They held on to their carefully groomed beards and their neatly brushed hair. Ellen would snort whenever she came across one.

"I love it here," was a line they would include in the first four sentences they spoke to anyone who entered their shops.

"Yeah," they would drawl, chewing a bit on the inside of their lower lip as though playing with a wad of Skoal, "been here, oh, 'bout five years now."

"Almost a native," you were expected to gush, and most visitors to their shops did.

On Ronnie the boots and the Western-cut shirts with the snapped-to-the-cuff buttons and the faded jeans were honestly worn. Ellen couldn't help herself. She was looking at Gary Cooper.

"I mean, we're talking cowboy here," she told the women in the newsroom. "We're talking down-home, back-forty, shit-kicking cowboy."

Since almost no one in the newsroom was native to the state or the Southwest, they were equally fascinated with Ellen's cowboy.

This was no tie-wearing PR grinner, no Paris affair, good for a year and nothing else, no boy to be charmed by Brooklynese. This man had family and a family history and a ranch and a love of the land. And, by the end of the second month, this man had something to say.

"Ellen, I think I need to tell you something and I know it's gonna seem a bit sudden."

He stood with one foot resting on the bottom rail of the white fence surrounding his mother's front two acres.

"Go ahead."

"I never said this to anybody before, Ellen, not really, but I think I'm in love with you."

She stared in shock and then burst into a laugh of pure happiness. She didn't tell him this was the first time anyone, man or boy, had said that to her. What she did say was a little less honest.

"I love you too. I do. I wanted to tell you, but I was afraid." She moved tight to his side.

"You don't have to say that," he said, putting his arms around her. "You don't have to say anything."

"It's true," she said, her arms around his waist. "It is."

It wasn't, not then.

31

It was the trip to the ranch up north that made her question all the decisions she had made about her life and her future. Up until that trip, she wanted to travel light. She didn't want the problems of possessions or relationships. She wanted the freedom to leave whenever she chose.

The next move, from Albuquerque to somewhere else, was close. She figured it would happen within the next six months. Love or not, this thing with Ronnie McBain could only last until the move. That's what she thought before the trip to the ranch.

"It's an easy ride," he told her. "About three hours."

They passed though a handful of towns where the main streets were a quarter-mile long with a few houses and maybe a store or a post office. Between the towns, the land was empty, free of people and their places.

"I used to go out there," Ronnie said, nodding to the seemingly endless expanse. "I'd camp and think about things for a week or so."

Ellen gave the statement a small smile. The emptiness was beginning to make her nervous.

Ronnie's twang seemed to deepen as he drove the white Ford pickup deeper into the country. He pushed his cowboy hat far back on his head.

"It sure is pretty," he commented to himself. He reached to pat her on the thigh.

"It really is," she agreed and wondered how it was that they passed only two cars in what must have been an hour since the last town. The few pickups they did pass earned a touch of his hat brim in greeting.

They got the same pseudo-tip in return.

"Not too many people up here," he told her. "You got to depend on your neighbors."

My God, she thought, trying to accept the strangeness of this day and this land, this really is the West. That is what the West is all about. Those New York morons with their clipped beards and their fat behinds in new blue jeans and look what I have, she told herself, look what I can learn.

"It is beautiful," she stated firmly, wanting to believe it.

"Over that range is Pedernal," he told her with a nod to the east. "It's a flat-top mountain. You see it in a lot of paintings by those artists who lived in Taos back in the Twenties and Thirties. It's like a symbol."

She stared out at the red line of mountains and the purple shadows beyond them.

"There's a lake up here we can go to if you want. I've been going up there since I was a boy. There's another one too, but I don't like it. Too many people from the city. Looks like this big old pond."

She nodded her agreement.

"There it is," he said, pointing to a cabin on a rise. "That's the house."

The small cabin faced the valley that stretched to the distant red mountains. The kitchen area had a hotplate, a single shelf, and a plastic ice chest. There was a double bed with a tarnished metal headboard in the tiny bedroom. In the main room, a card table had been placed in front of the large front window. They could sit there and watch the storms as they rolled over the red mountains and into the valley of the neighboring ranch.

"Watch," he said that night as the storms moved in.

The purple and deep black-blue clouds rolled low across the valley. Bolts of lightning, like the limbs of bare winter trees, slashed down to the earth and sliced the black sky with their thin white lines.

"Tomorrow I'll get some horses," he told her. "Johnny Shorter will let us have a couple. We can do some riding. We'll take a look at the dugout. Boy, my folks had it rough."

They stayed four days. They walked and rode the land. They met other ranchers at the bar with the massive hand-carved wood door. They searched for Indian arrowheads, cooked over a fire, listened to the transistor radio and the bible thumping out of Texas. And, they made love.

She said little those days. She didn't know what he wanted to hear and she didn't know how she could change herself so that she could stay here with this cowboy. How could she change to want nothing in her life but this?

He wanted this life, built it with his own hands, and she wanted to be part of it. For the first time in her life, she wanted to be part of something that did not move her on, something that stayed put for years, lifetimes. That's what she told herself.

"How much would it take to get this place working?" she asked, with a new drawl in her own voice.

"An awful lot," he said and shook his head. "The stock alone would cost and with the price of beef where it is, it would hardly be worth going into ranching right now. There's a lot of work that needs to be done, the fences, the cabin. It's miserable in the winter. At least we have electricity, but I tell you, walking out to the shithouse in the middle of January ain't no picnic and it can snow right through to June."

"Still, if you love it and you thought you wanted to make it a home, it would be worth it," she half-questioned, half-stated.

"Yeah," he said, gazing over the land the way his mother looked over her front two acres.

That he did this all himself, that is what so stunned Ellen, the fences, the cabin, building the shelves for the few paperbacks he kept there. He told her how he would finish the kitchen and how it would be with a sink, a stove and running water.

"Could be fine," he said. "Real fine."

"It would be fantastic," she pronounced.

She felt only a little bored after the four days and when they left she told him, "God, I want to stay."

"It is a good place," he said.

Now, she was in love. She was in love with Ronnie McBain, with his family, with his ranch, and with all of New Mexico. He showed her the New Mexico she never wanted to see. They rode the tram to the top of the Sandias. They camped in the Jemez Mountains and swam naked in a hot springs he found there years before.

"Up there, way up there," he nodded to the surrounding cliffs, "I found a kiva, you know, where the Indians had their ceremonies. I damn near fell into it. It was a cave up there." He pointed up to the mountain behind them.

"Everything was intact, pots, everything. I rode in three days and stumbled into it. Nobody else had been there and nobody else would ever find it, not for a long time. These pots," he stretched his hands wide and round, "they were like this. Not broken, all painted. Unbelievable."

"Could you find it again?" She was excited by the thought of seeing such a place.

"It would take pack mules and a couple of days and even then it wouldn't be easy. The land looks different now with all the logging going on. New roads, that sort of thing. But, yeah, I could find it again."

"Let's," she said. "Let's go up there and find it."

She wanted to see the Indian bowls with their black geometric patterns. She wanted to find the kiva, the room where they did their secret things. She wanted to spend the days riding with Ronnie McBain.

"Leave it be," he said.

"Why? It would be fun."

"I don't want to," he said and she heard a hint of anger in his voice. "Let's leave it alone."

No. That meant someday somebody else would find it, stumble into it. They would take the pots and sell them or keep them and she would never be there to see the secret place, to be the first reporter there, the one who could tell the story. She would not be able to have one of those black patterned pots, those priceless pots.

"How come?" she pushed.

"Forget it, Ellen. There are some things you have to learn to leave alone."

He took her to the state fair, to the Indian dances, to the pueblos.

"I love this place," he would sigh on their trips. "I surely do."

So did she, she told him but she knew what she really loved was Ronnie McBain, the cowboy who would build a good, safe, Western world around her.

"You'd go crazy living on some ranch out in the middle of nowhere," her mother told her on their once-a-week call. "Yes, you would, Ellen. You'd be bored to death in a month."

"I don't think so," she responded. "This is different."

"You were made for love," he told her as they lay together. "You make me understand what it means to be willing to die for someone you love. Because I would, Ellen. I would die for you."

She knew she had finally found the man she could trust, a man she could love forever.

"You could come here and live with me," he said from the guesthouse bed.

"It might be a little crowded," she said.

She didn't want the guesthouse. She wanted an adobe house in town with red chilies hanging by the door at Christmas. She wanted a garden and a pickup truck. She wanted to work in the feed store with the farmers and the horse people. She wanted to talk about the ranch, her ranch. She wanted to learn how to fix fences. She wanted to be so busy with a new life, his life, that she would never have to worry about being bored.

"It sure is miserable up there in the winter," Joan McBain commented. Ellen said nothing. She knew how warm it could be in that bed with Ronnie.

"You're a sweet thing," he said. "Such a sweet thing. Little skitty sometimes," he drawled, and she melted. "And, I do like that in a girl. Good for breeding too," he said as he ran one rough hand across her belly and her hips. "Wide and strong."

The first time she steeled herself and brought up their need to talk about the future, he turned from her and shook his head.

"Everything is fine now, Ellen. Why do we have to talk about changing it?"

How could they not talk about changing it, she wondered. What was she supposed to do, sit in a one-bedroom apartment for the next who knew how many years? Was she supposed to keep reporting in a town with no news, in a state with nothing to cover? Was she supposed to spend weekends in his mother's guesthouse, sneaking across the lawn after the rest of the family went to bed? Is that what was worth keeping the same?

"Things have to change," she told him. "That's the way it is."

"That's bull," he snapped. "Nothing has to change unless you want it to and I don't like changes."

Their first and only fight came soon after, following a day filled with too many hours of drinking. Drinking or not, she felt she was goaded into it.

They were at Carl's apartment, a friend of Ronnie's, when the men began making comments about the woman in the television movie they were watching.

"I always liked big tits," Carl said. "You did too, didn't you, Ron? Once, I mean," he said with a loud shout of laughter and a pointed look at Ellen's chest.

"Hell, why not," Ronnie agreed and reached for another beer.

"What about that little lady from Midland? Darlene, that was her name, Darlene the barrel racer."

Darlene's name and phone number were written on the wall above the guesthouse phone.

Ronnie laughed.

"She was built," Carl said.

"Remember her, Melissa?" he called over to his fiancé. "Like Dolly Parton."

"Sure, sure," said Melissa with a grimace.

"Like those big ones," Carl said again.

"Tend to drag a bit," Ellen commented.

Ronnie looked at her. Melissa smiled.

"Sure. About forty they are down to your knees," Ellen continued. "In fact," she sipped from her glass of wine, "women with big breasts have more breast cancer."

She didn't mean to say that exactly. She meant breast cancer was harder to find in large-breasted women. She let it stand.

"Really?" Melissa leaned forward in her chair.

"That's bullshit," Carl said, but he didn't look so sure.

"Could be," Ellen said and paused. She was about to pay them back for the breast comments along with the hours spent in a bar where she and Melissa had been ignored while the men swapped stories of mutual friends. Yes, she was going to tell the sportscaster's story.

"Let me tell you," she leaned close to Melissa, "what this sportscaster once told me."

"What's that?" Ronnie called from the kitchen.

"It's about this size thing," Ellen said to Melissa. "You know, this size thing men have about themselves. They all have it. This sportscaster told me they check each other out, even if they say it doesn't matter."

She could see Ronnie standing in the kitchen doorway.

"You know, all those magazine stories telling them it isn't the size that matters, not the size of the baton that makes the music. All that *Playboy* stuff. Well, the guy says it's all bull. He said he looked. I mean, he spent a lot of time in locker rooms, so he looked."

She gave a hoot of laughter.

"What, what?" Melissa demanded happily.

"He said it was exactly what you'd expect. He said the weightlifters have these real little ones." She made a measurement of about an inch with her thumb and forefinger.

Carl turned from the din of the television.

"What?" he demanded.

"They are tiny, really, really dinky. And he said football players are normal, no big deal, but basketball players are ..."

Ronnie now stood over them. Ellen looked up, met his eyes, and went back to Melissa.

"That basketball players are enormous. That's what he said."

They both laughed.

"What the hell are they talking about?" Carl asked.

"The size of dicks," Ronnie spat out. "Who has the biggest dick."

"Oh," Carl shrugged and turned back to the television.

Ellen looked up at Ronnie. There was no challenge in her eyes, no mocking, only a question. What would he do with her now?

"It was cheap, that's all," he said when they were back in the guesthouse bed.

"It was a story," she said. "You and Carl sit around and talk about breasts and old girl friends. That's okay, right?"

"It isn't the same thing, Ellen, and for some reason you don't get it."

"It is exactly the same thing. You talk about breast size and Darlene. Okay, I'll talk about men."

"And cocks," he spat. "That's real nice. That's the kind of woman a man wants to introduce to his friends."

She lay in the darkness. She did not remind him of Melissa's open laughter or Carl's indifference.

"You embarrassed me and you embarrassed yourself," he finished.

He raised himself on one arm and pounded his pillow into a desired shape.

"Ronnie, please." She put her hand on his shoulder.

"Ellen, go to sleep or go into the house. I want to get some sleep."

She waited for his touch, for him to roll over and reach for her. He did not.

"I had too much to drink last night," she told Joan McBain and Sara the next morning over coffee at the kitchen table. Neither of them responded.

Ronnie came in later and read the paper as she sat and stared at the table. She started to apologize, to give her mumble about too much to drink.

"It's not important, Ellen," he said from behind the paper. "Forget it."

She wasn't sure why telling the sportscaster's story was so wrong, but the hangover and Ronnie's words in the guesthouse bed left her resolved to be more careful. She would try to act the way Ronnie expected a woman to act. She would tell fewer stories and do a lot less drinking. She couldn't risk losing this man.

In the weeks that followed, she found herself trying to move closer to him, to be touching him, his back, his shoulder, his arm. She moved into him, watched him, waited for a sign that he had forgiven her and that she was doing things right, the way his woman should.

He gave no indication that his feelings for her had changed, but she sensed a difference. She believed he had seen something in her he didn't like and the damage could not be undone.

Not long after the sportscaster's story, she got the call.

"We want you, Ellen Peters," Jim Brown announced.

"You're kidding."

Months had passed since her interview at the station and even though Brown warned her it might take a long time before they had an opening, she never thought Carter would agree to hire her.

"The job is here if you want it, but we need to know right away," Brown told her.

She knew she had to give him an answer without a note of indecision in her voice, nothing that would warn him off.

"Give me twenty-four hours," she said. "That's all I'll need."

"No more than that, Ellen."

"Don't worry, I'll get back to you. And, Jim?"

"Yes?"

"Thanks."

She didn't ask about money or who would pay for the move or the hours or days she would be working. They could talk about that later. What she needed to know now was how the man she loved was going to stop her from taking the job.

"I think you should take it," he told her in the late afternoon quiet of the restaurant. "It would be good for you. It's what you do."

She nodded and then burst into tears.

"Come on," he said as she wiped at the tears with the tiny cocktail napkin. "It's not so far away. I'll come see you. It's where you should be, Ellen. You know that."

As they left, she saw the seated women looking up at him and the waitresses turning to him, the tall, handsome man with a cowboy hat in his hand.

"I do love you," he said on one of their last nights in the guesthouse bed. "You know that."

She nodded in the darkness, her face wet with tears.

"But, we've only known each other a few months."

"Six."

"All right, six, but I'm not ready to offer you or anyone anything permanent. I'm not ready for that."

And what about her? Where would she ever find another cowboy with a ranch and a cabin on a hill?

She didn't cry that last morning, but it hurt when she left him leaning on Joan McBain's fence. She knew he'd turn his attention to one of Joan McBain's horses when her car was out of sight. He'd stand there another five or ten minutes before going to the house or the tack room or to talk to Juan Moya, Joan McBain's man. And that, she thought, would be that.

It could have been the sportscaster's story or the way she denied the city he loved to that San Francisco art gallery owner. It could have been her strong opinions or the voice that sometimes grew too loud. It could have been any of those things or anything else that made it so easy for Ronnie McBain to let her go and she couldn't do a damn thing about it. He'd miss her, though. She knew that.

The first month they spoke twice a week, alternating calls.

"Love it here. Professional beyond belief," she told him. "Miss you," she would say.

"I miss you too," he would answer.

"I love you, Ronnie," she would say and hate the ring of childish pleading in her voice.

"I love you too," he would say and she would go to bed aching for him and crying herself to sleep.

Finally, after one month, he told her.

"Ellen, I think we better stop talking for a while. This isn't working."

"What do you mean?"

"It's too hard. I didn't think it was going to be this hard. We both have to get on with our lives."

"If we could see each other, it would be okay," she told him. "We need to see each other."

"No, Ellen, I don't think so. I think we need to stop this for a while."

"Are you seeing someone else?" she demanded. "Is that it?"

He gave a tired laugh.

"No, Ellen, but if I want to, I will. I told you I wasn't ready for anything permanent. You should be making a life for yourself out there, not waiting around for someone like me."

"Ronnie, please, I think we need to see each other," she pleaded.

"No. We have to stop talking for a while."

"For how long?"

"Let it go for awhile, okay? I need some breathing space and so do you."

She wouldn't argue. She would play this thing like the non-pushy, non-liberated woman he wanted and she would wait. If he didn't want her, it would be because there was something wrong with her, something she couldn't hide and something she didn't know how to change.

Months later she sent a note to Joan McBain. She wrote about the wonderful weather and how much she liked her job. She did not mention Ronnie. Eventually, she stopped crying at night.

*

Ellen did have another story about size. It was a better story, a sweeter one. Thinking about this story made her smile but she never told it. In a way, it was too sweet.

She had a crush on an editor at the Florida station. She blushed if they passed in the hall. If they accidentally touched, she jumped as though burned. Finally, he took her into an empty office and shut the door.

"Look," he said roughly, "I'm queer. Do you understand?"

"Sure, I understand, but I don't like that word," she said, trying to hide the shock of his announcement.

"So, make it gay, but I am."

They remained friends, sharing a beer or two in the hours after work.

"I have something I need to ask you," he said on one of those nights. "It's really bad," he said. Beads of perspiration dotted his forehead.

"Look," he fumbled for the next words. "I mean, how do women feel about a man's size. You know, penis size?"

"What?"

"The size of his penis." His face was red.

"I don't know. Why are you asking?"

"Well, ah, this is really personal." He reached for her hand.

"It's that Chip's is bigger than mine." He whispered the words.

She knew his boyfriend and she didn't like him.

"How much bigger?"

"Well, I mean, I am normal but he is much bigger."

She gave a snort. "Unless he's the size of an elephant, it doesn't matter."

He looked stunned.

"No, really," she said. "Not to a woman. I don't know why it would matter to men. And isn't everyone about the same size when they're, you know, erect?"

"Not Chip," he said sadly.

"Does he ever say anything about it?"

"No, no," he assured her.

Oh, but she bet he did. She bet Chip said a great deal.

"God, that's no problem at all," she proclaimed.

He smiled hopefully. "So, it doesn't matter?"

"Not the size of the baton that makes the music," she recited without a trace of doubt.

32

"Some guy with a gun at St. Joe's, sniper maybe," Tony Santella yelled across the newsroom. "Debbie, get down there. Move."

She grabbed her pen and pad and slung her purse over her shoulder. "Who's going with me?" she called to George.

"Cappy."

"Got it," Cappy said. He walked toward the door to the garage, holding back the desire to run to the van and the story.

Throughout the newsroom reporters stopped their typing and phone chatter. Photographers moved into a listening position. This could be a big one. Cappy slammed out the door and the spell was broken. They all moved back to their work.

"He's on the third floor or something," Tony said.

"Okay," said Debbie.

"I'm sending out the remote truck," George called after her.

"What have we got?" she asked Cappy.

"Sniper, that's all I know, and everybody in town is going to be there."

She felt good again, alive, for the first time since the abortion. This is what she wanted to do, this kind of run-and-gun story. This is what she was proud to do for a living.

"Hell," Cappy swore and made a quick turn. "They've already got the streets blocked."

He had to get past the cops. He drove into an alley, across a side street and into an enormous empty lot.

"Over there, over there," he pointed to a break between two buildings. "You can see the hospital but it's a haul. Call George and find out what side the guy's on."

"George, which side is the guy on? North, south, which side?"

"What?"

"What side of the building, the sniper, what side?"

There was no answer.

"George, can you hear me?"

"Gee, I don't know," he mumbled. "Can you see anything?"

"Move," Cappy yelled, and threw open the van door.

"Here, here." He tossed her the box with the clip-on mikes and tucked an extra cord into the waistband of his pants.

"Let's go."

They walked quickly through the lot and, rounding a building, faced the flashing lights of a patrol car.

"Where is he?" she asked the officer.

"Up there," he nodded to the hospital across another empty lot. "You can't go any farther. This is as far as you go."

"Right," she said. "Anybody hurt?"

"I don't know. Hey, you, get back." His attention switched to a newspaper photographer who had moved into his line of sight.

"You too," he ordered Debbie.

"Everybody must be on the other side," she said to Cappy who was trying to get a focus on the multi-storied building.

"If we could get up there," she nodded toward a parking garage facing the east side of the hospital, "we could get a direct shot to the hospital."

Cappy looked doubtful. They would have to walk back to the lot, make a wide circle away from this cop, staying along the back of the buildings, then break and run for the garage. They would make it only if the cop didn't glance sideways and spot them when they made that run. Was it worth the effort?

"There has to be another door to that garage, the door for the stairs, one we can't see from here," she insisted.

"If we're lucky," he grumbled as they began their slow move away from the small crowd that had gathered.

They walked back toward the alley and began to make the wide half circle. They crept tight to the buildings before breaking for that run to the garage.

"Shit, it's not even finished," Cappy said, seeing the blue construction-site dumpster. Debbie disappeared around a corner of the building.

"Cappy," she called, "there's a door here. It's open. Come on."

"Yeah, yeah, yeah," he grunted behind her as they climbed the stairs.

At the third level, she slowly pushed the door open and peeked out.

"I think this is good," she whispered.

Cappy peeked out as well. "Looks okay to me."

Like children, they tiptoed into the empty garage, the unfinished cement floors crackling beneath their steps. Cappy went straight to the far edge that faced the hospital. He stood and stared and then fell into a crouch, yelling. "Goddamn, get down. Jesus, I think that's him. Right there. Do you see him? Over there, at that window. Oh God. Sweet Jesus God Almighty."

"Where, where?" She stretched to see the wall of hospital windows level with the garage.

"There, the next floor up, middle window. Wait a second." He lowered his head to the camera eyepiece. "Yeah, yeah, yeah. Not much light, not much," he muttered, "but that's him. Talk to George."

He unhooked the walkie-talkie from his belt and skidded it across the floor.

"I need a better shot," he said and, with the camera held like a rifle, he duck-walked forward, pulling the recorder behind him.

"George, Debbie. Do you hear me? George?"

"Go ahead, Debbie," answered Tony Santella.

"We've got a shot," she said, careful with her words. Every newsroom monitored every other newsroom's frequency. If they figured out where they were, an army of reporters and photographers would soon be pounding up the stairs.

"Good." Tony's voice was calm. "Find someplace to go live. We want to do a cut-in."

She didn't answer as she stared at the windows. How could Cappy see so far? Suddenly, she gasped. She could see a man, not his face but the shadow of him. She believed she could see a rifle in his arms.

"Debbie, did you hear me?"

"Oh wow," she laughed nervously.

"We need a live shot. Get some place where we can set up," he ordered.

"I'll be back." She clicked off.

"Did you hear that?" she gave a hoarse call to Cappy.

The door slammed behind her. She jumped in terror.

"What the fuck are you doing here?" the man shouted and waved a gun at her.

"Reporter," she shouted back, her arms raised. "Television reporter."

"Damn it." He shoved the gun back in his shoulder holster. "Get the hell out of here now."

"Hey, wait a second," she moved toward him. "We're okay up here. Come on."

She could hear the whirr of the recorder. Cappy was shooting and would not stop until he had what he needed.

The man hesitated. She saw the indecision.

"Please," she said. "We'll move back but let us stay up here."

"Cappy," she called, "move back."

Cappy waved one hand but never took his eye from the eyepiece.

Feet pounded on the stairs. The door slammed open. Behind it, other feet pounded upward.

"What the shit's going on here?" one of two uniformed officers shouted.

"Television," the first man said. "They are leaving."

"You get out of here now or I swear to God, we'll take you in," hissed one officer.

Cappy looked up and gave her a quick smile. He had it.

"No problem, officers," he said and moved toward them, still in a crouch.

"I should arrest your ass," someone shouted as they went out the door. "Arrest your sorry ass."

Twenty minutes later, the station broke into regular programming with a live report on the sniper. Debbie stood in a parking lot near the hospital. As she spoke and helicopters whirred, they rolled the tape fed to the station only minutes before with its grainy shot of the man at the window.

They had an hour before the six o'clock. Tony told her to come back in.

"We've got Burton out there now, talking to the cops. We'll go live with him at six. We need you and Cappy back here."

"It's my story," she argued.

"No, we want you in-set. It's going to be tight, so get back now."

"Shit, shit," she shouted at Cappy. "Do you believe that?"

"They want me too?"

"Yeah."

"Okay," he said. "If that's what they want."

It was also what he wanted. This thing could last for hours. Going back in was fine by him.

"Good story," Richard Ferguson called to her when she came into the newsroom.

"Yeah, but damn it, it's my story. They shouldn't have brought me in."

"They got him. They got him," Tony yelled from his position

beneath the scanners. "Somebody find out who the hell he is. Get Benton. Debbie, get that copy into editing."

Jack Benton kicked it off, going live from the scene with the cop lights flashing behind him. Debbie followed, reporting from the set. They used Cappy's shots in the newscast intro and in Debbie's voice-over along with other shots from the scene.

"Tight," Tony sighed with pleasure during the commercial break.

"Woo," Jim Brown exhaled. "Fantastic. We beat all of them."

"Good work," they all said to her.

*

That night she asked Ellen what she thought.

"It was a good story. Nice tape. I don't think anybody else had anything like it. And, your in-set worked. I didn't think it was going to, but it did. That one shot of Cappy's of the sniper, that was something else. You were lucky."

"Lucky?"

"Yeah, lucky to have that shot," Ellen concluded.

"Well, I think it was more than luck," Debbie stated.

"What do you mean?"

"I mean, I think I did a real good job, both of us did."

"You did," Ellen agreed.

"You didn't say that. You said I was lucky."

Ellen sighed.

"No, Debbie, I meant the shot Cappy got was lucky, that's all."

"I know, I know," Debbie sniffed. "I guess I wanted you to tell me how good I was."

"You were," Ellen laughed.

"You know, I felt proud of myself, like I was on top of everything. I felt like this is what we are supposed to be doing. Get the story, tell the people the truth. That's the reason I got into television."

She heard the click of Ellen's lighter and waited for the exhale.

"I thought television news was the one place where I could tell the truth. You are paid to find out the truth and report it and help people understand what's going on."

"I know, Debbie. You've told me that."

"All right, but that's how I felt tonight, like I did my job."

"You done good."

"You really think so?"

"Yes, Debbie, I do."

"Okay, then, well, I better go. I'll see you tomorrow?"

"Yes, you will," Ellen answered.

Two minutes later Ellen's phone rang.

"It's me again."

"Yeah?"

"I wanted to say thinks, thanks for everything, listening to me and all that. I know I can be a pain."

"No problem."

"Okay then," Debbie said. "I'll see you tomorrow."

Ellen stared at the phone, wondering, with a head shake of exasperation, how anyone could get so churned up over what actually amounted to about an hour of real work.

33

She told the group about her story with a shy pride.

"So what?" the younger woman asked. "So you're a big television star. So what? Does that make you better than the rest of us?"

"No," Debbie tried to explain, "that isn't what I meant. I meant it was a good day for me. That's all."

"You know," the younger woman went on with a toss of her head, "I don't know why you are here. You're so happy with your job and everything, why do you need therapy?"

"Yes, I sort of wondered that too," said the older woman. I still don't know what your problem is."

Bob nodded his agreement.

Because I need to be here," Debbie responded. "Because I need to find out why I get so depressed."

Now she called her sadness depression because the others in the room used that word to describe their own weekly conditions.

"You never seem depressed to me," said the older woman.

"Maybe that's good?" Dr. Waddell offered.

"You mean she feels good when she's here with us? Is that what you mean?" she asked.

"Yes, Maynell, I think that's what I mean. Debbie doesn't feel sad when she's with us and that's good, isn't it? Isn't it, Debbie?"

"I guess so," she said and smiled, but she felt the fear begin. "I hope I am getting better. No," she corrected herself, "I am getting better." She smiled at them. They would like that.

"Well, I don't know why any of us are here," the older woman said. "I mean, what are we supposed to be doing here?"

The younger woman ignored the question and went back to Debbie.

"You are unbelievable," she told her. "The only thing we've talked about since you came here is you. You're depressed. Big fucking deal. Could we please talk about something else?" She flung herself back in her chair.

Bob looked at his hands. The older woman folded her arms across her chest. Dark glasses hid Terry's eyes.

"You asked me the questions," Debbie said plaintively.

"Because you never stop whining about being so fucking sad," the younger woman yelled, her face swollen with anger. "I've got no job. Terry's an addict. Maynell," she nodded toward the older woman, "has two kids who live off of her. We don't know what he's here for," she nodded over at Bob. "Who cares about your shitty little problems?"

"Why does this make you so angry, Carol?" the doctor cut in.

"Why can't she be angry?" the older woman asked. "Aren't we supposed to talk about how we feel?"

Debbie was fighting back the tears. She didn't know how to be part of them. She didn't know what they wanted her to be. She didn't fit in anywhere, not anywhere, not even this room. They would be happy if she left. Yes, they would. What was wrong with her?

"I don't care what we talk about," the younger woman stated, "as long as it's not about her."

Bob shook his head.

"How's Terry?" the older woman asked, her voice like a chirp from a bird.

"Well, man," he pulled out of his couch slouch, "I guess it's okay. Yeah, everything is going fine."

"You trying to convince us or yourself?" Bob asked.

"Hey, man, no. I mean, you ask how I am and I'm tell you I'm fine." He gave a quick smile. "But, hey, I don't want to talk about it. Okay? I don't feel like talking today. That okay?" He looked at

Debbie. She tried to smile.

"Let's talk about something else," he said.

They all seemed to nod, to smile back at him. That is what Debbie saw. She looked down at the floor. She would not let them see her cry.

34

"You talk to Debbie much?" Clifford asked Ellen "I mean, in the past couple of weeks?"

"We talk in the station and on the phone. Not that much."

"I think she's in trouble," he said, not talking his eyes off the road.

Ellen shook her head. She was tired of the phone calls, tired of the little-girl voice pleading for reassurance. She was keeping those late night calls short. Sometimes she didn't bother to answer the phone.

"Remember when she first got here she was having all those dinners and things?" Clifford asked.

"Uh huh."

"Well, I went by there last night and a couple of times last week and I knew she was in there, but she wouldn't answer the door." He turned to Ellen, his eyes wide.

"You don't know for sure she was in there."

"I know," he stated firmly. "I know because of that peephole. I know because I see a light in that peephole and then somebody was looking through it, blocking it. That's how I know she was in there. And, her car's there."

"So what?" Ellen snapped in annoyance. "She's okay. I've talked to her. Let's talk about something else."

"Whatever you want."

After a moment of silence, he commented, "Sure is nice today."

"Only one more month and we turn on the air conditioners," Ellen reminded him.

"Not me. Uh uh. I ain't staying in this sweat hole one more summer."

A Greyhound bus pulled alongside them.

"I once traveled across the country on a bus," Ellen said, looking up at the bus windows. "It was an interesting trip."

"Ain't no way I get on a bus," he said. "Eating my kneecaps all the way to Philly? No way."

"I went all the way from Boston to Albuquerque on a bus," she went on. "I wanted to see the country instead of flying over it. I did get nervous once, in Washington D.C. Wouldn't you know, the nation's capital."

"What happened?"

"There were some mean-looking people in that bus station."

"Brothers?"

"Yeah." She nodded, remembering the pointed black faces, the skinny bodies leaning against the walls, the slick suits. They were waiting for young girls, the runaways, waiting for somebody who didn't look like they knew the scene.

"We are a mean bunch of motherfuckers," Clifford said with a laugh.

"You know," she said as they drove, "Debbie's okay. She gets too involved in things, that's all."

"She's had some bad times," Clifford said cautiously.

"I know she's had bad times,'" Ellen said. "And, I know about the latest one. She told me."

"You know about the abortion?" he blurted it out.

"Yeah," she nodded.

"Man," he sighed with the relief of finally being able to talk about it. "It was bad. There wasn't any blood or anything. I would have died right there. Still, it was bad, man, and there I was, my big, black self hanging around this place, thinking she's inside half-dead with some coat hanger or something."

Ellen broke into laughter. "Oh, Clifford."

"Go ahead, you can laugh. You weren't there. I was there and the whole time I'm thinking what am I going to do if this girl dies. Who's going to believe me with some dead white girl in her bedroom?" He shook his head.

"I ain't never been through anything like that before and I ain't never doing it again."

"She's okay now," Ellen said.

"I guess so," he said but he sounded doubtful.

*

He never told anyone, not anyone. That's what he promised her and he kept his promises. But, man, did he want to call Jason and tell him to get his white ass over there. He was the one who should be taking care of her. It was his mess. And where was he, Mr. Wonder Bread boy? Not taking care of his mess, that's where.

All Debbie said when he brought her home was that she wanted to sleep and he should go home. No way he was leaving her alone. She could die, they did sometimes, he knew that. He checked on her, every hour or so. He tiptoed into her bedroom and held his breath, and listened for the sound of her breathing. He watched the body beneath the sheet for the rise and fall that meant she was alive. Each time it came, he exhaled in relief and tiptoed from the room.

"What are you doing here?" Debbie asked the next morning, standing over the couch.

He hurried to button his pants.

"I thought it would be a good idea if I stayed, in case you might need something." His words were as rushed as his fingers.

"I'll make us some breakfast," she said, rubbing at her eyes.

"No, no, I gotta get home." He fumbled with the laces on his sneakers.

"I think you should stay in bed," he told her. "That might be best if you stayed in bed." He couldn't meet her eyes. He had to get out of there.

"You gonna be okay?" he asked.

"I think so. But, you need breakfast, Clifford. Let me make you something to eat."

*

"Yeah, it's gonna be hot soon," he grumbled to Ellen. "It's gonna be hot and stinky and this is one brother who ain't gonna be here."

"Where are you going?"

"I'm going to New York," he pronounced. "I'm going up there to NBC and I'm going to sit there until somebody looks at my tape and gives me a job. And, I ain't leaving until I got that job."

"It gets cold up there," she said.

He shook his head. That's what they all said. All he had to do was mention New York and they all started flapping their lips about the cold and the snow.

"Shit, I can buy me a goddamn mink coat," he yelled. "I can stay warm in New York with a goddamn coat, but I can't stay cool here, no way."

"So, go," she said, her head bowed over her notes.

"I will, you can bet on that. I'm going."

35

Debbie didn't tell the group about the abortion. She didn't tell them anything. She only listened and smiled when they spoke. She nodded and agreed and helped them, she believed, by being positive about them and what they were doing.

At one session she did cry out when Bob suggested they all go out for a drink after the meeting.

"No, no," she protested. "That's not right."

"Why not?" the older woman asked. "That would be fun."

"That's not why we are here," Debbie said. "We didn't come here for instant friendships, did we?" she pleaded to the doctor. "We are here to work, to get better, right?"

"Well," he paused to light a cigarette.

"What are you afraid of?" the younger woman sneered.

"I'm not afraid," she said, although she felt sick with fear. "I just don't think it's right."

The nurse named Jane who had come to a few meeting wearing her clean white slacks and crisp flowered top, opened her hands wide.

"I don't have time for a drink. I barely have time to be here. This time is terrible. Couldn't we change it?"

Debbie could feel her fear of these people and this room growing. She was afraid they would reach out and physically touch her. Why? Why was the fear getting worse?

She could call her doctor back home and tell him about the room and these people and her fear, couldn't she? No. He would tell her there was nothing wrong with them, that she needed a tune-up, that's all. She needed a tune-up.

She had to fight the fear. The fear was wrong. These people weren't bad people. They wouldn't hurt her. That's what she told herself over and over again, until she heard the voice.

"You should be afraid," the voice told her. "You must get out of this room."

How could that be true? Coming here was the only thing that could help her. But what if the voice was her instinct? Isn't that what the doctor told her after Baja? The voice was her instinct, warning her.

She looked at Terry. It helped calm the fear, seeing him there in his dark glasses, but it did not make her feel safe. The only time she felt completely safe was when she was alone in her apartment. She would sit in the dark, holding onto herself and ignoring the ringing of the phone or doorbell. She knew it was Clifford. She knew he was watching her.

"I'll go out with her," he'd tell George Harding, as though it didn't matter one way or another. "I ain't got anything better going on."

He'd ask her if she wanted to grab some dinner after work or if she wanted to meet for a few beers and talk about doing a series together. He'd try anything to keep an eye on her. He knew she was in trouble. He could feel it tight in his chest whenever he looked at her.

*

"She's seeing a doctor," Ellen told him. "If there is a problem, she'll work it out with him. She's not asking for your help, Clifford. Leave it alone."

Clifford couldn't do that. Neither could Jim Brown. He got the phone call from Sue in the front office, an old hand at the station.

"One of your people was asking about our insurance coverage for group therapy," she told him. "Thought you might need to know."

He called Debbie into his office. He shut the door and sat down in his high-backed chair, his hands folded atop his belly.

"Debbie," he said, "is there something wrong, something we can do to make you happy?"

"No, no," she said with a quick shake of her head. "Nothing is wrong. Why are you asking me that?"

"You seem a little down lately. I thought there might be something you want to talk about."

"No, really, Jim," she insisted. "Everything is going well." She smiled wide.

"How about a few days of vacation? Would you like to take a few days off? That wouldn't be a problem, Debbie. We care about you. You know that."

"I know," she said, nodding. "I know."

He left his chair and walked around the desk. He went to her, putting one hand on her shoulder.

"You're one of the family. You matter to us. If there is anything I can do to make things easier for you, you tell me, okay?"

"I'm fine," she assured him. "A little tired, but it's nothing important. I'll try to get some rest."

"Promise?" He gave her shoulder a squeeze. "Promise?"

"I promise." She smiled but pulled her shoulder away. That squeeze hurt.

He went back to his chair and, as she stood up, he asked, "Debbie, have you talked to a doctor about it, this being tired?"

"No, no," she answered quickly.

"No?" he asked, his eyes surprised. "Well, maybe you should. Don't forget," he said, his voice firm, "we all love you."

36

Jean Ann Maypin had three standard speeches for the many groups that requested her appearance. She had one on how to dress and act for success, one on how to organize time and one, she loved this one, about being a feminine woman in a man's world.

"I call this speech 'Grin and Bear It,'" she would start. "It's about being a woman in a man's world."

There would be giggling and clapping almost before the first sentence came out of her coral-glossed lips.

"She reminds me of my granddaughter Heather," one would whisper.

"Reminds me of that sweet Jane Pauley on the *Today Show*," another would chime.

"No, no, she's much better than that Jane Pauley," would come from the row behind.

They all knew the truth about Jean Ann Maypin. They knew she became a star without being coarse and rude and mannish. She did her best in a man's world and one day, they all knew this, she would meet Mr. Right and spend more time at home. She wouldn't have to give up television completely, but she would definitely be happier spending more time at home and raising a family. They all knew she wanted that. All real women did.

Jean Ann was dating a psychologist. She called him "my analyst" and giggled with the hint that perhaps she did see him, or had, on a professional basis. Then, she would roll her eyes to show how absurd it would be to think that she, Jean Ann Maypin, would ever need an analyst.

She loved his name.

"Gregory," she said and rolled her eyes at Paige Allen. "Isn't that cute? My analyst. We date, you know."

She liked Paige Allen knowing how desirable she was. Paige might be sexy and blond but she was no Jean Ann Maypin.

She met him at the station when he came in to talk with Jim Brown about doing mental health tips to fight holiday season depression. That idea didn't appeal to Brown but he was glad to add a presentable psychologist to his list of people they could use for a sound bite or two in future stories.

Gregory took her to dinner before the ten o'clock newscasts. He chose places with candlelight where Jean Ann could allow herself a single sip of wine from his glass. He would hold her hand and listen to her talk about her day and about television news. They were, he found, one and the same.

He smiled patiently when people stopped by the table.

"We watch you every night," they would tell her.

"Well, how sweet of you to say so," she'd say, and sign the scraps of paper they pressed on her.

Sometimes, after giving him a long look, her admirers would say, "and you too." He would smile and give a short bow of his head.

"I've told everyone I have an analyst," Jean Ann told him one night.

He shook his head.

"Oh, pooh. That's what I tell them. Everybody's got one, don't they? I could need one, couldn't I? It could be exciting. I have so many stories to tell. I wouldn't be boring."

He smiled.

"And, you know, I do need someone to talk to. Television is such a hard business. Oh, I have the most wonderful job in the world. I wouldn't change it for anything, but it can be difficult for a woman."

He nodded and smiled, watching her mouth as she chewed her

veal. Her knife scraped the plate as she cut another bite. He could sense the others in the restaurant staring and smiling and nodding in their direction. Jean Ann Maypin, gosh.

*

At the end of every speech, they asked the same question. It usually came at that too quiet moment with no hands waving with questions to be asked. Finally, one of the bravest, the most determined of them, would giggle and raise her hand and stand.

"Jean Ann, what's Tom Carter really like?"

"Yes, yes," would come the excited chorus.

She gave that question her warmest smile and she always said the same thing.

"Ah, Tom, he's quite a guy. I don't know what I'd do without him. He's helped me a lot and working with him has been a wonderful opportunity for me."

A sigh of contentment would fill the room. Was there ever any doubt?

SEGMENT THREE

"And finally tonight ..." Carter allowed for his thin smile. This was the light story, the kicker. Made them feel good, that's what those pricks Back East said anyway.

"We have a report about some very, very," he moved into a smirk, "special dancers." He had no idea what kind of dancers they were. Could be belly dancers, for all he knew. He didn't know. He read.

"Our arts and entertainment reporter," God, he hated that, "Harold Lewis, brings us the story."

He held the prim mouth smirk without moving, staring into the camera, waiting for the tape to take over.

That son of a bitch director wasn't fast enough. Too many times he left him hanging out here with a stupid fucking look on his face. He'd see about that.

He held the pose a second longer, the eyes narrowed. Next to him, Jean Ann turned to watch her desk monitor. She liked Lewis' little stories. She could smile after them.

37

Jim Brown decided to throw the problem to Tom Carter at the Wednesday management meeting. He had learned that every so often Carter needed something to stew over, something to get him into the newsroom. Once there he caused trouble, true, but the more the newsroom disliked Carter, the more they turned to him. And, that's exactly the way Jim Brown wanted it.

The three of them, Tony, Brown, and Tom Carter went down the list of reporters and photographers, stopping at certain names with comments about stories or output or, when it came to photographers, overtime. George Harding sat quietly to one side.

"Those pricks," Carter spat, "they're padding their goddamn time sheets. You bet they are and it's going to stop."

"Somebody has to shoot the stories, Tom," said George Harding.

"Well, find somebody to do it on our time, not theirs," Carter ordered. "You bring that goddamn overtime down or I'll do something about it."

Brown smiled an apology to George Harding. Every Wednesday meeting was the same.

"Who's low on story count?" Carter demanded. This was the part he loved, the story count. The count showed how these little bastards tried to rip off the station.

"Allen and, I guess," Brown hesitated as though examining the list, "Debbie Hanson. But, you know," he seemed to rush to explain, "Debbie's been down, a little sick, no big deal."

Carter began to swell with anger. Why was Brown making excuses?

"Allen's a fucking bimbo so who cares about her but you tell Miss Hanson to get on the stick. She's been here less than a year. Right, George?"

George Harding nodded. He had no idea.

"And she hasn't done anything worth talking about," Carter concluded.

"Ah, she's done some good stuff, Tom," Brown argued.

"Not enough, buddy," Carter spat back. "We ain't no goddamn nursing home. What do you mean she's sick?"

"Stomach or something," George Harding mumbled. No one had said anything to him about her being sick but that sounded harmless enough.

"Maybe the bimbo is preggers," Carter sneered.

"Well, that's an easy one to solve," Tony said without thinking.

"What?" Carter yelled.

"I was joking, Tom."

"You better be, boy. We don't put up with that shit in my newsroom. You got that?"

Brown looked at Tony. There was nothing they didn't find out sooner or later. Even if they only guessed at something, they were usually right. Every newsroom rumor he ever heard turned out to be true.

"I ain't having no pregnant gashes in my newsroom," said Carter.

George Harding flinched.

"Tom, Tony was joking," Brown stated.

George Harding sat like a schoolboy before an exam, all of his papers on his lap, his knees held close together.

"Are we almost done?" he asked. "I should get back out there."

"Go ahead," Carter said, "but you keep that goddamn overtime down. Who's the worst one on that overtime stuff?"

"Ah," George Harding was on his feet, holding his papers in a tight fist. "Ah, maybe, ah, Clifford Williams. He's usually high."

"He's high, ten, fifteen hours," Tony commented, then added, "He does good work."

He made it a practice to balance a criticism with a compliment. Something he learned from Brown.

"Not on my back he doesn't," Carter shouted. "You get that overtime down or I will."

George Harding nodded and left the room.

"That it for me too?" Tony asked.

"Yeah," Carter said.

"So, what about this Hanson thing?" he asked Brown after Tony left.

He liked a problem with the staff. They hadn't had any serious problems in a long time and he liked handling them, the overtime, the story count. That was his area. What he didn't touch was the newscasts. He didn't have any idea how those things got put together and he admitted it.

"I couldn't put a newscast together to save my life," he told Ellen Peters as they watched Chuck Farrell lay out the script on the long table. He put it down page by page, in five vertical rows, each row representing one section of the newscast.

It had all gotten so goddamn complicated, tapes, mini-cams, microphones, earpieces, somebody always waving at you, yelling in your ear. Oh, he could handle it out on the set. Who cared what the director said or the producer or the people on the floor? On the set he was in charge and if all went to hell in a handbasket, he was the man who made damn sure the right bastards got theirs.

He handled the staff and that is what kept it all together, not any goddamn row of scripts. It was The Best because he built the best goddamn team in the state. He built it, from Bakersfield to Omaha to wherever the hell that goddamn Polack Kowalski came from.

"I'm going to have to have a little talk with Miss Hanson," he told Brown to show him who was really in charge.

"Couldn't hurt," Brown agreed.

"Damn right. If something needs to be straightened out with that young lady, we better do it now. And I don't like this talk about her being pregnant. Who's she screwing anyway?"

Brown shrugged. He heard some talk that she and Jason were dating but after he tied him into Ferguson and the medical stories, there couldn't have been much time left for Debbie. It was a hard life, television, a lot of tough choices had to be made. As he once told Ellen, it wasn't good for relationships.

"Destroys marriages, yes, it can, and relationships," he told her.

"Doesn't have to," she countered.

"It's tough," he said, shaking his head. "Nobody understands what it means, nobody who is not in the businesss,"

"Sure," was her answer.

*

"So, what are you going to do?" Clifford asked as they drove to their story. "You plan to stay here forever?"

"No, not forever," Ellen said.

"Well, what are you going to do?"

"Clifford," she warned. She didn't want the questions today. No more questions.

"Like I said, I'm going to New York," he told her. "I can make it there. I'm good."

"A lot of people are," she said. She wasn't going to build up his dream today. She was tired of that too.

"Not as good as this nigger," he replied strongly.

"Well, it's too big for me. Too many people."

"Then where?" he demanded.

"I might pack it in and go back to New Mexico."

"Any jobs up there?"

"Yeah, but they don't pay."

"I'm already there in the don't-pay-me-nothin' place. I ain't going to another one."

She laughed.

"Nothin' as bad as this place," he shook his head. "Nothin.' It's March and I'm already sweatin' like a pig."

"And it's freezing in New York."

"You and that freezing in New York. So what? At least I'm going somewhere, sister."

She gave him a sharp look. He was staring straight ahead, his profile innocent of criticism.

"Well, at least we didn't get the prison story," she said.

"I hear that," he said, nodding with the words. "I hear that."

38

The prison story went to Debbie with Jason as her photographer. She pleaded with George for someone else. She had managed to avoid Jason for months, conniving and manipulating to work with other photographers.

"Clifford would be good on this one," she told George. "Or, how about Cappy? We work well together on things like this."

"Nope. Jason's it. Everybody else is out."

"Ah, George, doesn't Jason need to work on some series?" she tried.

"Debbie, go out and do the story," he said in frustration. What was wrong with these people? First they wanted to work together. Now they didn't. Well, they could forget it. He didn't have time to juggle the schedule first thing in the morning.

"How's everything been with you?" Jason asked her as they started the hour drive to the prison.

"Fine."

"I haven't seen much of you."

"No," she said, staring out her window. "I've been busy."

"Yeah, right." He turned on the radio. Rock and roll blasted through the van.

"You haven't gotten any shorter," he yelled over the music.

She said nothing.

He turned off the radio.

"Missed you," he said, looking over at her..

She continued looking out her window.

"Have you ever been in the prison?" he asked.

She shook her head. "I've never been in any prison."

"It's bad," he warned her. "We'll get in and out as fast as we can."

For Jason, prison stories were the worst, county, state, city, any prison. And, it wasn't only because they were hard to shoot, no faces allowed, and the light was bad. It was the noise, the sounds of metal on metal, cell doors closing, the strange screams of laughter.

"We'll get out fast," he promised.

He tried before, being friendly, talking to her in the newsroom. She would give him a smile but not much more.

"How's Ashley?" she asked suddenly.

"Working in Washington, as far as I know."

"Poor you."

"Come on, Debbie."

"Let's not talk," she said. "I really don't feel like it."

He turned the radio on and they rode the rest of the way without speaking.

They signed away any special consideration for their safety at the front gate. If anything happened to them, if they were taken hostage, they should not expect anything to be done for them. The gate slammed behind them and they stood in the open yard. Jason set up the tripod. The man from the warden's office stood with them.

"You can go up there," he said and pointed to the walkways running atop one fortress-like wall. "Would that be good for you, a good view?"

The legislature was in session. Any story about prison overcrowding could mean more money. The warden told him to give the television people what they wanted.

"And we'll need to go inside one of the cell blocks. Is that okay?" Debbie asked.

"Already set up."

The warden told him to take them into the three-story square brick jail built back in Territory days. They wanted shots of a prison system in need of money, they'd get them there.

"That about does it," Jason said, straightening up from his stance over the tripod. "Anything else you can think of, Debbie? Out here, I mean?"

"No. I guess we should go inside."

"Now remember," said the man with the short-sleeved white shirt, "stay back from the cells. Stay in the middle."

He shouldered the recorder so Jason could carry the tripod with the camera screwed into position. They passed into the gloom of the brick block.

"This is where we put the men who need protection from the general population," he told Debbie.

Her eyes moved across the high rows of cells.

"Do they ever go outside?" she asked in a whisper.

"When the other prisoners are inside, sure."

Jason moved to the center of the cellblock. The warden's man turned back to the guards at the door. Debbie moved further into the dark of the building.

"Hey, hey," the voices called to her. "Hey, lady."

They came from a dark corner of the old brick building.

"Hey, hey, come here," came the soft plea from the dark. "Come closer."

She took a few steps toward the cells and peered through the gloom, trying to find the face that matched the voice.

"I can't see you," she cried.

"Whatcha doin', lady?" came the voice of a black man lost in the blackness.

"We're doing a story about overcrowding down here," she said and tried to turn in the direction of the voice but she was confused. She turned again.

"Where are you?" she asked.

"What station you work for?" This seemed to be another voice.

Jason worked far from her, raising the camera and his eyes to the highest tier.

"Can we see it? When?" came the first voice.

"Tonight, probably. Maybe again tomorrow at noon." She tired to talk to all of the cells in that corner, like an audience. She smiled shyly.

"You never really know, but probably tonight."

"What station?" asked a voice.

"What she say?" came a faraway call.

"Hey, hey, lady," The first voice softly begged for attention. "Hey, you know that Jean Ann Maypin? You know her?"

"Yes," she said. "I work with her. Same station."

"She a nice lady? She looks like a real nice lady."

"You fool," came a laugh. "What a motherfuckin' fool."

"Shit," echoed down the cell row.

Jason signalled to her.

"I have to go," she told the wall of darkness.

"Hey, hey, lady, what's your name?"

"Debbie Hanson," she said without hesitating.

"You're on television, lady? Can we see you on the television?"

"Almost every night." She gave a little laugh and turned away.

"You got everything?" she asked Jason.

"Everything I can get and it ain't much. I hope you don't plan more than a minute on this story because we don't have squat."

She looked up to the top row of cells. There was more light up there. It wasn't so terrible. They weren't so bad, the people in here, only sad and lonely.

Jason picked up the camera and the tripod. The man in the white shirt moved toward the recorder and she looked up again.

"Psst, psst," insisted the call. She found it, the voice, in the cell on the second row. The lower half of the cell was covered with a sheet, a privacy constructed by the man within. She smiled a greeting.

Then, she saw it. His penis was poked through a hole in the sheet, full and red. He was masturbating. She saw his eyes as he watched over the top of the sheet. They were wide and staring, floating above the white sheet. She turned away and quickly followed after Jason.

"Bye, lady, bye-bye," cried the voice from the darkest corner of the cells.

She walked into the sunlight.

"We'll go up to the activity rooms," their man was saying. "You know, we've got our own television station, right here. Only problem is nobody really knows what to do with it. We have a prison news show, stories about classes and things that are going on. They really like that." He and Jason walked ahead.

*

"Stop, stop, please," she pleaded. "Please stop now."

"Sure, okay," he said, and turned the van onto the shoulder of the desert highway.

She ran a few steps, bent over and vomited.

"Oh, God," she gagged. "Oh, God, please."

"Debbie, what's wrong? What can I do?" He stood behind her,

She waved him away. "Don't look at me, please. Go back."

"Debbie, please." He moved to take her arm.

She shook her head and fell to her knees. She threw up again.

"Tell me what to do."

"Get me something to wipe my mouth, please, Jason," she said, reaching out one hand without turning her head.

He ran back to the van and grabbed a handful of the tissue sheets they used to clean the camera lens.

"I'm okay," she told him as she wiped her mouth. "I am, really."

She tried to laugh as she stood up and brushed at her skirt.

"I didn't have anything to eat this morning. I guess I don't feel so good."

"You want to stop some place? A doctor, emergency room?"

"No, no," she assured him as they got back in the van.

"We'll get you something to eat," he said. "Don't worry. That's what you need, food. Don't worry about getting back to the station. Fuck that. I'm going to get you something to eat and then you can go home. I'll take care of George."

She leaned back in the seat. "No." She sighed. "I'll be fine in a minute."

"Don't argue with me, Debbie. I'm taking you home. Between the heat and that goddamn hole and not eating, you've made yourself sick." His voice was strong, confident.

"Please don't worry, Jason."

"I am worried, damn it," he shouted. "At least let me pull over for some coffee or something. A soda, that might be good. You might need some sugar, right?"

He gave her a quick worried look. Her eyes were closed, her head resting on the seatback.

"It was that place," she said hoarsely. "It was so dark in there. It was so strange. It was like cages and animals. I just want to forget it."

"Okay," he said. "Right."

He knew it. It was that place. Prisons could have that affect on you, like your first operation.

"I know what you mean. I hate these stories. I don't feel so good myself and I'm so macho," he joked. "Yeah, I'd rather cover a good cancer operation any day," trying to make her laugh. But, he meant it. Cancer over prisons any day.

39

Four people came to group that night, the older woman, Jane the nurse, Terry the addict, and Debbie.

"I suppose we should start," the doctor said.

"Where is everyone?" the older woman asked.

"I don't know. No one called." He gave them a tired smile.

Debbie tried to return it before going back to staring at her patch of the world beyond the small window.

"So, how is it going?" the doctor said to no one in particular.

"Fine," Debbie said, making her voice bright. "Good."

"I think my job is going to be better now," the older woman said. "I think my boss is going to retire and that's good news."

They looked at her.

"It means I'll be working for someone else. That's got to be better."

"Do you know for sure he's leaving?" asked Debbie.

"No, but that's what people are saying, that he is going to take early retirement."

"What if he doesn't?" Debbie asked gently, trying not to sound critical.

"I don't know. I mean, I don't know." The older woman's eyes became confused, frightened.

"You don't have to think about that now," the doctor told her with a pointed look at Debbie.

"But I thought she was going to make a decision about her job," the nurse joined in. "Him leaving doesn't mean she's made a decision, does it, Doctor?"

Terry moved on the couch, shifting his position, then shifting again.

"Why shouldn't I hope he leaves," the older woman asked. "What's wrong with that? It would be easier for me."

Debbie looked over at Terry. He had been off drugs for almost three months. Every session she told him how great that was. She felt proud of him and thought she may have helped him by being in the group.

"I gotta tell you," Terry cut in. "I mean, I don't have to but ..." He looked at each of them before stopping at Debbie. "But, I am going to anyway."

The black circles of his glasses faced her.

"I shot up before I came here. I am high right now," he announced in a loud voice.

Debbie's mouth fell open.

"Terry," the doctor gasped.

Terry shrugged and folded his arms across his chest.

"No," Debbie cried out. "That's wrong. That's all wrong."

The others turned and stared.

"It's wrong," she told Terry angrily. "You are supposed to be stopping this. That's why you are here and you're high. You couldn't wait an hour?"

"He did tell us, Debbie," the older woman said strongly. "That counts."

"That's right, Debbie," the doctor said with a look of doubt.

"That is not right," she yelled, the panic, the fear, growing in this horror of a room.

"What are we doing here week after week? What are we doing here?" she demanded.

"At least he came," the nurse said, reaching for a cigarette from the doctor's pack. He nodded his permission.

"Yes," he said to Debbie, "Jane is right. At least he felt he could come here."

"So what? He's high. He's on drugs," she protested. "He couldn't even wait an hour. You couldn't even wait," she cried to Terry.

"I knew it!" he shouted, jumping to his feet. "I didn't have to say anything. I didn't even have to come here." He stomped out of the room.

The doctor went after him.

"Don't you see what's wrong here?" Debbie begged of the two women in the room. "We are coming here to get better. This is the one place we are supposed to come and try to get better so we can leave. And he comes in here on drugs. Don't you see how crazy that is? Don't you?"

"Terry will be in in a second," the doctor said as he came back into the room. "He is outside trying to calm down." He glared at Debbie, his face blotched red.

"This is terribly hard for him," he told her. "We asked him to be honest with us. He's doing his best and we aren't making it any easier for him."

Pure terror suddenly enveloped her. He was telling her she was wrong, all of her feelings were wrong. They were all telling her that. But, no, she wasn't wrong. She couldn't be wrong.

"I think we should ask him to come back in now," said the doctor. "And I think we should be gentle with him. He was in trouble and he came to us. Okay?"

Debbie felt the bile moving high in her throat.

"Terry, come on in. Terry?" the doctor called.

He walked in, head lowered, and sat back on the couch. He folded his arms across his chest.

"I will never forgive you for what you said," he told Debbie in a cold voice. "And, I'm never going to forget it."

"Terry," the doctor warned.

"No. At least I came here. I didn't have to."

"That's right," agreed the older woman thoughtfully.

Debbie was taking short, fast breaths. She put one hand to her forehead.

"I don't think this is right, any of this," she said as though speaking to herself. "This isn't why we are here. We are here to get better, not to stay the same way forever."

"I don't know why we are here. I never really have," the older woman sighed.

Debbie looked to the tiny slit of a window. It couldn't be much longer now.

*

Brown caught Jason as he was leaving the station.

"What's this I hear about Debbie getting sick?" he asked.

"Ah, you know. It was hot. She hadn't eaten much. She got sick. End of story."

"That's all?"

"Yeah."

"I am really worried about that girl, fella," Brown said as they walked to the parking lot. "I am really worried about her."

"Ah, she's okay," Jason told him.

"Something has been wrong with that girl for a couple of months now," Brown said. "I can't figure it out what it is."

He watched Jason's face as he added, "Maybe she needs to talk to a therapist or something?"

"Oh come on, Jim. It's only the job. You know how it can get to you. It gets to everybody once in a while."

"Yes, it can," Brown agreed. "But I get the feeling there is something else going on. You have any idea what it could be?"

Jason shook his head.

"Yeah, something else. We really have to help her," Brown pronounced solemnly.

*

She rocked on the couch, arms pulling her legs tight to her chest, swaying back and forth as the television sent soundless pictures back to her. Outside Clifford waited, staring at the peephole. He rang the bell once, twice.

"Hey, Debbie," he called. "Debbie, you in there? It's me, Clifford. Debbie?"

The bell rang again.

She waited and believed she heard a soft sigh as he moved away from the door.

40

She answered the phone on the first ring.

"Ellen, it's me, Clifford," his voice was blurred by background noise.

"Where are you?"

"Some bar. Hey, listen. I went by Debbie's and she's not answering the door. Could you give her a call or something?"

"Why don't you call her?"

"I tried, but she didn't answer the phone and I know she's there. I know it and I heard she got sick up at the prison today. She was throwing up or something."

"What?"

"Somebody said she had the flu or something, but I'm worried."

"She's probably unplugged the phone so she can get some rest. It's nothing to worry about."

"And George told me I had to take the next few days off."

"Why?"

"He said I was too high in overtime and I needed to give it a break. I was supposed to work this weekend and he told me to forget it. You believe that?"

"I believe everything."

"Can you meet me for a pizza or something?"

"Clifford, it's eleven o'clock. No way I'm leaving here. Tell me what else George said."

"Hell with it. I'm tired of this shit. I'll talk to you later."

He went back to his seat at the bar. On either side of him, two stools away, sat a white man.

He sipped his scotch.

"Doing okay?" the bartender asked with a tight-lipped smile.

Clifford wondered if he got the word to keep the blacks down at the bar. You didn't want too many, did you, not on the busy nights. A few were okay on the slow nights but not on Friday and Saturday nights. Too many blacks sent the young white businessmen with the money someplace else. He bet this bartender knew how to make it rough on blacks on weekends.

"Hey," Clifford asked, "can I get something to eat?"

"Too late. Kitchen's closed. Sorry."

Yeah, thought Clifford, sure.

"That's okay," he said. He was tired and he was lonely. He hadn't had a date in months. The couple of clubs he went to were filled with brothers wearing button-down white shirts and talking about how it was at the old fraternity and how it was now at the big corporation. What was that? Those brothers were whiter than anybody in this honky town.

"Who do you like for the game?" the bartender asked as he wiped down the counter.

"I don't follow college ball that much."

"That's smart. This town never had much of a team."

Clifford nodded. Man, he had to get out of this place and he had to do it soon. He motioned for a refill.

There he was, picking up the scraps, George's raggedy old stories. No big medical series for him. Oh, no. Mr. Jason gets the good stories and what he didn't get Steve got, and then Cappy. And what did that get him day after day? He got shit. That's what he got, shit.

And now this thing about overtime.

"How am I supposed to pay my bills?" he yelled at George. "You're taking money out of my pocket. Am I working for free here or what?"

And, what did he get?

"It's not my fault. Talk to Brown."

That's what he got.

Steve heard it all and what did he say?

"Nothing is going to change. Nothing is ever going to change."

Oh yeah, something could change. He could get out of there. Yes, he could. Other photographers did. They came in one day and said, "I'm out of here. I got me a job in Denver," or San Diego or Miami.

Look at Jason. He'd be going to DC or New York. He didn't say anything, but he was looking. They all knew that, and he'd go. Cappy too. Steve would stay. He'd been big time once. Now he was drinking quiet and keeping his mouth shut.

And him? He was busy flapping his lips and going nowhere, no how.

He studied his reflection in the mirror behind the bar. He was the blackest thing in this room, in this town. Now, what was that?

41

Tom Carter wasn't about to forget Tony's so-called joke. He knew these people too well. Tony makes a joke about someone being pregnant. George Harding says something about a stomachache. Brown makes excuses for her. They all knew what was going on and there was only one of them he could trust to give him a straight answer.

"Everything okay with you?" He tried to smile at Ellen Peters.

"Why not?" She knew he wanted something and he wasn't going to get it from her. He never did, not unless she knew it would annoy him and not hurt anyone else.

"I've been checking your file," he said. "I see you got a couple of vacation days from last year."

"I know."

"You should take them soon."

"When I get a chance, I will."

"Better make it soon," he warned.

He nodded toward the room beyond the blinds. "Everything okay with that mob out there?"

"Same as usual. Everyone trying to get the hell out."

"That so? Well, missy, they ain't going to find any place better than The Best."

"Probably not," she muttered.

"What's that?"

"I'm agreeing with you, Tom. They won't find anyplace that's any different from this."

"Yeah, well, you've been around, haven't you?"

"Yes, I have." She looked up at the ceiling.

"Debbie Hanson called in sick today," he told her. "You know anything about that?"

She gave a small sign of relief. She was right. Debbie was under the weather. Clifford had gotten crazy about the whole thing.

"I heard she had been having some flu problems or something," he continued.

What was it he wanted?

"That better be all," he added

"What?"

"I said," he raised his voice, "that better be all it is. I don't want no pregnant women in my newsroom."

She stared.

"We ain't that liberal here, missy. No unmarried pregnant women in this newsroom."

She gave a short laugh.

"What makes you think she's pregnant? She's not pregnant. God." She laughed again.

"Well, that's not what I hear," he leered at her.

Now her eyes were locked on his. Surprised, he thought, but not that surprised. So, there was something.

"I call 'em' like I see 'em," he said, "and it's my business to know what's going on out there."

"First of all, if it were true," she responded angrily, "it's nobody's business and second, you are all wrong on this one. Like the man said, consider your sources."

"Where there's smoke ...," he taunted.

"Tom, if you want to know anything about Debbie, you ask her, not me. And I'm telling you, it's none of your goddamn business."

"You watch that mouth of yours, missy," he warned, pointing at her. "It is my goddamn business. If I've got a pregnant reporter, I'd better know it. And, I don't want to hear talk about abortions either."

"Abortion?" She shouted the word. "Who the hell said anything about abortion?" What did he know and how? "This is crazy, Tom. You are making something out of absolutely nothing and somebody could get hurt."

"Yeah?" he smirked. "Well, I run this place and if you don't like the way I'm doing it, there's the door." He signaled with his thumb.

A stab of fear kept her silent.

"You watch that mouth of yours, Peters, and you take those vacation days. You take 'em soon. Take 'em or lose 'em."

"Fine," she said, getting to her feet. "I'll take tomorrow off and Friday and Monday. That should make George happy."

"Don't tell me. I don't keep the goddamn schedule. Gonna look for a job, Peters?" he asked as she reached for the door.

"I'll give you a great recommendation," he laughed.

She shut the door firmly behind her.

He reached for the phone. He was going to call that girl at home and she better be there, by God. He wanted to get this thing settled once and for all. He had other fish to fry.

42

She lay by the pool. A few people spoke to her as they passed her chair. Others sat down next to her.

"Nice day," they said.

"Yes, it is," she said.

"Been here long?"

"About a year."

"I'm from Detroit. This is fantastic, swimming in March."

"Sure is," she agreed.

"Can't wait to call home and tell them I'm down here by the pool."

She could do the same, call her father and tell him she too was sitting by the pool. The last time they spoke, he asked her about taking a week off and flying up there, or he might fly down.

"Maybe in May," she told him.

But, today, in the sun, she thought she could call him and tell him she was coming or, she smiled, tell him he should come here. He could come here and sit by the pool with the palm trees and the sound of people laughing.

The sun felt soft on her face.

"You like it here?" someone asked her.

"Sometimes," she said, her eyes closed.

"God, I love it. It is so much better than where I came from. Do you know anything about Nebraska?"

"No, I don't."

"Well, if you did, you'd know what I'm talking about. Swimming in March. Who would believe it?" said the young woman's voice.

"Boy, would I like to live here," a male voice told her. "This is the life. Me and my wife are going to look at places this afternoon. I figure, what the hey. This is the place to be. This is the future. What do you do?" He stopped to breathe.

"I work in television."

"Really? Could we see you on the tube? What do you do?"

"I do the news." She opened her eyes and looked at him. "I'm a reporter."

"No kidding?"

He was probably in his late forties. Black hair covered his chest and shoulders. He scratched at his belly.

"Me and the wife don't like that Barbara Walters, you know?'

"Uh huh."

"Nope, don't like her at all. How much does a house cost out here?"

The sky was a sapphire blue and the breeze moved through the palms. Beyond the splashing of the swimmers she could hear that breeze.

It was perfect, like a beautiful resort where people lived and talked and moved at an easy pace. Maybe if she slowed down and took more time to sit by the pool and read in the sun, she would feel different about this place. Maybe she would see it like everyone else did.

She left in the afternoon, driving east on the broad avenue that ran along the side of the mountain. Old ranch-style houses sat at its base waiting for the developers to buy them up and knock them down. Dirt driveways led up the mountain to the memories of adobe hotels where dudes once warmed in the sun. Big new yellow-brown stucco houses with rust-red tile roofs flowed down from paved roads to the avenue below.

She turned north to the highway where the resorts came one after the other, surrounded by flowers and lawns and sprinklers shooting water diamonds into the sun. East again past the quiet streets of the desert homes with their lawns of manicured dust and cactus.

She reached the small community where houses clung to the desert and the sides of the small hills. She drove past the empty parking lot of the shopping mall that had never been built and past the pond with the fountain that sent up an hourly shaft of water high enough to be seen for miles. It held some title of being the tallest, the biggest, the everything fountain in the world. She made a half circle of the town and pulled back on the highway.

She crossed the small bridge over the river. She saw hints of green and felt the quiet of a good place to fish or sit or eat a picnic lunch. She stopped at the small store next to the road leading into the reservation. She bought a can of soda from the glass case. The Indian woman with the thick black hair smiled at her as she took her money.

"Can I drive in there?" she asked, gesturing in the direction of the reservation.

"What?"

"Can I drive onto the land, the nation's land?" She was embarrassed by her words. The nation's land, that sounded strange, uncomfortable.

"Sure, yes," the woman looked confused.

"I can drive on it? No problem?"

"No, no problem," she said and turned to wait on the tall Indian boy wearing a white cowboy hat with a single feather.

"Thank you," she said.

The woman did not answer. She and the boy were laughing together.

Outside, she took a deep breath. The air smelled of trees and fields. It was so quiet, only the birds singing, only a car passing on the highway. She smiled. She was going to make it. Damn it. She was going to make it. She began the drive back.

The key was this land, this being out on the land, away from the city. That's what she loved. Next week she would drive into the reservation, look at the small farms and the animals. Or, she would drive to the mountains, up to the small towns. She could stay in a little inn. She could do that. Yes, she could. She would be all right. She knew that now.

There would be no more doctor or group or drug addicts. Without all of that she would, for once, be fine. All of that craziness would be out of her life. She would clean it all out, get away from the bad things.

A car passed her, big, faded with the sun. It flew around her going seventy or eighty miles an hour. She thought the driver must be angry in his old rotting carcass of a car.

The job wasn't bad, not really. She had to relax, not take it so seriously. Isn't that what Jason told her, not to think so much about things? She could make sure to come out on the land, go to the mountains, get away from work every chance she got. That's how you survived. Learn to love this place. It was a good place, warm and good. Everybody thought so.

The camper in front of her was going less than forty miles an hour. A Confederate flag covered the back window. She took a chance and pulled out. She saw him as she passed, an old man hunched over the steering wheel.

Maybe there was something else at the station she could do, another type of job. She gasped. The thought stunned her. She didn't have to be a reporter. There were other things she could do, better things. Wow.

She could do some producing or work on the assignment desk. She had good story ideas, lots of them. This was a decision about how she was going to live, how it could all be better. She exhaled deeply. She felt wonderful with this new idea. Assignment editor. Why not? They were the ones who really made the news. They were the ones who picked out the stories to be covered.

Two cars were coming at her, side by side. She caught her breath, waiting for the car in her lane to make the pass or to pull back fast. At the last second, when there seemed to be no chance he could do it, he made the pass and as he flew by she saw him, a wild, death's-head-grinning kid of a driver.

Tomorrow she would talk to Brown, to Carter. She would tell them her plan, tell them what she wanted to do. She wanted a career in television but no more reporting, not now, at least. Ellen was right. No wonder she was depressed. It was a depressing job.

Two cars sat crumpled and glass-strewn at the intersection that marked the end of the desert and the beginning of the city. An ambulance waited, doors open. A group of men had gathered. She could not see what was in the middle of their small circle. The cop in khaki and mirrored sunglasses impatiently waved her on.

All right, maybe in six months she could do a little reporting to keep her hand in. But right now, it wasn't good for her. She'd forget that vision she had of sitting at a typewriter, smoking a cigarette. That's what Ellen looked like, sitting in her cubicle, her sunglasses pushed on top of her head and her fingers flying across the keys, punching at the letters. She could be that later or never. Now, she needed a plan. Now, she had one.

The traffic rushed by. In her side mirror she could see the angry face of the man tailgating her in his black Mercedes. Suddenly he swung out, passed and pulled in front of her sharply as though shaking his fist in her face.

Tomorrow would be different. For the first time she knew that. Tomorrow was, what did they say, the first day of the rest of your life. And, it was, it really was. Gosh, she told herself, she was happy.

43

"Ain't no flies on me," he said out loud as he turned on the engine. "No flies on this black boy."

He chuckled. Close to dawn and he was still running hard. His bags were in the back and his tapes on the seat next to him. He patted them. It took him only a few hours of editing and dubbing after the six o'clock news.

He did it fast, without thinking. He opened with spot news followed with a hard news package, sports footage, and a feature piece with some tricky editing. He closed with two of the medical stories he did with Ferguson along with a clip from the kidney transplant. The tape ran less than fifteen minutes.

A few people passed by the editing booth as he worked. He could see their shadows move to the small window, stop and move on. Steve was there, working late or coming in after a few beers to find some company. He knocked before opening the door.

"Late story?" he asked.

"Working on my escape tape."

"Gotcha," Steve said and closed the door.

He finished by midnight and went back to the apartment to pack his two suitcases. That's what he came to town with, two suitcases, and that's what he had now, and the stereo. He wrapped it carefully in his electric blanket and buffered it with his pillows. The whole muffled pile rested on the floor behind the front seat. The speakers went in the trunk separated by the suitcases.

He patted the tapes again, five tapes. He gave a laugh. That's all he had after more than a year of humping that camera all over the desert, up and down mountains, in and out of vans. That's all he had for all the heat and the sweat and the fifty-hour weeks and George mouthing off at him, telling him where to go and how to get there and expecting four stories a day and one at two o'clock in the morning, some house fire nobody but nobody cared about.

The rent was paid until the first. He had only used the oven a few times, not enough to eat into his cleaning deposit. He put a letter through the slot in the manager's door to let him know he was leaving and would call in a week.

So what if they decided to screw him out of the deposit? A couple of hundred bucks, he'd eat it. It was worth a couple of hundred to get out of this town. Like he said, he was going to New York and he would sit in that NBC office until they gave him a job. If they wanted references, they could call Steve and Ferguson, even George. Not Brown. Brown would screw him. He knew that. Brown would screw him good.

He thought about calling Debbie or going by her apartment but stopped himself. He was done with that.

He'd call them from New York and he'd say, "Well, here I am here working in the big time. How's it down there? A hundred and ten? My oh my."

He laughed.

The Buick started with a hum. What he needed was a map, a big one. He knew he had to head north until he saw the signs for Albuquerque then hang a right. That was all he needed to know for the next few hours.

He pulled out of the parking lot. He tightened the muscles in his shoulders, pushed them back, sat up straight as he hit the street.

He gritted his teeth. In thirty minutes, forty, there would be one less nigger in this honky town. Hallelujah.

44

"George had to go to some sort of prayer breakfast," Kim Palmeri told her.

"Where's everybody else?" Debbie asked.

"It's early. Can you do this?"

Debbie took the assignment sheet.

"It's no big deal, but we need stories today."

"You know what would make this good?" Debbie asked. "I could go out where people are dumping in the desert. Talk to these homeowners about people dumping in alleys. We could try to get an interview with the mayor.

"Obviously, if they are dumping it's because there's no place to put it or nobody is picking it up. We should ask him about that. Why aren't there more heavy trash pickups? You think we could get to him on this?" She was excited now. This was the way stories should be done.

"Carter's looking for you, Debbie." Mary walked over to them. "He called a few minutes ago to find out if you were in."

"Why?" she cried out as though she had been punched in the chest.

"I don't know. He didn't say. Probably nothing to worry about," Mary reassured her. "He's on his way in."

"Ah, no," she moaned. "I've got to get out of here."

"I already told him you were here. I'm sorry, but you know how he is."

Debbie searched for hope, any hope there could be. "It might be nothing," she told them. "And, I need to talk to him too." She tried to make her voice strong.

Maybe she could get to Brown first. He would help her. She would tell him her plan, that she wanted to do assignments. He would help her.

"Is Brown in?" she asked Kim.

"Not yet."

"Well," she said, "it will be okay, won't it?"

The other women didn't answer.

Ten minutes later Mary called.

"He wants you in his office."

She looked down at her hands. They were shaking. All the resolve, the joy that came with the drive yesterday had disappeared. She was filled with with terror. What was he going to do to her?

"I tried to get you at home yesterday," Carter told her. "All day. Where the hell were you?"

"I wasn't feeling well so I unplugged the phone, so I could sleep."

"Listen, honey," he sneered, "we're on call twenty-four hours a day in this station. We don't unplug our phones and we don't take them off the hook. You got that?"

"Oh," she said and gave a small smile of relief. "I am sorry. I wasn't thinking." Was that all it was? Okay, then.

He narrowed his eyes.

"And we've got another problem here too. I want to know what the hell this talk is about your personal life. I don't like that going on in my newsroom."

"I don't understand." She reached for the edge of his desk.

"You heard me. There is some talk about your personal business and I want it stopped now."

"What do you mean?"

"I mean," his eyes narrowed, "this station is made up of ladies and gentlemen."

She nodded, still confused.

"And I don't want any dirt in this station."

"Please," she begged, "I really don't know what you're talking about."

"What I'm talking about, sweetie, is some talk about you making a mistake in your personal life, one that affects this station. Is that true?"

Oh no, he knew about Jason and the abortion. What else did he know? Did he know about the doctor and the group and her breakdown? How could he know? Who would tell him that? Who? Ellen? Clifford? Who else did they tell? They must all know, everyone must know what she was and what she had done.

She stared at him, her face white with fear.

He smiled. She was scared. This one was scared.

"If there is something dirty going on, you clean it up," he ordered. "I don't want to know about it and I don't want to hear anything else about it." He tapped his fingers on the desk. "But, you get this and you get it right." He pointed both index fingers at her. "Everything you do reflects on the rest of us. You are always on the job. Always. And, from what I've been hearing, you better shape up, young lady, and that means your work too." Yeah, she should be scared. "I had my doubts about you right from the beginning. I didn't think you were ready for us but...."

She jumped to her feet, cutting off his words.

"You are a vile, evil, old man, and you're lying!" she shouted. "You don't know anything about me. Nothing. I have to get out of here!" she yelled as she ran from his office.

He jumped after her, yelling from his doorway, "You get back in here, young lady. I'm not finished with you. You get back in here now."

She was grabbing things off her desk. Tapes fell to the floor, coins and lipstick fell from her purse.

"No, no, no," she was crying as she scooped everything back into her bag.

"Listen here, missy," Carter was marching toward her, "you better get yourself under control."

"No, no, no!" It was a scream of terror as she ran toward him.

Kim came around the corner of the row of cubicles, her eyes wide with excitement.

"No!" Debbie screamed again as Carter reached out as though to stop her. She pushed him aside. "No more." she cried.

Throughout the room, across the desks, the early morning phones rang and rang.

*

Dr. Stanley Waddell puffed on his cigarette. He took another drag and checked his address book for her number. She missed her appointment yesterday.

Predictable, he nodded to himself. She was upset over the group session. Well, he was upset too and he had a right to be. She risked months of work with Terry, months.

All right, perhaps he had been a little hard on her, but he expected more from her. She was strong, much stronger than Terry. This could set Terry back months, he puffed, months.

The group worked better before Debbie came. Yes, it did. It certainly had been a more pleasant weekly experience. Now, no one wanted to come. It was too intense. People got too upset. That's what they told him in their individual sessions.

Oh, they explained it in different ways, of course. They claimed it was financial, that they had to choose between private sessions and group. That was Carol.

Bob said he couldn't make either the private session or the group, using his job as an excuse. Jane said she had shift change at the hospital and couldn't make the group sessions. He wondered if she hadn't made the shift change herself, if there even was a shift change.

Maynell called and said she would rather not come to group anymore but would if he wanted her to. Terry said he would never come back. He said he wouldn't talk about it and didn't want him to bring it up again.

He reached for the phone.

Of course, she could have forgotten about yesterday's appointment. Sometimes, as the great man pointed out, a cigar is only a cigar. He crumpled the empty cigarette pack.

If only there was someone to talk to, someone who could tell her she was all right, that everything would be be fine, that she wasn't crazy. She could never go back to the station, never. They talked about her, laughed about her. Yes, they did. She was just one of their stories. Even Ellen, she thought, even Ellen.

And the group? The thought made her stomach turn. If she went back to them and that horrible room she would have to stay there forever. They didn't want her. There was no one to call and no place left to go.

She went into the kitchen and began to clean. She could not call her father. What could he say, come home? She couldn't do that again. She couldn't start over again.

She ran a dust cloth across her grandmother's hutch. She licked her finger and wiped at a spot on the dining room table. She looked in the bathroom. The towels hung straight on the rack. In the bedroom, she dusted the top of the dresser and moved her father's picture slightly forward. She picked up her mother's picture and rubbed her finger across the glass.

"Oh, Mommy," she whispered. "Oh, Mommy."

In front of the dresser mirror, she brushed her hair. It was long now, blond and full to her shoulders. She pulled it back into a small ponytail. She found a pink ribbon in the top drawer and tied a bow around the curl of hair.

She stopped in the kitchen and took an apple from the basket on the counter. She rubbed the apple hard on her jeaned thigh. Today she was going to do something she had never done before. She was going to climb a mountain.

Juan Moya waved as Ellen came up the long driveway. Joan McBain watched from her kitchen desk.

"So," she said to Ellen after the mugs had been filled, "you thinking about coming back here?"

"I have thought about it," Ellen said with a nod.

"I thought you liked it over there."

"No, not really. As a matter of fact, I don't know if I ever liked it. I have to get out of there and soon."

"Well, it's your life and you better enjoy it while you can," Joan McBain commented. "Although, I don't know if coming back here is the answer. It wouldn't have to do with Ronnie, would it?"

Ellen shook her head.

"I haven't talked to Ronnie in two years. This doesn't have anything to do with him."

"Just as well," Joan McBain said with a sigh. She looked to the wide window. "I don't think that would be a good reason for coming back here. There's a lot going on in his life."

"Yeah?"

"Yeah, he's doing real well. He's talking about buying a second feed store over in Bernalillo and he's looking to buy a house."

Ellen sipped at her coffee.

"He's also been seeing this girl Linda for a couple of months now. She's got a good job with the city. Comes from a local family. She's a nice girl and I've got a feeling they might get married." The words were delivered as though of little importance.

Ellen sat frozen in shock.

"I believe marriage would be good for him," Joan McBain

continued as she poured more coffee. "You two ever talk about it?"

"I'm sorry," Ellen said faintly. "I didn't hear you."

"Did you two ever talk about getting married?"

"Not really," Ellen said. "I would have liked it."

"No," came the emphatic response. "No, I don't think so. You two were too different. You know that, Ellen, when you think about it."

"Sometimes different works."

"Not often, honey. You gotta have something in common, something big."

But they did, Ellen thought. They had this place, this kitchen and the mornings drinking coffee and the window to the fields and the horses. They had this woman in common and Sarah and Bob Junior and young Phillip. They had the ranch, the big sky, rolling ranchland up north.

She wanted to see the ranch again, to see the cabin as she first saw it from the road, small and waiting. She wanted to see the red ridge of the mountains and to see him, tall and lean, walking the land.

"How's the ranch?" she asked.

"Up north?"

"Uh huh."

"I think we've finally got somebody interested and it's about time."

"Interested how?" Ellen asked.

"In buying it, honey. We've been trying to sell the dang thing for years," Joan McBain said, lighting a cigarette

Ellen stared in surprise. "You're selling it? What does Ronnie think about that?"

"He's the one who wants to sell it the most. We'll both be sorry to see it go, sure, but land needs to be worked. You can't let it sit idle for too long. And Ronnie sure as hell ain't going to work it. The other boys don't care one way or the other."

"But I thought Ronnie loved the ranch."

"He likes to get up there every so often but Ronnie ain't no rancher. You know that." She laughed.

"But all the work he did up there," Ellen insisted. "The fences, the cabin."

"He didn't do all that, Ellen. It was Bobby that built the place and kept it up while he was alive. Sure, Ronnie helped his dad but no, it was Bobby. Ronnie's a town boy, honey, like his mama."

Ellen rubbed her face with her both hands.

It hadn't been him at all. It hadn't been her cowboy who looked so right in his jeans and boots. She made it all up.

"You weren't thinking about you two getting back together, were you?" Joan McBain asked, a worried note in her voice.

Ellen shrugged.

"You know what your problem is, honey?"

"You tell me," Ellen said, her voice suddenly cold.

"You're afraid of success. Oh yes, you are," Joan McBain said to Ellen's grimace.

"You're damn good. I used to watch you. You were the best thing going in this town. You'd be good anywhere."

Ellen stared up at the ceiling.

"Instead, you spend your time going from one rinky-dink town to another and now you're thinking of coming back here? Honey, you should be going to a big city, not back here. Nothin' here for you. Nothin'." She paused for a pull on her cigarette.

"You plan to see Ronnie while you're here?" she asked with a smoky exhale.

"I don't know."

"He'd love to see you, Ellen. I know that. He's down at the store. You could catch him there."

What was she supposed to do, walk into the store and wait until neither of them had anything left to say or until it was time for him to leave to be with this new woman, the nice girl, the one he was going to marry? That wasn't the way she pictured it on the long drive up.

She had pictured how she would walk into Joan McBain's kitchen and he would be there and she would smile at him. He would lift her up the way he used to and say, "Hell, what do you weigh, girl?"

He'd put her down and pick her up again by the loops of her jeans.

"You don't weigh as much as a sack of feed," he'd say.

That is the way she wanted it to be by the time she reached Gallup, the way she knew it would be by the time she passed Grants.

"I really care for him, you know," she said softly.

"I know, honey. He is easy to love. Hey, look at that little sweetie." Ellen followed her gaze.

"She's my prize, my little princess."

Outside in the pasture the spindle-legged foal bounced after the mare.

"Cute baby, isn't she? She's going to be somethin' great."

Before she got into her car, Ellen stopped and took a deep breath. There was a biting chill in the air. There might be snow tonight. She looked up at the clear, cloud-free sky. No, not tonight, but maybe tomorrow.

It would be a day to sit and read and watch the snow and the Sandias as they turned black-green with a dusting of white. Or, if she got lucky, the mountains would disappear in thick gray clouds that would billow close to the ground like sails.

"How are you, Elena?" Juan Moya moved to her side.

"Lo mismo, the same," she said. "You think it will snow tonight?"

"I think tomorrow," he said.

"Be nice to see snow."

"It don't snow down there where you are, does it?"

"It's already hot," she laughed.

"You like it?"

"Not much."

"I was there once. It is a big city, no? And it was hot. I remember that." He shook his head sadly.

"It hasn't changed."

"You like it better here?" he asked.

"I think I do."

"You come back, Elena?" he asked with a shy smile.

She could go by the store. She could see him, say hello. She could call him tomorrow and tell him she was in town. He would know. Joan McBain would tell him and he would know she was at Dale's. If he wanted to see her, to talk to her, he would know where to find her.

Ellen knew how this night would go. She would wait for the sound of his truck. She would wait through the wine and Dale's stories and the station gossip. She would wait and jump if the phone rang, which it would, but not for her. She knew that too.

"You should come back," Juan Moya said strongly. "I never liked that city. Too hot."

There was that wooly wet smell in the air, that catch of breath in her throat, the moving sense of a hard change coming. Yes, it might snow tonight.

"We'll see," she said.

She got into her car without glancing back to see if Joan McBain watched. She didn't want to know.

47

Nancy Patterson faced another weekend without news and she didn't care. Between sick photographers, bored and surly reporters, out-of-commission vans, interviews who canceled or never showed up, she didn't care. She would use what she had. That was the job of a weekend producer, to use what you had or could find. She had two newscasts today. She'd be out of the station, home free, really home free, in about ten hours.

She counted her possibilities. Two crews were out. That meant three stories, four if she was lucky. She could pull a few stories from the network feed. She had wire copy to rewrite and a package she could pull of the hold sheet. Add sports and weather and she had her newscasts. She opened the morning paper. She only needed two minutes of state news, tops.

As she read, the scanners clicked and chattered away. If something out of the ordinary came across she would hear it whether she was reading, writing or answering a phone. She could be in the bathroom and hear something that would make her run, if no one was looking, or walk quickly if someone was.

They all did that, reporters, photographers, producers. They heard the fire call, the shooting report, over the chaos of a working newsroom five screaming minutes before a newscast. They were tuned in that way, waiting for the big story.

Like Ellen would tell non-news people, "On slow days we sit there and pray for a plane crash."

Nancy wasn't praying for any tragedy today, not when she was alone with the scanners and the phones and the two crews who didn't want to be wherever they were. She didn't want anything to ruin a slow and simple day.

"Let me get through these two newscasts," is what she prayed. "Let it be smooth."

The call for Brian Rafferty, the helicopter pilot from Across the Street, came at three o'clock. She would remember that. She looked up at the clock thinking it was time to start rewriting the wire copy when she heard his name on the scanner. The Department of Public Safety wanted him.

DPS called him first for the rescues and the searches. Rafferty would fly upside down to get a story or a body. Reporters at The Best said Rafferty should wear a badge. That's how tight he was with the cops. The Best's pilot, Ken Davis, was lucky to be second on the scene, if at all.

The two-way on her desk buzzed.

"Nan, heard a call for Rafferty. Might want to check it out." Cappy's voice was emotionless.

"Yeah, I heard it. What's your ETA?"

"Ten minutes. Rodriguez is on his way in. He got his own car. Over and out."

"Ten-four," she said to the dead mike. Crap. If DPS wanted Rafferty there was a problem and that meant she might have to find someone to cover it.

"Some problem up on Padre Peak," the DPS dispatcher told her.

"Somebody lost or fell? What?"

"That's all we got."

"Come on," Nancy insisted.

"We don't have any information. Call back in a few minutes. We might have more then."

Damn it. Rafferty was already up. She heard him clicking his own messages across the scanners while she was talking with the dispatcher. She would have to find Ken Davis.

She tried his pager and his home phone. No answer.

"News Base to Sky Eye. Base to Sky Eye. Ken?" she called on the helicopter radio.

Oh Lord, this would blow the whole day.

Cappy was back on the two-way.

"What's going on?" he asked.

"Something on Padre Peak."

"Want me to swing by? I'm right there."

"Yes, do that. I can't find Ken. Let me know what's happening."

Charles Adkins and Steve slammed into the newsroom. Adkins carried bags of hamburgers and French fries.

"What's up?" he asked. "We heard a call for Rafferty."

"Something on Padre."

"Ken up?"

"Can't find him."

"Shit," Adkins said before turning to his hamburger and the sports section, "that guy is unbelievable."

"This is News Base to Sky Eye. Base to Eye," she tried again.

"Any problem?" asked Jim Brown over the two-way. His voice was soft, disinterested.

"Some sort of rescue or something on Padre. Trying to reach Ken."

"Rafferty up?"

"Yup."

"Have you tried Ken at home?"

"Yup."

"Try the airport. You've got the number for the hangar?"

She flipped through the first of the Rolodexes. Cards fell out, yellow with age and blue and black with penned notations.

"Let me know what goes on." Brown clicked off.

Adkins stood over her, his fingers spinning through another Rolodex.

"Here, here," he tossed a card at her. "Try this."

"Unit Eight to Base. Eight to base."

"Go ahead, Cappy," she answered.

"Got some cops out here. Some hikers spotted something." She could hear the excitement in his voice.

"What?"

"Don't know. Ambulance here. Rafferty's been called to do a flyover. Where's Davis?"

"News Base, this is ..." The call letters were lost in static.

"Sky Eye to Base," it came again.

"Hold on," she told Cappy. "He's on now."

"Talk to him," she ordered Adkins as she turned to the speaker that gave her Ken Davis.

"What's up?"

"Something up on Padre."

"I'm there."

"Hey, tell him to come here first and get me," Adkins ordered

"You got a story ready?" she asked.

"Nothing out there," he said. "Nothing to it."

"I need whatever you have."

"From a fucking puppet show?" he demanded. "Come on, Nancy."

Steve walked toward them with Mark Cunningham a few paces behind.

"He can pick me up," said Steve. "Charles can drive out there and meet Cappy. That will give us someone on the ground and I can be shooting from the copter."

"Hey, what's going on?" Ken shouted on the speaker.

"Okay. Steve, get your equipment and get up to the pad. Charles, take a van and go out to Cappy," she ordered.

"Ken," she called over the radio, "get in here and pick up Steve."

"Everything under control?" Brown was talking again.

"Should I take the live unit?" Charles Adkins shouted from the newsroom door. "We might need it."

"Take it," she yelled back. "Everything is fine," she told Brown.

"What have you got?"

"Don't know. Ken is up and is going to pick up Steve. Adkins is on his way out to meet Cappy."

"Okay. I'll be at home if you need me."

"Yeah, yeah," she mumbled. She had to build the newscast.

"What can I do?" asked Mark Cunningham.

"Edit when we've got something to edit," she told him.

Tommy Rodriguez ambled into the room, a friendly smile on his face.

"Where have you been?" she demanded.

"I've been on my way here," he said, the smile gone.

"What have you got? What stories?"

"What's wrong with you?"

"I've got everybody and their brother out on a rescue or something and I don't have a newscast. What have you got?"

"What kind of rescue?"

"Just tell me what you have!" she shouted.

"A couple of nothing pieces. I want to kill that day-in-the-dog-park thing."

"We're not killing anything. Get it together and give me the times."

"Okay, but what's going on?" He followed her to the wire machine.

"Get the stuff to Mark," she ordered. She ripped the paper and marched back to the desk, a long stream of wire copy trailing behind her.

Tommy was right on her heels.

"Somebody dead or what?" he asked.

"This is Cappy to Base. Cappy to Base."

Tommy beat her to the desk.

"Go ahead," he said.

"Looks like somebody fell. We've got some witnesses here. Who is this?"

"Tommy."

"Can I get a reporter out here?" Cappy asked.

"He wants a reporter," he told Nancy. "Says he has witnesses or something."

Nancy looked up from her typewriter. She frowned. Those witnesses would stay there until hell froze over if they thought they were going to be on television.

"Tell him Adkins is on his way."

She turned to the sound of the helicopter beating the air above the building.

"Adkins's on his way," Tommy told Cappy.

"Tell him I'm in the park. The entrance is on the north side. He knows where it is." He doubled-clicked off.

"Hi, how's it going?" Scott Reynolds was standing next to her. Dependable and pleasant, he was the perfect weekend anchor.

"Oh, God, Scott. I don't have anything done. Would you check on the feed? Pick something up for the ten o'clock. Something is going on. A rescue, I think. That might be my lead, but I am going to need a few things off the feed. Something hard, something soft."

"Okay," he smiled.

Five minutes passed before the next interruption.

"Live to Base. Live to Base." It was Charles Adkins' voice.

"This is Base. Go ahead," Tommy answered.

"We're going to do some interviews with the people who think they found a body," Adkins said. Other voices interrupted.

"Oh, yeah, well," Adkins continued, "They saw what looked like a body and called the cops."

"Somebody dead, alive, what?" she demanded as she tore a script page from the typewriter. "Geez!" she cried. "I'm going to need an engineer. Tell him we'll send out an engineer in case we go live."

She was breathing hard, like a runner. What if there wasn't an engineer in the station? Those guys were never around. But, there had to be one, had to be. Sports usually had a live'er on the weekend and they had to have another engineer in the station to make sure everything was working.

"Would an engineer please call the newsroom," she called over the public address system.

"And?" came the quick telephone response. "What can I do you for?"

"I need an engineer out to my live unit. I may want to send something back and I might need a live'er tonight on the six."

"Why don't you send somebody out to pick up the tape?"

"I don't have any time or any people," she shouted. "I want an engineer out there."

"I am supposed to do a live shot for sports," he reminded her.

"I don't care. Go out there and send the stuff back or bring it back."

"No can do right now," was the singsong reply. "Nobody else in right now and I have that sports live'er from the arena. You can't cancel that."

"Then find another engineer!" she yelled.

"Double time," he sang.

"Pay it, damn it."

She slammed down the receiver. You couldn't argue with an engineer. They did exactly what they wanted.

"So, what do you need?"

The short man who belonged to the telephone voice now stood over her. Damn, he must have been only a few feet away when he called.

"I need," she said through gritted teeth, "an engineer to go out to the live unit at Padre Peak."

"Why didn't you say so?" He grinned.

She stared at him. This is what she needed now, an engineer's moronic sense of humor.

"They're in that park on the north side of the mountain," Tommy told him from the seat he had taken at the assignment desk. "You know where that is?"

The engineer nodded and stepped back as Nancy stood up and grabbed the pile of script papers. He followed her to the long empty table in the front of the room. He watched as she began to lay the lines of the newscast. Where a script page was missing, she inserted a sheet of yellow paper. Her movements were slow and deliberate.

"You can't get a live shot from there, you know," he said from his position behind her. "Mountain's in the way," he said, clasping his hands behind his back.

She ignored him and stared at the lines of white and yellow paper.

"Your show," he commented as he walked away.

"How long is your story?" she called to Tommy Rodriguez.

"That thing on the park will be about fifty seconds but you should toss it," he said. "I also have that piece on the new sewage plant. I figure it at about one-thirty."

"Fine. Write the intros." Her mind was now on her times. After a long stare at the table, she began to rearrange the sheets. She threw two yellow sheets to the floor. Like she needed this. Depending on what Adkins got, she would be standing here shuffling the script, exchanging yellow papers for white, right up until the last five minutes before the newscast. One yellow sheet headed the top of the first vertical row. That was her lead.

"This is Sky Eye to Base. Sky Eye to Base."

"Go ahead, Ken."

"We got Rafferty lowering some guy on a rope. We got the body coming up on a stretcher."

"Body? You said body?"

"That's an affirmative. No doubt about it."

"Dead? What?"

"I don't know."

Great.

"Get in as fast as possible," she ordered. "We need that tape."

She turned to the two-way.

"Cappy, you there?"

"We got what we can out here," Charles Adkins responded. "What do we do now?"

Oh, crap, did she need that live'er now?

"An engineer is on his way. Wait for him and trade units, then come in." She gave two clicks on the receiver button. What the hell was the engineer's name?

"Could the engineer please respond?"

"You mean me?" the voice asked.

"Right. Trade units with Adkins and head out to the sports thing."

"Like I said," the voice sang. "I'm doing a live'er tonight for sports."

She could imagine the smirk on his face. Who cared? So far, so good. Sports was covered. She'd have Cappy's footage and Steve's. She had her lead, whatever it was. Good, she'd get out of here yet.

48

"Everything set up?" Rick Whalen, weekend sportscaster, stood at her desk.

"If you set it up, it's up," she answered.

He handed her script sheets.

"This is pretty much how it's going to go. I'll wing it, but make sure they've got the scores."

He handed her another pile of sheets with the numbers and names that would appear on the screen.

"You got anything good going?" he asked.

"A hiking accident, maybe, something."

"Nice," he said.

It would be a good newscast, not that he cared that much. What he cared about were the big-money men who were in town during the winter months. All those guys from New York and Chicago were right now sitting around the hotel pools tanning their guts.

At six o'clock, all those big time boys would be getting out of their showers, reaching for a drink from their mini-bars, and watching the news, especially the sports. And, he'd be there for them to see. Who knew where that could lead.

"You know where to reach me," he told her.

She managed to type two pieces of copy before she had to reach for the phone.

"Who is this?" The voice was low and urgent.

"Who is this?" she demanded.

"Brian Rafferty."

"Hey, Brian," she brightened. "It's Nancy Patterson. How's it going? Still working hard?"

"Shut up and listen," he ordered.

"What?"

"Can you get to Brown?" His voice was muffled as though he was cupping the mouthpiece, hiding the movement of his lips from whomever might be watching.

"Why?"

"Listen, I shouldn't be telling you this. This isn't public yet, but I think Brown needs to know."

"Okay." She waited.

"You've got to get to Brown and tell him something and if you ever say where you got it, I swear to God I'll say you're lying. You got that?"

"Okay, okay," she agreed. She'd worry about that after she heard what he had.

"It was one of yours," he said. "That body I picked up was one of yours."

She felt the hair rise on her arms.

"What do you mean?"

"It was Hanson. Debbie Hanson."

"Oh my God," she gasped. Tommy Rodriguez, back in his cubicle, looked up from his typing.

"Listen, damn it," Rafferty demanded. "Nobody knows, not yet. Not anybody who is saying anything. I had to tell the cops, but it's not official. I can't even tell my own people yet. Do you hear me?"

"She's dead?"

"Yeah. They don't know what happened. Look, I'm sorry. I met her a few times. Nice kid. I thought you guys should know before anyone else got it. I gotta go." He hung up.

"I can't believe this," she muttered, still holding the receiver.

She took a deep breath and then turned to the two-way.

"Get in here. Get in here now," she yelled. "Cappy, Adkins, I need you now."

"What the hell is wrong?" demanded Tommy Rodriguez, standing over her again.

What did she do? Tell him first or get to Brown?

"Sit down, now," she ordered as she checked the middle Rolodex for Brown's home number. He answered on the first ring.

"Jim, this is Nancy. I've got to talk to you."

"Go," was his calm reply.

"It was Debbie. That body Rafferty brought down, it was Debbie and …" She stopped abruptly. She could not hear him breathing. Tommy had jumped to his feet.

"Jim?"

"I'm listening," he said quietly. "Go ahead."

"Rafferty called. He recognized her. No question about it." Who cared if she told everyone it was Rafferty? Who cared now?

"Do you have confirmation, DPS, hospital, anybody?"

"No, we're not supposed to know. Nothing is confirmed."

"Don't call anybody. Don't use the two-way until I get there. You understand?"

"Yes, I understand."

She took another deep breath. She knew what she had to do. She had to put a newscast together, a new one. She had less than two hours. She looked up at Tommy Rodriguez.

"You have those intros?" she asked.

"Are you kidding me?" His face was ashen.

"Do them. We might not use them. I want them done, in case."

"What are we going to do about Debbie?" he cried.

They stared at each other.

"What the hell were you yelling about?" Cappy called out as he marched into the newsroom, Charles Adkins close behind him. "We were practically in the garage."

"It was Debbie," Tommy blurted out. "That person they found was

Debbie. The body up there."

Adkins's knees seemed to buckle. He grabbed for the desk. "Jesus Christ. What are you talking about? What happened?"

"Brown's on his way in," Nancy said, her eyes going from one face to another. "We have to sit on it until he gets here. Nobody is supposed to know."

"No way," Adkins stated. "We should get it on the air right now. Do a break-in. It's our story."

"What about her family?" Cappy asked, looking from face to face. "Does anybody know her family?"

Where was her family, Nancy wondered. Who had the phone numbers? Did they have to get someone in from the front office to handle this?

"What about Carter?" Tommy asked. "Are you going to call him?"

"Scott!" she shouted to the newsroom. "Scott, are you in here?"

"Scott Reynolds," she called over the PA system, "Scott Reynolds to the newsroom."

"What do you have?" she asked Cappy. "We have to get something together."

"We have those interviews with those people who saw the body. A couple of shots of people walking up the trail. You know," he said without meeting her eyes.

"Steve will have the shots from the copter," Charles Adkins added.

"Where are they?" Tommy vied for his own position in front of her.

"There," she said, and they all looked up at the noise of the helicopter making its rooftop landing.

"What do you need?" Scott Reynolds walked to the desk.

"That search-and-rescue was Debbie Hanson," she told him. "We don't know how or why. We don't know anything, but it was her."

"No. How is she? What happened?"

"She's dead," she said bluntly. "And we don't know what

happened. Brown is on his way. We have to get ready for the six. What do you think we should do about Carter?"

Let him decide. He was the weekend anchor. It was up to him to decide if the newscast should be turned over to Carter, at least until Brown arrived.

"I can't believe this," Scott Reynolds was shaking his head. "Dead? She's dead?"

"What about Carter?" she demanded. She didn't have time for this.

"I guess I can call him," he said. "What will I tell him about Debbie?"

She shrugged. Tommy Rodriquez and Charles Adkins also waited for her instructions. Cappy stood next to them, his camera resting on the desk.

"This is ..." Brown's voice rattled through the call letters.

"Go ahead."

"Who's there with you right now?"

"Rodriguez, Adkins." Both of their voices were light, unconcerned, for the benefit of anyone else listening.

"We don't you get Tommy on some sort of look-back piece, not too long. We'll save that for later." It almost sounded as if he was smiling

Tommy nodded.

"I'll be there in ten," Brown said and clicked off.

"Scott, call Carter," she ordered, "and don't tell him anything over the two-way."

"What do you want me to do?" Adkins asked.

"Get the rescue piece together with Steve."

Cappy's face fell. What about him?

She turned to him. "You work with Tommy on the retro about Debbie. And move. We've got about an hour and a half."

"And," she instructed all of them, "no phone calls out on this.

None. You got that?"

Fat chance, she thought, fat fucking chance.

*

Across the Street they had been listening to the calls. The weekend producer sat back in his chair, tapping on his chin and wondered why Jim Brown was on his way into the station. Something was breaking. Christ, what the hell was it? He sure didn't have anything except the body Rafferty brought in. A good lead story, but nothing major without more info.

"Slow day without that dead hiker," he said to the few people who sat in his newsroom. He went back to his typing. He'd get whatever they had, eventually. He'd get it.

49

"Can't get Carter," Scott told Nancy Patterson as Jim Brown came through the door and marched to toward her.

"No Carter," she told him as she got up from her chair.

"Keep trying," he said and put his arm around her shoulders.

"We'll make it," he said softly. "It's bad but we'll make it. Let's get this newscast together." He hugged her. "For Debbie," he said. "We'll do it for Debbie."

God, that was it. He nodded. That was what this day and this night were all about.

"Get Tony in here," he ordered as he took the chair at the producer's desk. "Use that phone." He pointed to the assignment desk.

"Does anybody know what happened? I'll get Martinez at DPS. We have to have that confirmation."

In the time it took Jim Brown to walk through the newsroom, wrap his arms and his words around Nancy Patterson, they had the news Across the Street.

"It was Debbie Hanson, the body Rafferty picked up, Debbie Hanson," the weekend producer yelled.

"Who the hell is Debbie Hanson?" the sportscaster asked as he walked through the newsroom. A photographer shrugged.

So, that's why Brown was on his way in, the producer nodded to himself. Well, he had some footage from the mountain and the rescue, but how the hell was he going to get anything on Hanson, even a photograph, for his newscast? He'd have to call Brown. Good grief.

At The Best, Brown was talking to his people.

"It was our Debbie," he said, looked at each face, searching for the shock, the sadness.

"Our Debbie's dead and we don't know exactly what happened but we've got to pull this one together. We've got little more than an hour but we're going to do it. We have to."

"Tommy?" he called to Tommy Rodriguez who was running toward editing.

"No time," Tommy yelled. "Gotta find tape."

"Cappy?" Brown turned to the photographer who stood in front of him, his arms folded across his chest, "you gonna make it?"

"Sure, Jim," Cappy said. "I'm fine."

"Okay then," Brown said to no one in particular. "Let's move." He reached for the phone.

"Jean Ann, this is Brown. We need you in right now. Right now for the six o'clock. Don't ask any questions. Come in now." He hung up.

That would burn Carter. Well, it was his own fault. He was the one always yelling that no member of the news team should ever be out of contact, day or night.

He made the call to the media liaison man at the Department of Public Safety.

"Sam, this is Jim Brown. I need some help."

"Go ahead," said Sammy Martinez. He knew what Brown wanted, but how did he find out so fast? Who the hell told him?

"Let's not kid around, Sam. We know it was Debbie Hanson you brought in off Padre, but we need your confirmation."

There was no response.

"We're going with it, Sam," Brown warned.

"Jim, we just got it ourselves," he lied. "We don't even have next of kin. I was getting ready to call you about that."

"Public figures, Sam. This is different."

"A reporter is a public figure? Not in my book," Martinez told him.

"Look, I'll get you what you need, family names, numbers, all that. Her father is a judge or something up in Oregon."

"Oh, shit," came the groan.

"I'll have that number to you in five minutes," Brown promised. "Do you call or what? I mean, do you do this?"

"We get somebody up there to take the message to the family or we call direct. Nobody wants that job."

"Sam, we have to go with this. You understand. She's got no family here except us. We're her family. So, it isn't going to matter if we announce it on the six o'clock, is it?"

"You gonna contact the family before we do?" Sammy Martinez wanted to know. "I'd rather you didn't."

"If that's what you need to do, do it. I'll get you the information, but we are going with the story on the six."

"That's your call."

"It's rough," Brown sighed. "It doesn't get any rougher. What happened to Debbie, I mean. A fall, right?"

"We won't know for some time. That's up to the medical examiner."

"But it looks like a fall, right?" Brown insisted.

"Can't say," Martinez told him. He won on that point, at least.

Brown sent Nancy over to his office to find the personnel file with the contact information and started rearranging the paper lines on the long table.

Jean Ann slammed through the newsroom door.

"Dear Lord, what's the matter?" she demanded.

"Debbie Hanson is dead," Brown told her. "She fell on Padre Peak."

"Oh, my God," she cried, one hand clutching at her throat. She swayed backwards.

"Whoa, hold on." Brown reached for her.

"Sit down. Somebody get Jean Ann some water," he yelled.

"You have to pull this together for us," he told her. "We can't find Carter. You'll go in-set with Scott."

"I don't know. I don't know if I can do this." She shook her head as she rummaged through her purse.

"I know, I know," he soothed. "It's bad but we have to do it. For Debbie," he said. "You can do it. I know you can."

"Yes," she said and dabbed at her eyes with the crumpled tissue. "This is horrible. I really loved her, you know. I really did."

"We all did, Jean Ann. That's why we have to do this right." He was almost overwhelmed with the emotion he felt, "It's her last story, Jean Ann, her last story."

It hurt him to say it, to hear it. It was that goddamn beautiful. He knew he would say it again.

Jean Ann raised her eyes to his face. She nodded.

"I'll get ready," she said.

*

Fifteen miles away, Rick Whalen waited impatiently on the players' bench. He had an hour before he would be on air. The engineer moved around him, carrying cables back and forth across the floor.

"I can't do anything without a camera," the engineer told him.

"Yeah, yeah, yeah," Rick Whalen chanted. They'd get him on the air somehow, cameraman or not. And where the hell was the photographer? He'd give him five more minutes and then he'd call the station.

He patted his jacket pocket to assure himself the round of pancake makeup was there.

Now, how was he going to get into it? He liked starting with a smile and a joke. He'd have to think of something funny to say to Reynolds.

He took a deep breath and exhaled slowly. He had nothing to

worry about. He was a natural, everybody said that. He was a natural.

*

At the station, another engineer began to sweat. He had no tapes for the newscast, not even a fucking rundown. What the hell was he supposed to do without tapes?

"Where the hell are the tapes?" he called into the control room. "Is anybody there?" He tapped on his headset microphone.

"Jesus H. Christ, is anybody listening?"

He tore off the headpiece. He knew about Hanson. They all knew about Hanson. But, what the hell was he supposed to do? He didn't have the tapes. How the hell could they get a newscast on the air? Nobody sent over any tapes.

Down the hall in the dressing room, Jean Ann Maypin started into the mirror. She did not judge her beauty or lack of it. She did wonder, for a few seconds, if she should have her ears pierced. They would let her wear those small button earrings. It was the big dangling ones they didn't like.

50

Thirty-five minutes before the six o'clock newscast, the weekend producer from Across the Street called.

"All I can say is that we're really sorry," he told Brown.

"Thanks, fella," Brown said. "We appreciate that. We really do."

"Is there anything we can do?" The producer tried to match the low and emotionally drained tone of Brown's voice. As he spoke, reporters and editors stood around him making frantic hand motions.

"No, I think we can handle it," said Brown. "Hey, guy, thanks for asking."

"You're going with it, of course?" the weekend producer asked.

"Have to. She was our baby," said Brown.

So, thought the producer, the bastard was going to make him ask. He wasn't going to give him a break.

He asked. "Next of kin notified?"

"It's being taken care of. That's the tough part, isn't it?" said Brown.

Did that mean next of kin had been told or not? Smarmy bastard.

"That means we can all go with it," he stated. "That's the way I see it."

"Guess so," replied Brown.

The producer gave a thumbs up to the people around his desk. They broke away in a run.

"Look," he said to Brown, "I know this is hard on your people, but I'd like to put something together about Debbie, something short, maybe pull something from one of her stories, some background on her." He waited.

"I think that's great," said Brown. "Why don't I send a tape over with some of her work. It will take a little while," he warned. "And we don't have any still photos of her."

Prick, he wasn't going to give him even a shot of her for the lead. Well, what the hell. They had Rafferty's pick-up on the mountain, the body coming up. Get something from Brown for the end of the newscast and they had more than enough.

"That's okay, Jim. Anything you've got will be fine," he told him. "Don't worry about sending it over. I have somebody on his way right now. Should be there any minute." He smiled to himself. The guy he was sending would kill to get that tape.

"And listen, we're sorry about this. Real sorry." And, they were.

*

The Best kept the story at one minute fifty-five for the Saturday six o'clock. Re-edited for the ten o'clock news, it ran two minutes. The story ran a third time on the Sunday six o'clock.

The other stations had complete packages for their Saturday ten o'clock newscasts, with footage and information supplied by Jim Brown. The Sunday newspapers carried the story on the front page. A picture was added for the Monday edition, but the story was now front-page. second section.

Jim Brown spoke to Judge Hanson at eight o'clock Saturday night. He assured him the station would do anything they could to help him during this terrible time.

"You know," Brown said to the father, "we thought of Debbie as a member of our family here. We all loved her. She was the best."

Brown wondered if he should organize a memorial service in town. They had a minister they used for stories on religion. He could put together something uplifting. Wait. Did he really want to do that? It would have to be soon, within a few days, and who could make time on a weekday? Not in this business. Next weekend would be too late.

People move on, they forget. Only natural.

What mattered was what they did for Debbie right now, and they did it well. Yes, they did. They pulled it together. There had been only one problem, and that one he expected.

*

Tom Carter flew into the newsroom ten minutes after the six o'clock ended. He was purple with rage.

"Why the hell wasn't I told?"

All right, he was out of contact for the first time in years, but it couldn't have been more than an hour. He needed to pick up his new Jeep. On Monday, they would outfit it with all the radios and scanners, but he wanted it home this weekend. He liked driving it, nodding to the people who recognized him and waved. The open Jeep gave him that rugged, in-charge look.

Then, he gets home and turns on the news and look who's there, that dumb bitch practically bawling on the air. She actually had a piece of Kleenex in her hand when the newscast opened. He saw that, that quick wipe at her eyes one second before she was full on camera. Like she didn't know she was on camera. Right. That bitch.

Almost as bad was that son of a bitch Reynolds right next to her. Couldn't wait to get his job. What the hell was going on?

"I should have been called!" he shouted at Jim Brown. "Why the hell wasn't I called?" He waved an accusing finger in Brown's face.

Brown waited until the finger and the hand rested flat on the desk.

"We tried calling you, Tom, every way possible. We tried every five minutes."

"Yeah, I just bet."

"We thought it was important that one of you be in-set so we called Jean Ann," Brown said, his voice calm.

"Oh, yeah, I saw her weeping and crying. I saw that," Carter spat back.

"We're all broken up about this, Tom. We had to think about getting the story on the air. That was our first concern, Tom," Brown reminded him.

"You should have gotten to me no matter what you had to do. I'm the one you call first, and don't you forget it." The finger was back up again and pointing.

*

On Sunday police climbers confirmed that from what they could see, and it wasn't much, Debbie Hanson fell.

They saw no signs of a struggle. Nobody was reporting any problems, no note or a goodbye phonecall. Anyway, she wasn't wearing the right shoes for hiking. Sneakers, come on. She slipped, fell, hit her head, and died. People did. All the time. If there was anything else going on, the ME would figure it out.

"Why did they even send us out here?" one of them asked, kicking a piece of broken glass off the trail.

"You know, television reporter. They want to make sure they close it down nice and clean."

As they hiked back down the mountain, an old blue and white Volkswagen van with Indian print curtains on the windows was being towed from the parking lot.

*

On Monday morning a call from a Dr. Stanley Waddell was transferred to Jim Brown's phone. Mary took the message and left the pink slip on his desk. It was only a name, a date, and a phone number. Jim Brown did not return the call that day but he did plan to get to it, and all the others, when he had the time.

51

She stood in the doorway staring at him, arms folded across her chest. He couldn't read any emotion on her face, only eyes staring, a slight downward turn to the mouth. He wondered about that short hair of hers. Why didn't she let it grow? It had been long when he hired her.

"Come on in," he said.

He smiled and nodded as she sat. He felt good about her. She may not have been there for the nightmare of the past few days, but he knew that she too had suffered. Of course, she had.

Neither of them spoke for a few seconds. He waited for her. She seemed to be searching for a comfortable position in the chair. Finally, she leaned forward, resting her arms on his desk, hands folded, and he saw the beginnings of a smile.

"Tell me," she said. "What happened?" It was a gentle question, friendly.

"With Debbie?"

She nodded.

She got the news Monday night. She had only been home a few minutes and had reached for the phone to call Debbie. This was a night when she wanted to talk to her. She wanted to tell her about the decision she made. She wanted to tell her that as much as she loved New Mexico, and she did love it, she wasn't going back. She was going to make the phone calls to those big cities of Joan McBain's. Debbie would be happy for her. Yes, she would.

The call to Debbie went unanswered. Ten minutes later her own phone rang. It was Chuck Farrell.

"She must have been hiking or something," he told her. "She fell about forty or fifty feet. They say it was a head injury. Must have been immediate. At least, I think so. I hope so."

So did she.

Brown's deep sigh brought her back to her question.

"Yes, Jim, what happened to Debbie."

"Gosh," he shook his head, "it's been rough. I wish you'd been here. We needed you. I didn't know where you were, nobody did. Not until Monday, anyway." He paused.

"She was quite a gal, quite a gal," he said and rubbed at the corner of one eye.

She nodded pleasantly.

"Have you had a chance to see the stories we did? We did our best." He raised his gaze above her head.

What was it she wanted? She did want something.

"So?" He opened his own hands wide and shrugged.

She shook her head, making a tisking sound with her tongue.

"Hey, you know, we want to make some sense out of this, make some good come out of it. And, you can help us." He could see the interest in her eyes.

"What we need to do is some sort of series on the dangers of living here. But," he stopped, searching for the right idea, "but not everyday dangers. We'll do it on the dangers of things that seem like fun, recreation."

He nodded sagely. This was a good idea.

Her slight smile and nod signaled her agreement.

"You know, the dangers of swimming pools and going out on the lakes."

"Exploring," she added. "Camping."

"Right, right, you've got it," he exclaimed happily. "People going out in the desert. We'll tell them the dangers and how to avoid them. A desert-survival handbook sort of thing. Maybe we'll even put together a booklet. People can call in and get one."

He liked it. He liked it a lot.

"Of course, we wouldn't get rolling on it for a month or so. We'd run it around summer vacation time, but we should be thinking it now."

"And, we have some great footage," she said.

"Hmm." He nodded.

"We have all that footage of people being hurt while they're out having fun in the sun," she offered with a wry smile.

He didn't like that smile or the tone of her voice.

"We have some footage, yes," he said with a warning note of his own, "but that's not the point."

She gave a short laugh. "Oh, I think that is exactly the point. Think about it. We could do one part on the dangers of hiking without ever leaving the station."

"Ellen, is there something you want to say?" he asked, annoyed.

"No. I'm here to find out what happened to Debbie."

"You know what happened."

"No. I know what happened on the mountain, I guess." She shrugged. "But I don't know what happened here."

"What are you talking about?"

"I have a feeling something happened here at the station, something not so nice. Now, why would I feel that way, Jim?"

She leaned back in the chair and crossed her legs. She ran her hand along the crease in one leg of her black slacks.

"I hear Debbie had some trouble here before she went on her little walk," she said, playing with the crease.

He swallowed hard.

"I hear there was some problem with Tom and she ran out of here in tears," Ellen continued.

His face went tight, the fear starting low in his chest.

"It's the little things that make a story interesting. Don't you think?" She smiled.

"Ellen, I don't know what you're getting at, but you're wrong, whatever it is," he stated strongly.

"Really? And here I'm thinking it might make it a better story, a little extra something nobody's talked about. Isn't that what makes it news, even now? And we do love our news, don't we, Jimmy." She grinned. "So why don't we talk about what happened to her here that set her off that morning?"

"Nothing happened here," he declared firmly to hide his growing fear.

"Of course," she went on," nobody really cares, but if they did, all you would have to do was tell them how much we loved good old Debbie and how much she loved her job and how happy she was here, like all of us. Right?"

Suddenly, she felt incredibly tired. All the other things she wanted to say, all the anger she put into the words she rehearsed, had faded away. She stood.

"What's it to you, Ellen?" he demanded, sensing the weakness. "How much did you ever care about Debbie, or anybody else, for that matter? What kind of a friend were you to Debbie?"

Now he could have his own smile.

"I think you're in shock, Ellen. You go home and cool off. When you come back, we'll have a talk about how you see your work and your future here."

She left his office without shutting the door.

He waited for a few seconds before going to the doorway and looking out. He could see her, the top of her head over the cubicle partitions. He quickly pulled back and closed the door. He sat in his chair. He was shaking.

She could cause some trouble. Yes, she could, with that big mouth of hers. She'd make a few phone calls and he'd get the questions. The whole thing was supposed to be over and done with. He heard about the argument with Carter. Carter said it was nothing. Both of them letting off some steam.

"I only asked her where she had been and why she wasn't answering the phone," Carter told him. "What the hell? If you ask me, the girl was always a little loose around the gills."

And now there was this other thing, this phone call from Clifford Williams. Steve told him he called and said he was halfway to New York.

"Said he was going to buy a fur coat," Steve said and grinned. "Though you might like to know."

The only black in the newsroom leaves, no explanation. It might look bad to the people Back East. Then again, maybe not. You could never tell with those guys.

*

Chuck Farrell watched as Ellen threw papers and tapes into a box. "What's going on?"

"Nothing. Don't worry about it." Another tape clattered into the box. "He wants me to do a series on hiking accidents, but frankly, I don't think I want to."

"Where are you going?"

"I don't know and I don't care, Chuck, but I have to get out of here."

"You know, Ellen," he said softly, "we're all just trying to earn a living. That's all. We're people doing a job. We're all trying to survive."

"Good for you, Chuck, but I can't, not this way." Her voice broke with the words. "I'm definitely not tough enough for this."

She picked up the box and walked down the cubicle row. She paused at Carter's office. He wasn't there.

52

The night air was soft. A good night, she thought, March and still cool.

There wasn't too much noise, some traffic moving in the distance, the gentle hum of a hundred television sets filtered through screened windows and open patio doors.

She sat in the car, her legs outside, feet on the ground. It never took long to move. She looked at the sky, black as that night in the forest. She had been so sick with fear that night, sick that the men who killed four or five people were there, hiding in the dark, waiting as she waited with her dolt of a photographer.

"Look," the officers told her, "if these guys come, you run. Get into the woods. They'd love to get their hands on some television people." They both nodded their blond, short-cropped heads.

She tried joking with them.

"If I hear anything, I'll dive under your car."

"There won't be any room," said one of the twins. "We'll be there first." He wasn't smiling.

They told her, off the record, that the baby these men had killed had been tossed in the air for target practice. No one was going to make that official, they told her. It was too horrible.

God, she was scared that night. She didn't want to die there, not for that story, not for any story. She shuddered with the memory of the fear and the cold. She wondered if she told Debbie about that night and how frightened she had been.

Tonight she'd drive north and keep going, north, maybe northwest. She would go someplace where it was cold, where there were great chucks of empty land, few people, and television sets filled with snow. She'd go someplace where they didn't know what *The Today Show* was and didn't care.

*

"That's the news for now," Carter gave the audience his lips-closed, corners-curled, smile.

"We'll be back at ten o'clock with more of the news of our state and our nation." Jean Ann Maypin smiled wide as she spoke. Her lips were dry.

"And so," Carter took it back, "from all of us, good evening and good news."

Jean Ann nodded her agreement. She tightened the crossing of her ankles.

Carter picked his script and turned to her as though to smile, to chat, to relax. He tapped the script sheets on the desk.

In the control room, the director called for the wide shot, and producer Tony Santella gave a crooked smile to all those in the room.

"Piece of cake," he said. "Piece of cake."

In his office, in his high-backed vinyl chair, Jim Brown sat, hands folded over his belly, and stared at nothing at all.

EPILOGUE

There is a perfect view of the city from the park at the foot of the mountain. Here, sitting in your car or resting against the side of the mountain, you can see how the night begins, how the sky turns red and gold and blue and then fades to black.

You watch the city lights come on, cooling even the hottest night with their sparkling white promise. There are other lights as well, those from the cars speeding on the road below, back and forth from a thousand places. At night, it is a city of the future, of prosperity, of all you could ever dream.

There is only one problem with all of this. The park closes at dusk, the same time the city and the sky turn beautiful. Of course, you could watch the coming of the night by standing outside the park gates. You could, if so inclined, jump the fence, climb a short way up the mountain and sit and wait for the night to begin. But, more than likely, you know that inside the park or outside the gates, the view is about the same. Besides, you can see the city lights quite well from a moving car on the road below.

KATHLEEN WALKER spent ten years as a television reporter and producer covering the news for network affiliates in New Mexico and Arizona. She moved on to freelance writing after her last position with PBS in Tempe, Arizona. *The Best in the West* is based on her experiences in television news.

Her freelance work includes numerous articles for *Arizona Highways* magazine. Her two studies of the Spanish Colonial mission system in Arizona and California—*San Xavier: The Spirit Endures* and *A Place of Peace: San Juan Capistrano*—were published by its book division. Her first novel, *A Crucifixion in Mexico*, was published by Black Heron Press. She is also the author of a book of short stories, *Life in a Cactus Garden*, and a collection of humorous essays, *Desert Mornings—Tales of Coffee, Cactus & Chaos*.

She did her undergraduate work in Latin American History at La Universidad de las Americas in Mexico City and earned her master's degree in Corporate and Political Communications at Fairfield University in Connecticut.

She resides in Tucson, Arizona.